What the critics are saying

"This was a great story and the secondary characters make it even better. I look forward to more tales." - *4 stars, Romantic Times Magazine*

"THE PRICE OF PLEASURE is a fast paced, racy novel filled with intrigue, villains and incredibly erotic love scenes that will keep the reader hooked." - *Catherine Loney, Romance Reviews Today*

"Ms Wylde's first novel at Ellora's Cave is definitely a 5 star winner! From the first page I was hooked! If you want to read a story that is guaranteed to make your temperature rise, and possibly curl your toes, then THE PRICE OF PLEASURE is a must read." - *Charlene Smith, Sime~Gen, Inc.*

"Joanna Wylde has woven an intricate web around a galaxy far away, evenly balanced with erotic scenes, villainy and a wonderful love story." - *4 1/2 stars, A Romance Review*

Ellora's Cave Publishing, Inc.

Discover for yourself why readers can't get enough of the multiple award-winning publisher Ellora's Cave. Whether you prefer e-books or paperbacks, be sure to visit EC on the web at www.ellorascave.com for an erotic reading experience that will leave you breathless.

www.ellorascave.com

Ellora's Cave Publishing, Inc.
PO Box 787
Hudson, OH 44236-0787

ISBN # 1-84360-447-7

Edited by Martha Punches.
Cover art by Darrell King.

THE PRICE OF PLEASURE

Written by

Joanna Wylde

For my editor, Martha Punches, and my husband, David.
Thanks for everything.

Part I: The Station

Chapter 1

The House of Lilies was busy tonight.

Jax sat in a corner booth watching the activity around him. The large, dimly-lit room was filled with his brothers-in-arms, Saurellian warriors enjoying the charms of the newly conquered women of the mining station. The pleasure house, with its lush red fabrics and gold accents, was a place designed to make a man forget his cares. Jax was ready for that forgetfulness, the kind that only came in the arms of a beautiful woman. He sighed with satisfaction, sitting back, sipping his drink and thinking about which one of the many pleasure workers filling the room would be his that night.

It was good to be here. They had been fighting for months, beating the Emperor's troops back star sector by star sector. Their forces had taken almost a quarter of his vast territory before a truce had been called. The Saurellians hadn't started the fight, but by the Goddess they'd finished it. Now Jax and his comrades had been assigned to this remote system, babysitting the troublesome Discovery station. In Jax's opinion, "Discovery" was too optimistic a name for the grotty outpost.

There were millions of asteroids surrounding the small sun at the center of the system, containing enough ore for a thousand ships; all of them had to pass by Discovery station sooner or later. Losing the system had been a crippling blow to the Empire's economy, and there was little doubt that they'd try to re-take it if the peace talks fell through. *They'll have to get through me first,* Jax thought savagely. A scowl momentarily marred his near-perfect, olive-toned face.

One of the waitresses at the table next to him caught his expression. He watched as her eyes widened in surprise. She made a pretty, pouting little *moue* of concern with her mouth. Never one to disappoint a lady, Jax flashed her a quick grin, then ran a hand quickly through his tousled, black hair–the "nervous" gesture never failed to catch a woman's attention, something he'd learned early on.

The waitress smiled seductively at him in response, and started sauntering toward him until Gelvar, another of Jax's squad-mates, grabbed her from behind. She squealed in pleasure, dropping her tray. With a growl, Gelvar buried his face in her neck and she shrugged her shoulders helplessly at Jax.

He grinned back at her, more than willing to let her go to Gelvar. There were plenty of women to go around; one was much like the next. He would never consider letting a female get between him and his fellow warriors. Turning his attention back to the room at large, Jax downed another shot of the pleasure house's finest black market *bakrah* in satisfaction.

His squadron was one of the toughest in the Saurellian armada. The Imperial forces would not find them an easy target if they chose to return to the mining station. Until then, it was time to relax and enjoy the pleasures of conquest.

A roar from the crowd roused Jax from his thoughts. One of his friends, Daaron, had been lured up on to the circle-shaped stage that thrust into the center of the room, and the warriors in the crowd were going crazy. A pleasure dancer dressed only in a filmy sarong and matching band across her breasts had dropped to her knees in front of Daaron, running a finger suggestively up and down the length of his bulging crotch.

Jax recognized her as a crowd-favorite from the night before, her shapely and well-endowed body easy to remember. The thought of her performance then, complete with three volunteers from the audience, was enough to make him shift in his seat uncomfortably. His pants seemed far tighter than they had earlier...

"What should I do, boys?" the woman called out loudly, flashing a broad grin at the audience. Their crude suggestions rang through the crowded club.

The men were feeling wild tonight, Jax thought.

Laughing, she responded by yelling, "Well, then, what's it worth to you? I think I need some motivation!"

Instantly credits started raining down on the stage. Another woman, naked except for a series of strategically-placed leather straps, started walking around leisurely, bending over at the waist to pick them up. Apparently the men liked the view she gave them, because another shower of credits came flying toward her.

"I can see you men know what you want..." the dancer called to the rowdy crowd. "Fortunately, I'm a woman who knows how to give a man what he wants!"

With that, she rose a little on her knees and used her teeth to slowly draw down the fastening on Daaron's pants. The crowd roared again, growing louder as she paused dramatically. Then she pulled the zipper all the way down with a flourish, freeing the warrior's enormous cock from the imprisoning fabric.

It stood out straight from his body, the head flushed red with excitement. Reaching out delicately with her tongue, the woman swirled it around the helmet-shaped tip. The warrior gasped, reaching one hand down to grip the back of the dancer's head. Encouraged by Daaron's grasp, the woman slowly drew him into her mouth, then pulled back teasingly.

As Jax watched with interest from his seat, Daaron gave out a groan, and tried to pull the woman's mouth back over him. She resisted, however, standing up instead. Music with a slow, pulsing beat began to sound.

"Darling, I think we can give them a better show than that," she said, looking to the crowd for approval. The answering shouts from the crowd agreed with her. Turning away from the man, she rotated her hips, then slowly started pulling at the skimpy little sarong she wore around her hips.

"Take it off!" rang out a voice, and the crowd went wild. She winked broadly at the audience, then slipped the sarong off, kicking it into the audience.

As Jax and the other men watched, she slowly dropped to her knees, facing the audience and turning her back to the aroused male standing behind her. Her large breasts strained against the confines of the brief band holding them. The crowd urged her on as she removed the band and flicked her hardened nipples with her fingers. Then she glanced flirtatiously up at the man standing behind her, and rubbed the back of her head sensuously against his aroused penis. Daaron gasped audibly at the sensation.

Slowly leaning over toward the audience, the woman placed both hands firmly on the stage, thrusting her round bottom up at the warrior.

Daaron didn't need to be asked twice. Kneeling down behind her, he grasped his cock in one hand, rubbing up and down its length several times. Then he lined himself up against the woman's moist cunt, pressing against her.

She looked out at the crowd and licked her lips, pushing gently back against him. "Let's give 'em a show they won't forget," she said over her shoulder.

Daaron grunted in agreement, then grasped her waist with both of his broad hands. Holding tightly, he thrust into her. The sensation must have been intense, because her gasp was loud enough for Jax to hear it all the way across the room.

The music rose in volume, and the crowd quieted as Daaron pulled almost all the way out of the woman, then slammed his cock back into her. She gave another cry, and Daaron started pumping in time with the music. The dancer's ass slapped back against him, and her breathing grew fast. Daaron and the warriors in the audience weren't the only ones enjoying the show, Jax noticed with amusement. The dancer looked like she was going to explode at any minute.

The feel of a hand sliding along his leg distracted Jax from the stage. A woman slid into the booth next to him. He recognized her–it was Dani, a pleasure-worker he'd been with just the night before. She smiled at him, her bright blue eyes full of promises.

"Hey, Jax, back for another round?" she asked, purring softly in his ear. Her hand reached his crotch, wrapping itself around the aroused length of his dick. He pushed herself against her hand, enjoying the almost-painful pressure of her grip.

"What do you think?" he said, giving her a slow smile.

"Why am I not surprised?" Dani laughed. "You guys have only been here three weeks, and I haven't met one of you yet who isn't always ready to go. It's almost inhuman."

At least some of the locals weren't afraid of them, Jax thought wryly. Dani and her co-workers had been more than eager to welcome them to the station. The rest of the inhabitants hadn't been as happy to meet their new overlords.

"So," Dani asked with a wicked smirk. "Why is it that you're such a lusty crowd? Even Imperial soldiers need a rest now and then, but not you guys."

"It must be all the beautiful women here," Jax said, looking over Dani's lovely features. She had a fair complexion, with white-blond hair and radiant blue eyes. He had met many pleasure workers who tried to duplicate that coloring, but Dani's was natural.

Dani laughed at his answer, enjoying the compliment. He was lying, of course. Her clients always were, but she still liked to hear it. He hadn't satisfied her curiosity, though, and she wanted a real answer to her question. The Saurellians were definitely wilder than any other group of men she'd met in her line of work. Their sheer stamina had made her curious enough to press him further for a real answer.

"Seriously, what is it with you guys?" she asked again, running one finger around the head of his penis. The combination of the stage show and her hand had hardened him sufficiently that the entire length was outlined against the fabric. Slipping down the fastener, she allowed his cock to slip free. It was thick and hard, just the way she liked it.

"Well," Jax said, settling back in his seat under her ministrations, "If you really want to know, we aren't fully human, not like you, ummm–damn, that feels good. A little harder there, please…"

Dani smiled at his request, then removed her hand. There was nothing she loved more than a man squirming under her. "Go on, I want to hear what you were saying," she said encouragingly. Slipping one leg over his, she straddled Jax's lap.

His eyes closed and his head dropped back against the seat. Reaching around her waist with both arms, he attempted to pull her down on him on to his waiting erection.

"I want to hear what you were going to say," Dani said playfully, teasing his cock-head with the lips of her cunt. The poor man looked like he was going to have a heart attack at any minute. "Now tell me," she laughed. She relaxed her knees and slid down on him hard, engulfing his entire length at once. *He was huge*! It felt like he was thrust halfway to her throat. Dani took a second to savor the moment. The feeling was fantastic!

"Hmmmmf," Jax grunted.

"Now, you were saying?" Dani asked, playfully squeezing him with her inner muscles.

Jax groaned in pleasure. "Um…I was saying that, uh, part of the reason we have such strong sex drives is that we're only truly satisfied with one of our own women. We can fuck as many non-Saurellian women as we want, but the hunger never ends. We'll always want more. Nothing really stops the hunger."

"What?" Dani asked, forgetting for a moment to continue her movements. It wasn't the answer she had expected, certainly not from a man who looked like he might explode from pleasure at any minute. Then her professionalism kicked in, and she started moving again.

"Well, if you can't really be fully satisfied with us, why don't you bring your own women?" she asked. "In the Empire, legionnaires bring along their wives and families. Why don't you? Are your women too weak to fight with their men?"

"Hardly," he said, lifting her by the waist with his powerful arms. He started pumping her body more strongly against his, thrusting up into her flesh so hard it made her gasp. "Our women are a force in and of themselves...ummmmfff...there simply aren't enough of them–to, umm–to go around. For every female child born, there are three or four males. The lucky ones find mates. The rest of us...ohhhhh...make do. Goddess, you feel good."

"What do you mean, 'make do'?"

"Well, most of us leave the home world," Jax said somewhat breathlessly as her body once again came to a rest on his. He tried thrusting against her again, but she was too preoccupied with what he was telling her to respond. Her breasts, however, formed an easy target directly before his face.

She wore only a brief halter and he pressed his mouth into her cleavage, laving the soft flesh with his tongue. She gave him a little push away, and he could tell from the look on her face that she wanted to hear the rest of his story. He contented himself with reaching under the halter instead, searching for her ripe nipples. He found them, then rolled one of the tight buds between his thumb and forefinger. Dani gasped slightly at his ministrations, but she didn't start moving against him again.

With a sigh, he continued his explanation, "We realize at a young age if we aren't one of the lucky ones to have a mate. We mate fairly young, so most of us ship out by the time we're 25 or so."

"What did you do?" asked Dani, fascinated. He pressed her nipple again, and her muscles tensed around him in response.

Gasping in response, she grunted, "I mean, how did you end up here?"

Jax squirmed restlessly against her and said, "I think that we could continue this conversation at a later time. I'm feeling kind of distracted."

"You know," Dani said slyly, "For someone who can't possibly be satisfied by a human woman, you seem awfully willing to keep trying." Her internal muscles clenched him tightly and he gave an involuntary moan. The sound made her smile in satisfaction.

"What can I say? I'm an optimist." Jax said, grinning up at the beauty straddling him. Dani wrapped both arms around his neck and pulled him forward to kiss her. His penis pulsed within her, and she knew he was close to coming. Fortunately, it would take more than just once or twice to tire him out. Jax had to be the best lover she'd ever had, and she'd had quite a few.

"Let's go up to my room," Dani whispered in his ear.

Jax didn't even bother to answer. He just picked her up and started across the crowded room to the stairs without even bothering to pull out of her. As he'd told Dani already, he was an optimist. A human woman might not be enough, but she was certainly something. Like every unmated Saurellian male on the station, he'd take everything he could get.

* * * * *

Their conquerors certainly were strange, Calla thought, carrying her basket of linens through the hostel's narrow upper corridor. For such rowdy men, most were remarkably clean. They had taken over Mistress Jenner's Hostel when the station surrendered nearly a month ago, yet during that time she hardly saw them. They spent much of their time patrolling the station shipping docks and manufacturing plants, or running reconnaissance trips through the asteroid belts. At least one was always on guard at each of the hostel's entrances, but Calla had never dared to even really look at them, let alone engage them in conversation. They were large, heavily-armed men who seemed to take their work very seriously.

They also took their play seriously. During the evenings she could hear them in the hallways, although her owner would never have let her out where she could watch them. Mistress Jenner was something of a religious fanatic, a member of the strict "Pilgrims of the Apocalypse." The Saurellians' carousing was disgusting to her, and she would never dream of allowing even a slave such as Calla to become polluted by their presence.

Calla made her way through each of the rooms, changing linens and straightening what little there was to straighten. They had very few personal possessions, so she hadn't gleaned much information about them in her cleaning. Usually she was able to tell a great deal about the guests by what they left in their rooms.

The final room, at the end of the hall, was actually a small suite. According to Jess, her best friend and crèche-brother, the squadron's commander was staying here. Mistress Jenner seemed to hate him more than all the other Saurellians combined. Calla had heard her blame the man for everything from the recent rise in food costs to the timing of transport take-offs, which caused a shudder to run through the entire space station. Last week, Jenner had spilled hot tea all over her hands during a rough launch.

According to Jenner, the commander was the most disgustingly licentious Saurellian of them all. He even had pleasure workers spend the night with him at the hostel and hosted parties in his suite, something which never would have happened if they weren't under martial law. Mistress Jenner wasn't brave enough to stand up to their conquerors, but there was no question as to what her opinion about them was.

She believed they were evil, pure and simple. Not that she had held a much higher opinion of the Imperial troops, of course. As far as Calla could tell, the only people Mistress Jenner actually liked were her fellow Pilgrims. Given the choice between accepting Saurellian money or being turned out of her own home, however, Mistress Jenner had opted to take the money.

When she reached the suite's door, Calla didn't bother to knock before placing her hand against the palm plate to open it. There was never anyone there during the day, anyway. As she walked in, she banged her basket on the door frame, dropping several towels on the floor. Carefully balancing the large basket against her small, compact frame, she knelt down, reaching for the towels.

The action was just enough to loosen the knot dark brown hair at her nape, and the entire mass of unruly curls came off her head and down before her eyes. She fought with it for a few seconds, then gave into the inevitable and set down the basket. She'd have to braid it to get it out of the way now, she thought with disgust. She hated doing that, because braids, combined with her youthful features and the smattering of freckles across her nose, always made her look like a 12-year-old. Not that she had anybody to impress, anyway, so it really didn't matter she reminded herself wryly.

As she braided the long mass with swift fingers, she heard a sound come from the other room. She froze in place, heart thumping. After a moment's silence she laughed nervously to herself, convinced she had imagined it. Perhaps the long hours were getting to her...

Moving quickly and efficiently once her hair was out of the way, she set her basket on a low table, picked out a set of linens and headed toward the bedroom. As she opened the door a pair of strong arms grabbed her from behind, and she was pulled back against a large, unyielding form. Calla tried to scream, but the noise was instantly muffled by a hand that covered her face. Something sharp pricked her neck, and she knew she was in big trouble.

"What are you doing here?" a deep voice whispered harshly in her ear. Calla tried to answer, but her captor's hand still covered her mouth. "I'll let you speak, but if you scream I'll cut your throat. Don't try to play games with me."

"I-I-I'm C-C-Calla," she said, stuttering slightly in fear. The blade pressed more sharply against her neck. "I w-w-work here, I clean the rooms."

The man's hand and arm slipped lower, clasping her across her chest and effectively pinning both her arms. His body was hard against her back, his arm a band of iron trapping her. Even if he wasn't holding a knife to her throat, there was no way she'd be able to get away from him.

"I gave strict orders to Mistress Jenner not to have anyone come in here today. I'm going to check your story out," he said, arms not moving an inch. "If you're lying, this is the time to tell me. Otherwise I'll kill you."

"I'm not lying," Calla whispered. She could scarcely breath, she was so frightened. He would do it, he would actually kill her. She could tell from his voice that he was serious.

The man keyed a small comset attached to his shoulder with his chin. "Tiernan, this is Seth. I've caught a woman going through my room," he said. "She claims to work for the hostel. Her name is Calla. Can you confirm this for me?"

"Yes, sir," Tiernan answered, his voice sounding tinny through the tiny speaker.

Calla assumed he was one of the men guarding the hostel's entrances. He should be able to confirm her identity, although he couldn't go quickly enough for her comfort … Until then, it was clear that the man had no intention of letting her go. His arms remained inflexible as steel–there would be no escaping.

She could feel the entire length of his body against her back, solid as a wall. His breathing was steady and sure, although every muscle was tense and ready for action. Then she felt something pressing against the small of her back. With a shock, she realized her captor was becoming aroused as he held her against his body. Fear swept through her–if he wanted her, there was nothing to stop him. Mistress Jenner certainly wouldn't come to save her, even if orders hadn't been given to stay out of the suite. *Stay calm,* Calla told herself. *This will pass if you just stay calm.*

Seth's erection was quite obvious now, jutting insistently against her. She tried to edge her lower body away from him slightly, but his grip tightened instantly.

"I told you not to move," he said in a menacing tone. His breath was coming a little faster now. Holding the knife steady at her throat, he moved his hand from her upper arm to slide slowly down her chest. It slowed at her breast, cupping her gently. Using his thumb and finger, he plucked softly at her nipple, sending a whisper of sensation through Calla's body. It felt exquisite. There was something strangely sexy about being held like this, she thought. The realization was simultaneously disgusting and compelling.

After a few seconds, his hand left her breast to slide lower, stopping just below her slightly rounded belly. Pressing with the palm of his hand, the man rubbed her body gently against his cock. One finger reached down toward her clit, and even with the layers of cloth between them Calla gasped slightly at the touch. She was afraid of him, but excited, too. He still held a blade to her throat, and she didn't doubt that he'd use it if he needed too, but he was also attracted to her. He held most of the power in the situation, but some small part of it was hers–he wanted her, Calla, the slave.

With a shock, she realized she wanted him, too. A tendril of sensation coiled through her at his touch, and she could feel moisture gather between her legs. Without pausing to consider the consequences of her actions, she relaxed against him slightly, allowing her legs to shift restlessly. It surprised him, Calla could tell, because he stopped breathing for a moment.

She watched as he moved the knife from her throat. He set it down on a small table beside them before reaching back to her aching breast. He started rocking the aroused length of his cock against her again, one hand massaging her breast while the other focused attention between her legs. His large fingers moved back and forth, pushing the rough fabric of her undergarments across her most sensitive spot. It felt so good it was almost painful.

A pressure was building in her body, and while she was still far from coming, she let out a little moan. She simply had to have more. Without thinking, Calla whispered, "I want to do more than this."

The man holding her must have felt the same way, because he groaned into her hair and thrust sharply against her with his cock. Using both arms, he crushed her against his body, lifting her so that he would be cradled against her butt.

The feeling of him there, so close to where she wanted him, was almost too much. Calla moaned a little, trying to convey her urgency. She wanted him. *Now.*

Spurred on by the noise, Seth carried her toward the large bed in the center of the room.

It was still mussed from his sleep the night before and the thought of his body lying there caused a rush of moisture in between her legs. In mere moments she would be experiencing that body for herself, and she was ready. His hard length pressed against her with every step; Calla's muscles clenched involuntarily in anticipation.

When they reached the bed, he pushed her roughly forward and she fell on her stomach. Before she could even start to crawl into a different position, her skirts were up around her head, tangling her hands and immobilizing her. His large, fingers felt roughly for the moist entrance to her cunt. Calla moaned and pressed back against him. She was ready for him.

Then his fingers were replaced by something much larger and his cock pushed against her opening. Both of his hands went to her hips, lifting them high and bracing her slight frame for what was to happen next. Calla couldn't see a thing, but he felt enormous and she briefly wondered whether he would fit.

Then her question was answered as he gave a powerful thrust against her. Goddess, he was huge. It felt like someone was shoving a battering ram up her cunt, and she cried out in pain and shock. She'd never felt a man like this one before.

At her cry, the man withdrew partially and paused to massage her clit. The feel of his fingers was heavenly, and within in seconds Calla was squirming against him. Somehow she managed to free her arms enough to raise herself on to her elbows, and she used the leverage to push back toward him with a whimper, yearning for him to fill her again. It was unlike any sexual experience she'd ever had. She needed him, wanted him, had to have him.

Seth starting thrusting again, moving more quickly as the tide of lust swept through them. He pushed into her again and again, grunting harshly with the effort.

Something was building in her body; she needed more, had to have it because the pressure was too much. Then it crashed through her, and she screamed out in shock and pleasure. Her arms, unable to support her weight, collapsed, causing her upper body to fall forward. Her hips remained high, held in the man's strong hands as he continued to pump his large cock into her. He moved faster and faster, squeezing her hips with his hands almost to the point of pain as he shouted out his own pleasure. Calla could feel the hot spurt of moisture deep within her body, then the weight of his spent body came down on her, all but crushing her. His breath was hot against the back of her neck, arms splayed on either side of her.

They lay there for a second, both struggling to regain their composure. Then the door crashed open and Calla heard someone call out, "Seth, are you alright? I couldn't raise you on the com!"

"I'm fine," the man said. He raised himself up on one elbow to look at whoever was in the room with them, the fingers of one hand slipping beneath her body to absently toy with her clit.

Little curls of pleasure at his touch coursed through her, and she shuddered lightly. Then Calla realized with sudden horror that she was still naked to the waist, completely exposed to both men. She started struggling upright but the man–Seth– was still fully imbedded in her and far to heavy to shift.

"Did you check on the woman's identity?" Seth asked, comfortable in front of his subordinate despite his partial nudity.

Calla moaned, a combination of pleasure and embarrassment, as his fondling continued.

"Yes, sir," the young man said. "She's a slave here. Apparently no one remembered to tell her not to clean today."

"Thank you," Seth said. "You're dismissed."

The door closed and they were alone again. Calla wished she could sink into the mattress and disappear forever, she was so embarrassed. Instead she said firmly, "Please let me up now."

"Of course," he said, sounding far more relaxed than when he'd caught her entering the room. His hand moved from her clit, and he pulled out of her. "I'd like to take a closer look at you. I haven't had a fuck like that in years."

Calla fought to keep in a hysterical giggle. She hadn't had a fuck like that in years, either, but she was horrified with her situation. Not least of her worries was whether Jenner would find out. The mistress had strong feelings about how unmarried women should behave, and those feelings didn't leave any room for encounters like this one. Not even for slaves.

More than one woman had been sold to a brothel after being caught in bed with a guest–and not a Guild-owned pleasure house, either. The last girl had been sold to a pimp who worked out of a seedy bar near the space port. The poor thing had been dead within a week. Jenner couldn't find out about this no matter what it took, Calla thought with conviction. She had to get out of here and pretend nothing had happened. She needed to keep the commander quiet about the encounter, too.

Sitting up, Calla reluctantly faced the man whose seed was still warm in her body. He sat next to her on the bed, trousers open and pulled slightly down. Her eyes strayed down to his still-stiff cock, then quickly flew up to his face. His skin was slightly dark-toned, and his shoulder-length hair was almost black. His eyes were black as well, and they stared at her intently. He reached one finger out and gently pulled up her chin.

"You're a cute one, Calla," he said. "I may have to keep you for a while."

There was no way Jenner would go for that, Calla realized, clamping down firmly on another hysterical giggle that threatened to escape. Oh no, not a good idea at all ...

"I need to go, I have work to do," she said. He frowned at her. Unable to help herself, Calla's gaze was drawn to his mouth. His lips were full and soft looking, a little grin playing at the corners. What she really wanted, Calla realized, was to lean over and bite the lower one ... Another bad idea. Things were definitely out of hand.

"When can you come back?" he asked bluntly. "I'm not done with you."

"I can't come back," Calla said. No matter how much pleasure this man had given her, she couldn't afford to anger Jenner. His hand grasped her chin hard now, forcing her to meet his eyes. He had lost his open, pleasant smile. She had to think of a way to get rid of him and keep him quiet, too.

"Why not? I'm prepared to compensate you."

"I'm married," she said, thinking quickly. "His name is Jess, and if he finds out what happened here it would kill him. I didn't mean to have sex with you, it was an accident." It was a stroke of genius, Calla thought. Or at least it would be if the Saurellian was willing to respect a slave's wedding vow. Jess was like a brother, they'd been raised together in the same crèche. He would lie to protect her without question. Since slave marriages weren't recorded, the Saurellian would never know the difference. Seth's hand tightened on her chin, and a dark look swept across his face, scaring her with its intensity. He was angry, she realized. His eyes flashed.

"I see," he said tightly, then abruptly let her go and stood up and paced across the room. His intense gaze followed her, and a muscle worked tightly in his jaw. "Get out."

Calla quickly stood up, not about to argue. It seemed like she might yet escape this horrible situation–she certainly wasn't going to give him time to change his mind. Moving quickly, she paused to pick up her basket and gather the fallen linens. Seth watched for a few seconds while she collected her things. Then he repeated his terse order.

"I said get out."

Dropping the linens, Calla did as she was told.

* * * * *

It took every ounce of Seth's strength to let Calla leave. He couldn't believe she was married. The mere thought of another man touching her made him want to smash his fist through the wall. He'd kill him, Seth thought. He'd kill him, and take Calla.

Then he caught himself, disgusted by his own thoughts. It wasn't as if she was his life mate, he reminded himself. She was just a slave on a third-rate, back-world mining station. He could have any woman on the station he wanted. What use did he have for one little slave? If anything, he should feel sorry for the poor bastard she was married to. After all, he'd just fucked her silly and she hadn't exactly protested. In fact, she screamed her pleasure when she came. Who knew how many times she'd done the same thing with other guests? Seth could probably have her again if he really wanted, but he didn't get involved with married women, even if they were only slaves. He liked his relationships open and simple, preferring to pay good money to get good service.

Seth prowled around his room another hour, then decided he needed to get out. He'd hoped to catch up on his reports to the Saurellian High Council. He was concerned about rumors that some mining camp factions calling themselves "pilgrims" were hoarding weapons. With a snort of disgust, Seth realized he wasn't going to be able to focus after his romp with the cleaning slave. Instead he'd go and check the patrols, and maybe even head over to the House of Lilies. He'd find a woman there who'd make Calla look like the little nothing she was. It was definitely time to seek out the services of a professional.

Chapter 2

When Calla collapsed, exhausted, onto her pallet in the kitchen that night, she couldn't fall asleep. Just thinking about Seth's hands on her hips, holding her while he pounded into her from behind, sent little shudders of pleasure through her. She was still sore from that morning, yet she ached from wanting more. He'd watched her with an intensity she'd never seen before. When she'd told him she was married, he'd looked ready to hit something. Or someone. She couldn't afford to have him find out she'd been lying to him. For all she knew, he might kill her.

The Saurellians were crazy, everybody said so. They fought hard, they fucked hard and they were ruthless with their enemies. Without being told, Calla knew that a woman who lied to their commander would be one of those enemies. Rolling over on her pallet, she pillowed her head against her arm, willing the pleasurable sensations in her body to go away. It didn't matter how much she wanted to go back to his room. It was too dangerous. Even if he didn't kill her, Jenner would sell her in a heartbeat if she found out what Calla had done. Even death would be better than spending the rest of her life on her back in a mining-camp crib.

Calla slept restlessly and woke up tired. She had plenty of work to do. Even conquering warriors had to eat, and it was her turn to check on the availability of supplies at the market. The bulk of their food at the hostel was delivered each week, but since war had come to their system Mistress Jenner had sent Calla or one of the girls each day to see what was available on the black market. Supply lines were up and running now that the Saurellians had occupied the station, but there were still good deals to be found if you were resourceful enough. Calla was very resourceful.

Slipping out the back of the hostel, Calla pulled a shawl over her head and made her way down a side corridor toward the central market. It was always safer to go out covered; she might not be much to look at, but more than one slave woman of even average appearance had disappeared in the station's back corridors. It was best not to take any chances. She was also concerned about running into Seth, but once she thought about it, she realized she had never seen him before yesterday. He was probably too important to spend his time on guard duty at the hostel, anyway. Bumping into him wouldn't be a problem, she assured herself.

The marketplace was centrally located in the station, making it easy for Calla catch a ride with one of the small transports that regularly moved through the station's main corridors. In less than ten minutes she arrived at the market, where she quickly hit all of her usual stops and arranged for the deliveries. Jenner gave Calla full bargaining authority, but no one got their credits until the goods arrived at the hostel. A slave might be trusted to run errands and negotiate for supplies, Calla thought bitterly, but she would never be trusted with actual money.

Checking the time, she realized there was at least an hour before she needed to be back to the hostel, enough time to visit her friend Dani. Dani's apartment wasn't far from the marketplace, although it was on the opposite side of the station from the hostel. That was fine with Calla, because it made it less likely that Jenner would ever run into her and Dani together. Dani was a pleasure worker, a profession that Jenner and her fellow pilgrims despised. According to Jenner, any woman who had sex outside of marriage was a dirty slut and deserved to be treated as such. In Calla's opinion, Dani had things pretty good.

Dani was a member of the powerful Pleasure Guild, highly trained and well paid for her services. She was completely free to come and go as she pleased, working in any pleasure house she chose. Upon retirement, she would have her pick of suitors and a healthy cash settlement, more than enough to support her for the rest of her life. Unfortunately, the Guild only accepted extremely beautiful girls in their early teens as apprentices. Calla was too old to join even if she wasn't a slave, she thought wistfully.

"Dani? It's me, Calla," she said into the little com outside Dani's door. It was still a little early for Dani to be up after working all night, but Calla knew Dani wouldn't mind her stopping by. They got very few opportunities to visit, especially lately. Things had simply been too chaotic.

"Calla?" Dani's voice floated out through the speaker. "It's good to hear your voice. Come on in."

Pressing her palm to the doorplate, Calla waited for the door to slide open. When it did, the scent of Dani's perfume wafted out into the corridor. Dani stood in the doorway, dressed in a luxurious silk robe tied around the waist. Her long, blond hair fell to her waist in fat curls. Calla knew she must have just crawled out of bed, but she still looked like a vid star. Dani always looked perfect–whenever Calla asked how, Dani would simply wink and whisper "trade secret."

"Come in, come in," Dani said, engulfing her in a warm hug, then gesturing toward the low couch in her living area. Dani's apartment was tiny, like every apartment on the cramped station, yet somehow it seemed like a different world to Calla. Everything was draped with silk and soft pillows, and there were holo pictures on the walls from all over the galaxy, one from each of the places Dani had lived and worked. She'd been everywhere.

"It's so good to see you, Dani," Calla said, smiling warmly at her friend. "Things have been so strange since the occupation started. You know, almost all of the Saurellians are staying at the hostel. They've taken over the whole place."

"I'm surprised they even bother to get rooms anywhere," Dani said with a laugh. "I'd swear they spend all their free time at the House of Lilies–though they're hardly sleeping there," she added with a wink.

"Really?" Calla asked, curious despite herself. Dani's stories of the pleasure house always intrigued her. Not that she was interested in learning any more about the Saurellian commander, of course, she told herself. She needed to keep her distance from him. But it was interesting to learn more about their conquerors.

"Oh, yes," Dani said. She sighed dramatically and draped herself back against the pillows. "You wouldn't believe what those men are like in bed. They're *insatiable*. I've never experienced anything like it. I have to say, if I wasn't a card-carrying member of the Guild, I'd do it with any of them for free… I swear the credits are just a perk."

"I see," Calla said. For once, she felt like she truly understood what Dani was talking about. She'd certainly never experienced sex as wonderful as what she'd had with the commander. If it wasn't for Jenner, she'd have taken him up on his offer in a heartbeat.

"Last night I was with one named Seth," Dani said. Calla's breath caught. Was Dani talking about her Saurellian? "He's like a machine. He fucked me twice in a row! I must've come something like five times. I can hardly walk this morning, yet I know for a fact that he had at least one other girl last night after me."

Calla's brow furrowed. Seth had sex with two other women last night?

"Was he, um, one of the ones staying at our hostel, do you think?" she asked, trying not to sound too curious. It didn't matter of course. Seth could never be hers, even for a few days. Only a slave who was a complete fool would allow herself to get involved with a free man like him. He'd have to leave eventually, and then she'd be left to Jenner's tender mercies. No man was worth it.

"Probably," Dani said. "He's the commander, so I would imagine that he's staying there."

It was him, Calla realized. If he'd left her to head straight for the pleasure house, then he must not have been as interested in her as she had originally thought. He'd seemed so angry when she told him she was married, but maybe that was just his way. He was Saurellian, after all. They were all crazy. It was stupid of her to think she'd actually been anything special to him, she thought in disgust.

"Um, Dani, I have a question for you." Calla said after a brief pause. Dani was probably her best source of information on the Saurellians–she might as well take the opportunity to learn as much as she could about their new governors. "What do you think of the Saurellians, other than just what they're like in bed, I mean?"

"Well, I like them," Dani said, after pausing for a minute to consider her answer. "They're open about what they want. They're here, they're leaving soon, and they aren't interested in playing any games, especially with women like me. I hate it when men pretend to be emotionally involved in sex."

"What do you mean, they're leaving?" Calla asked, confused. "I thought they were going to keep the station. I mean, they fought hard to take it. They must want to keep the mining belts."

"Well, from what I hear, they'll be leaving soon," Dani said, lazily leaning over and picking up a fruit from the basket on the table. Dani offered the little basket to Calla, who took a citrus.

She didn't get these very often, so they were a special treat. Calla suspected Dani realized that, because she always seemed to have them on hand when Calla came to visit.

"The *warriors* will be leaving, that is," Dani clarified. "They're sending a governor or something, with a regular occupation force. Their military is totally separate from the civil authority. From what Jax tells me–he's one of my regulars–the soldiers really hate it when they have to stay put for too long like this. They like action, and this isn't cutting it."

"That doesn't make sense," Calla objected. "The imperial troops liked action, too, but that didn't stop them from occupying the station for years."

"I don't think it's quite the same with Saurellians," Dani said. "It's kind of weird, but these soldiers are different from the imperial soldiers."

"What do you mean?"

"Well, this is going to sound strange, but I think they're just kind of sexually frustrated and restless all of the time," Dani replied, laughing a little. "According to Jax, they can only really be satisfied when they get a life mate, and there aren't enough of them to go around. I guess that only about one female is born for every four or five men in their home system, and while they can mate with human women, they can't bond with them. Once they bond, they bond for life, but the poor saps that don't get one of the women are just out of luck. Jax told me that by the time they're about 25, they pretty much have to leave the home system because they tend to get out of control, even violent."

"That's horrible," Calla said. "And they can't bond with anyone outside their home system?"

"Nope," Dani said. "They can fuck all they want, but it's never quite enough. According to Jax, most of them won't live past their 40th birthday. They get into too many fights. When they send a governor to the station, he'll be bonded and stable, a family man. Otherwise their occupation would never last."

Calla licked the last drop of citrus juice from her fingers, then looked longingly at the little clock hanging on Dani's wall. It was past time for her to go. With a sigh, she pushed herself off the couch and stood up.

"I need to get going, Dani," she said. "I'm sure Mistress Jenner's watching the clock again, just waiting for me to be late."

"I hate that old bitch," Dani said, disgust written all over her lovely face. "She's such a hypocrite–condemning pleasure workers like me, yet keeping you as a slave and dealing on the black market. I wish I could buy you, but the Guild forbids us to purchase slaves, even to free them. I doubt she'd sell you, anyway."

"You're too good to me," Calla said, standing up and giving Dani a hug. "You're right, though, she probably wouldn't sell me. Unfortunately, she almost seems to like me in some sick way. She's told me more than once that the only way I'm getting away from her is to die or get sold to a port-side pimp."

"Bitch," Dani hissed with feeling, then sighed heavily. "At the very least, take some of the citrus fruit with you. I know you love it."

"Thanks, Dani," Calla said, pocketing the fruit. She'd share it with the other girls at the hostel later. "I wish I had something to give you."

"Oh, I can always buy more citrus fruit," Dani said gently. "Good friends are harder to find. I count myself lucky that I ran into you in the market that day. You saved me from losing a fortune on that fake jewelry, you know. I still can't believe I fell for that guy's spiel."

Calla laughed at the memory. She'd seen old Gavin trying to sell Dani some of the same jewelry he usually sold to the drunken miners. Nothing but tin, with a coat of gold paint. Dani had been new to the station, however, and wasn't used to unregulated trade standards. Calla had stepped in and warned her just in time. They'd been unlikely friends ever since.

"Take care, and I'll see you later," Calla said, then stepped out the door. If she was lucky, she'd get home before Jenner realized she'd taken a side trip. Fortunately Mistress Jenner–while cruel–was not particularly smart.

* * * * *

It was nearly the noon hour by the time she arrived at the small, back-corridor door that was the service entrance to the hostel. A tall Saurellian guarded the entryway, and another was seated just inside the door. Both scrutinized her identity chit closely before allowing her to go through to Mistress Jenner's office, located off the kitchen. They'd seen her before, of course, but it didn't stop them from thoroughly checking her identity. The Saurellians might like to party, Calla thought, but they were all business when it came to security.

"I've gotten all the supplies," she said when her middle-aged owner looked up and acknowledged her with a grunt. Jenner was sitting at her desk, all three hundred pounds of quivering flesh tucked into a chair that was far too small for her massive body. Jess, with his dark sense of humor, had gone so far as to take bets among the slaves as to when the chair would break. "Here's the list," Calla said. "The deliveries should be complete by this afternoon."

Jenner reached up a hand for the small transaction pad Calla carried. Calla's fingers brushed against those of her mistress as she handed the pad over, and as usual she had to suppress a small shudder at the feel of Jenner's skin. They were cold and dry, like a snake's. Or at least like Calla imagined snake skin would feel. She'd always thought of Mistress Jenner as snake-like, with her staring eyes and stale scent. Her mistress was cold and cruel, something Calla had seen demonstrated time and again over the years. Jenner cared only for herself and her profit, no matter that she professed to be a devout spiritual Pilgrim. Of course, most of the Pilgrims seemed that way to Calla. Their religion was simply a way to justify their selfish actions, as far as she could tell.

"You've done all right," Jenner said grudgingly after a minute, beady eyes darting across the list of purchases. "They'll be needing you in the kitchen. We're a little short-handed. I had to let someone go today."

Calla felt cold fear in her stomach. "Let someone go" was Jenner's euphemism for selling one of the slaves, all of whom were Calla's friends. Trying to contain her concern, Calla nodded submissively at Jenner and made her way down the hall to the kitchen. When she opened the door, conversation fell silent and suddenly everyone became busy with their tasks. Everyone except Hari, a young girl who cleaned the cooking implements and dishes.

"Calla, you won't believe what Mistress Jenner did!" Hari said with wide eyes.

"Shut up, Hari," said Karin, the cook. She was one of the few slaves who had been at the hostel longer than Calla. Calla's fear grew stronger. No one but Karin and Hari would look at her, and there was a sadness in Karin's face that boded ill.

"Mistress Jenner said she got rid of someone," Calla asked quickly. "Who was it?"

"Calla, I'm so sorry," Karin said, walking quickly toward her. "Come sit with me at the table."

Something was very wrong, Calla realized. The only reason that Karin would look at her like that would be if Jenner had sold...

"Jess," Calla whispered, comprehension dawning. "She sold Jess. He's gone."

"Honey, none of us had any idea," Karin said, pulling Calla to her. The horror of Jenner's actions was too much. Calla had never been away from Jess, they were born in the same crèche on the imperial slave farm. It was beyond comprehension.

"Where is he?" Calla asked, hoping Jess was still on-station. At least that way she would be able to see him.

"He's gone," Karin said. "Jenner sold him to one of her pilgrim friends, a miner. They came to take him just a couple of minutes after you left to shop this morning. I guess the deal's been done for weeks; they just waited to collect him until it was time to ship back out to the mining fields. He's already off-station. She just didn't bother to tell any of us it was going to happen," she added with disgust.

It was typical Jenner, Calla thought despairingly. No matter than Jess was her best friend. No matter that they'd been together their entire lives. The most horrifying thing was that it hadn't been deliberate cruelty on Jenner's part–Calla was sure it simply hadn't occurred to her that the slaves would want to know they were going to be separated. To Jenner, Jess and Calla weren't even real people. It was too much to bear.

"I hate her, Karin," Calla whispered fiercely, fighting against the tears that threatened to take over her whole body. "I hate that bitch. How could she do this to us? He's my brother!"

"I'm so sorry, honey," Karin said.

Calla leaned heavily against her, almost dizzy from shock. Jess was gone, and she might never see him again. She felt like vomiting.

The rest of the day was more horrible than Calla could have imagined. All of them were upset, of course, but none had been as close to Jess as Calla. Each of her fellow slaves did their part to make Calla feel better. Karin saved a small tartlet from Jenner's own dinner for her, and Hari slipped her a chit worth half a credit the girl had gotten somewhere. It wasn't much, but even half a credit was a prize to a slave. Jenner herself betrayed no emotions when she swept into the kitchen for her evening inspection. Then again, why would she? Calla thought bitterly. In Jenner's mind slaves weren't fully human, a belief that was validated by her pilgrim religion.

By evening, the first shock of Jess' fate had worn off, and Calla was grateful for the comforting darkness of lights-out. She had been fighting off tears for the last several hours, and she couldn't hold them back any longer. Beyond the kitchen were the hostel's common rooms, mostly unused by their Saurellian guests, who preferred the atmosphere of the station's drinking and pleasure facilities. Needing some space for herself, Calla crept silently along the hallway and into one of the rooms. She crawled onto a low couch where she curled into a miserable ball.

She lay there, crying, for at least an hour before she came to a realization. She couldn't stay at the hostel any longer. Life had become too horrible. The only family she had ever known was gone. She and Jess had been born the same day on the slave farm. They had spent their entire lives serving others, trapped by the knowledge that runaway slaves were hunted down and swiftly executed by the imperial troops if caught.

But they weren't in the Empire any more, the realization came to her suddenly, and their new overlords were busy securing their conquests. This might be the best chance to escape she would ever get. If she could find and free Jess, they could escape into the chaos of the new political system and live out their lives with none the wiser.

Calla never seriously considered running away before, although Jess had been plotting escape for years. The obstacles were too high and the consequences were too terrible for Calla to try, and Jess would never go without her. But now that Jess was gone, she had very little left to lose. It was time for action.

With a new sense of purpose, Calla got up and crept back into the common sleeping room. The hostel had been her home for more than ten years, and she knew every nook and cranny of it. Now was the time to put that knowledge to good use, before she lost her nerve. Quietly gathering what few possessions she had, Calla placed them in a small rucksack and made her way to the storeroom. It was locked, of course. Jenner doled out supplies carefully, accounting for every credit's worth.

What Jenner didn't know was that Calla and Jess had managed to break the door's code years ago, programming in their own palm prints. As high-spirited teen-agers, they'd used the storeroom as a location for late-night feasts and planning pranks. As adults, she suspected Jess used the room to meet with his women; he was careful to keep that side of himself from her, but she'd heard rumors about his activities from the other slaves.

It was during one of their childhood feasts that they'd discovered Jenner's little secret–a trap door that let out into one of the station's ventilation tubes. At the time, they figured that Jenner's paranoia had finally gotten the best of her. After all, pilgrims were notorious for their survivalist tendencies, so it wasn't that strange that Jenner had a secret way to leave the hostel. Now it would give Calla a way to escape without any of the guards seeing her. Getting off the station would prove harder, but Dani might be able to help with that.

In the back of the room were several crates of expired emergency rations. Calla made her way over to them, picking her steps carefully so as not to kick anything and make a sound. Somewhere in the crates was Jess' emergency stash, everything he'd saved for their escape. Another stab of guilt hit her ten minutes later, when she found the pitifully small package containing Jess' hopes for their future. Inside were a few credit chits, two sets of dark clothing, and a fully-charged, palm-sized blaster pistol. Calla turned the weapon over in her hands several times in awe–how had Jess gotten it? She couldn't imagine...

It took another five minutes to replace everything and pull the dark clothing over what she was wearing. She didn't want to leave Jenner any clues as to how she'd escaped. Maybe, someday, another slave at the hostel would need to use the storeroom exit to get away. Then, grimly whispering, "It's now or never," to herself, Calla opened the trap door and lowered herself into the tube, carefully pulling the door back into place. For the first time in her life, she was free.

"I'm coming, Jess," she said quietly into the darkness. "I'll save you if it's the last thing I ever do."

Chapter 3

"Calla, I can't believe you've done this!" Dani said, filled with a mixture of horror and admiration at her friend's audacity. It was early morning, and she had returned from work at the House of Lilies to find Calla huddled in an alcove outside of her apartment. "Are you sure you want to go through with it?"

"Yes, I am," Calla said, meeting Dani's gaze firmly with her own. "I need to find Jess, and we need to get away from Jenner. He's always taken care of me–I can't just stand by now that he's in trouble. We both know what happens to slaves out in the asteroid mines. He'll die if I don't save him."

"You're right, he will," Dani said quietly, wishing Calla's logic wasn't so strong. A slave in the mines was lucky to survive a year.

"I understand if you don't feel like you can help me," Calla added. "I know the penalties for assisting a runaway slave."

"Calla, you're my friend and I'll help you," Dani said, tossing her hair defiantly. "Besides, I happen to be on *very* good terms with any number of our Saurellian landlords, and I have the Guild to back me up. Nothing's going to happen to me. I'm more concerned about you. Don't you have some kind of implant they can use to track you down?"

"Yes, but fortunately for me, Jenner's a cheap old bitch. She didn't want to spring for one of the high-end models that can pinpoint exact location. She'll be able to tell I'm on the station, but that's about all. Of course, getting off the station is another problem. It's programmed to release a toxin into my system if I leave the station's electrical grid, unless it's deactivated. That's the only way slaves who are sold are able to leave alive."

"I've heard of that," Dani said, a frown marring her perfect brow. "We'll need to get rid of the implant somehow."

"I've heard that there are surgeons who will do it, for a price," Calla said carefully. This was as far as she'd gotten with her escape plan–getting to Dani and asking for help. Everything was riding on what Dani said next. It would be almost impossible to get away without some kind of assistance.

"Oh, Calla, that's dangerous," Dani said. "Those things are supposed to be tamper-proof. Won't it release the toxin if someone tries to take it out?"

"It's a risk I'm willing to take, if I can find someone to perform the procedure," Calla said. "Jess and I talked about doing it lots of times, but I was always too afraid and he wouldn't go without me." She added bitterly, " Now I realize that staying a slave with Jenner was every bit as dangerous as escaping. She sold Jess knowing he would die–she just didn't care. If I hadn't held him back he would have gone years ago, but he thought he needed to stay and take care of me. Now I need to take care of him."

Looking at Calla, Dani could certainly understand why Jess had felt that way. Calla was had told her once she was 27-years-old, but with her small frame and freckled face she looked younger. If Dani didn't know better, she would have thought Calla was nothing more than a girl in her late teens. Perhaps they could turn fragility to their advantage.

"Calla," Dani said. Her tone was slow and hesitant, as though she really didn't want to even suggest her plan. "I have an idea how to get you off-station, but it's kind of tricky."

"What is it?" Calla asked, cautious hope in her voice.

"Well, first we'll have to get rid of your tracker. But I'm thinking that we could set you up with a protector, maybe one of the Saurellians. Even though you're not a member of the Pleasure Guild, there's some room in the field for promising independent contractors. You wouldn't make as much money as a Guild-trained worker like me, but it could be your ticket out of here. You've got decent looks, and you're young. There are lots of men who might be interested in a woman like you."

Jenner had threatened to sell her to a pimp a thousand times, but it had never occurred to Calla that she could sell herself. The idea was somehow appealing–for once she would be in charge of her own body. Still, there were potential problems...

"How would I protect myself?" she asked. "I mean, I've heard how rough spacers can get. I can't do Jess any good if I'm dead."

"That's where I come in," Dani said, smiling triumphantly. "I can help negotiate a deal for you. It's a trade secret, but the Guild keeps extensive records on all our clients. I can find you someone who has a good history and solid payment record. If you fulfill your part of the contract, you'll find yourself off-station. You'll have resources, and if you play your cards right, he may even help you look for Jess–some men will do anything for the woman they're sleeping with."

"I can't believe you'd do all that for me," Calla said. She'd known Dani was generous, but to negotiate a contract for her was more than she'd expected. Normally the Guild did everything it could to squash independent contractors.

"You know, Calla, I just wish I could give you enough money to go and find Jess by yourself," Dani said. "But the Guild puts most of what I earn in a pension fund, and I don't actually have access to it unless I resign. I just get an allowance until I cash out."

"Oh, Dani," Calla said. "I never expected that. I just didn't know where else to go."

"Well, I do have a little tucked away," Dani said, chewing thoughtfully on her lip. She did some quick mental calculations. "I think I have enough to pay a doctor, and to give you a little bit to take with you. You'll need it, especially if the contract doesn't work out. We'll need to buy you a new identity, too, and new finger and retina prints."

Calla nodded in agreement. Whenever Jess had talked to her about escaping, he'd listed everything they'd need. New identities were at the top of that list. She had to become a new person if she was going to have prayer of getting away from the station, let alone finding Jess.

"Dani, I swear I'll pay you back," she said. "I don't know how, but I'll do it."

"Honey, I just hope you don't get caught," Dani said, reaching her arms out to gather Calla close. It was all Calla could do not to cry at her friend's generosity.

"Me, too." Calla said. "But if I do, I won't let them know who helped me. I promise."

"Oh, you don't have to worry about that," Dani said with a wry laugh. "They wouldn't dare touch me. Being a member of the Guild does have some privileges. They may have the legal right to punish me for helping you, but if they do the Guild will pull right out and boycott the station. We protect our own, and our financial interests go well beyond the pleasure houses."

"I had no idea," Calla said, intrigued by the thought.

"Not even the emperor messes with us," Dani said. "At least not lightly. Neither will the Saurellians, if they know what's good for them. We're on both sides of the border, now, and we have a lot of influence. I'd like to see them try to come and get me."

* * * * *

The next month was one of the longest in Calla's life. According to Dani, Jenner had waited almost two days before reporting her missing, and the local station security force only made a quick, half-hearted search. Jenner wasn't well loved by the locals, and the Saurellians were hardly likely to get involved in the hunt for a lost slave. As long as she wasn't foolish, odds were good that no one would notice her presence. At least that's what Calla kept telling herself.

Getting rid of the implant proved more troublesome. It took Dani more than a week to find a surgeon willing to perform the procedure, and the price was higher than either woman had expected. Dani had enough saved up to take care of that, but not enough to do both retinas and fingerprints. They opted for the fingerprints.

Dani also arranged to have a new identity "created" for Calla at no charge. Calla didn't dare ask how she'd managed that. It was a pretty good guess that the average forger to be found on a mining station didn't often have the funds to visit a guild-trained pleasure worker. Dani had probably convinced him to barter his services for hers. Calla was now officially Devora Forester, Dani's distant cousin and an experienced pleasure contractor.

Once the implant was out, Dani disposed of it in the mining station's recycling system. It was their hope that when it was found and reported to Jenner, everyone would assume that Calla had been killed, and her body dumped. It certainly wouldn't be the first time a body disappeared into the depths of the unpleasant-smelling pit where station waste was slowly distilled into useable organic products.

The hardest part of the plan to put into action was the contract. Dani urged patience, reminding Calla that if they rushed into anything she would end up with a bad client. But clients wealthy enough to seek an exclusive contract were few and far between on the mining station, and Calla was starting to get worried. Each day she stayed there was another day she wasn't looking for Jess, and another day that Jenner might find her.

Initially, she'd been nervous about serving some man privately, but the longer it took to find the right client, the more worried she became that things would fall through. If it did, she didn't know what her options were. Dani was out of money, and Calla could hardly seek employment on the station.

In the mean time, Calla busied herself by studying pleasure training tapes. When she finally got a contract, she would need the sexual education to live up to her part of the deal.

It was nearly five weeks after Calla left the hostel that Dani came home bubbling with news. "You have a wonderful opportunity!" Dani said. "The Saurellians are finally sending a governor and long-term occupation force, which means all the men here will be leaving within the next few weeks. I think one of them might be interested in a contract with you."

Calla's hopes fell a little–most of the Saurellians had stayed at Jenner's hostel, so it was a pretty good bet they would know about a slave on the loose. Contracting with one of them didn't seem like a very good idea, and she said as much.

"Don't be silly," Dani said, giving one of her tinkling, trademark laughs. "They're not going to recognize a runaway slave who's turned into a glamorous pleasure worker. You've got a rock solid identity now. Besides, why should they care? Jenner hasn't exactly gone out of her way to make their stay pleasant. Even if one of them did recognize you, I hardly think they'd send you back to her. They can't stand her, and they can't wait to get off-station. Returning escaped slaves isn't their priority."

Dani was probably right, Calla thought. The Saurellians had interfered as little as possible with the day to day operations of the station. They didn't even pay much attention to the countless smugglers and black marketeers who roamed the station's ports and corridors freely. One escaped slave probably wouldn't matter to them.

"Okay, so this is my chance," Calla said, warming to the idea. "How do we go about arranging the contract? From what you tell me, they usually aren't into exclusive relationships."

"Well for one thing, any contract you make wouldn't be exclusive for your client," Dani said, a slight frown on her face. "You do realize that, don't you?"

"Oh, yes, of course," Calla said, blushing slightly at her naiveté. That's exactly what she'd thought, but she didn't want to admit her ignorance. "But don't they usually just visit a pleasure house wherever they're stationed? What makes you think one would want to take me with him?"

"Ha, that's the brilliance of my plan," Dani said smugly. "Usually they don't, but this is a special situation. Their squad is disbanding for now. They're going their separate ways. I guess peace negotiations with the Empire are going pretty well, and the commander is going to take some time to explore the asteroid belt or something. I guess he has an interest in mining.

"But this is the best part," she continued. "You see, he has a thing for women who look like you; he's been requesting small brunettes with freckles every night for weeks. It's actually kind of insulting," Dani added, pouting slightly. "He hasn't 'visited' me for quite a while.

"But it's the perfect set-up for you to look for Jess, and it's perfect for him, too. They can't go too long without sex, you know. Men really are weaker than us," she added with a laugh. "Especially Saurellian men. They think with their dicks."

Calla was no longer listening. As soon as Dani mentioned the commander, she got a tight feeling in the pit of her stomach. Was she talking about Seth? If so, Dani's plan couldn't possibly work.

"There may be a problem," Calla said quietly. Dani's smile dimmed a bit. "I've met their commander before."

"Tell me what happened," Dani said, seemingly unconcerned. "I'll tell you whether it's a problem or not."

By the time Calla had finished her story, Dani's jaw had dropped in disbelief. Calla stopped talking, and looked anxiously at Dani to gage her reaction.

"This isn't a problem, this is perfect!" Dani said. For once she wasn't smiling with innocent charm or seductive smoothness. The accomplished pleasure worker was grinning from ear to ear. "You already know he wants you, he's asked for girls who look like you ever since then."

"But he'll know I'm an escaped slave!"

"No, he won't even recognize you by the time I'm done with you," Dani said confidently. "He only saw you once, right? And not even your face, really."

Calla blushed again, but Dani didn't even notice.

"From now on you're an experienced woman who's worked her way across a hundred star systems. I'll provide you with a resume and references he won't be able to crack–another little Guild trick–and even if he suspects, he'll never be able to prove anything. All you have to do is get off-station and you'll be home free!"

"I'm not so sure, Dani," Calla said. "I think this may be a bad idea."

"We've come too far for you to get cold feet now, girl," Dani said sternly. "Besides, what are your options here? This may be your best shot at freedom and finding Jess. For love of the Goddess, the man's already headed in the right direction. All you have to do it convince him to take you with him."

"All right, all right," Calla said. "You're right. It's my best shot. So, how do we go about it? Will you just arrange everything, or what? It's not like I've done this before," she added with a nervous laugh.

"Well, since he isn't openly shopping for a contract, we'll have to convince him," Dani said. "He'll be at the House of Lilies tonight, so I'll arrange for you to meet him. You'll have to do the convincing. Don't worry about anything. I'll get you ready, and if you're too nervous I'll give you a little something to help things along."

"I'm not sure I like how that sounds," Calla said cautiously.

"Oh, you'll like it," Dani said enigmatically. "Just wait 'till you give it a try."

* * * * *

Later that evening Calla discovered Dani what meant. She definitely liked "it." There was something in the wine Dani gave her as they were preparing for her "interview", and Calla was feeling more than a little friendly by the time they were done. Dani had started her out with a relaxing massage with the specialist they kept on staff at the pleasure house. Calla had been hesitant at first, but Dani just gave her a knowing smile.

"Trust me," she'd said. "You'll like the massage. Kail has the most talented fingers..."

Dani was right about Kail's fingers, Calla thought lazily after an hour under his ministrations. She'd followed Dani into the dimly lit massage room unsure of what to expect. What she found was the most beautiful man she'd ever seen wearing only a brief cloth around his waist. He'd walked over to greet them, then gently led Calla to his waiting massage couch. Dani, smiling with satisfaction, reclined lazily in one of several chairs against the wall to watch.

Calla gulped, then turned to the man nervously. He was tall, with tightly defined muscles and a soft smile. He was also completely hairless, something she had never seen before. He noticed her look of inquiry, and laughed.

"I'm from Kelarus, we don't have any hair," he said with a smile as he pulled off her robe. It was disconcerting to have a total stranger remove her clothes, but not as much as she had thought it would be. "It's the wine, it helps you relax," he said. "Dani's own special recipe."

He gestured for her to lay down on the couch on her stomach. He left her side, and soft music filled the room. Then a drip of something warm hit her back. Kail spread flower-scented oil in small drops from her shoulder blades to the small of her back, then his smooth hands started running along her spine and she melted.

"Let your tensions and worries go," Kail whispered in her ear from behind as he manipulated her muscles. He spent long minutes sweeping his strong hands over her back and shoulders, then moved to the end of the table. Picking up one small foot, he worked his fingers over every inch of first the left and then the right before moving up to her calves. He gave special attention to the backs of her knees, tickling them lightly and laughing at her reaction. Then he reached the backs of her thighs.

Calla shifted restlessly. His touch was like warm honey, and she could feel herself growing moist as she realized he was slowly, inevitably, working his way toward the cleft between her legs.

He skipped where she wanted him to touch, however, moving to each of the soft mound of her bottom in turn, massaging and treating them to light, nipping kisses. All her nervous tension was long gone, but a new tension was coiling within her. Sexual tension. She wanted him to touch her, give her release, but she was too weak to move. His hands were hypnotic, she was captive.

After an eternity, he had her roll over on to her back, stretching her arms so that they lay high over her head. He started with her hands and worked his way down her arms to her shoulders. Then he reached her breasts, lavishing his full attention on each one until they were painfully tight, and her small red nipples felt as if they would burst. He dropped one slow kiss on each, then stood and walked once more to the end of the table.

Calla all but whimpered in pain as he left her, then felt herself tighten in anticipation as his hands grasped her ankles. Pulling her legs slowly apart, Kail started carefully rubbing again, moving ever closer to the center of her pleasure. She could feel the moisture rushing to her cunt, her legs twitching under his touch. She wanted him to move faster, harder. She gave a little gasp, and Kail laughed then stepped away.

"I think you're ready now, sweetheart," he said softly, and Dani giggled in the background. Kail held his hands out to her, pulling her up and off the couch. Calla simply stared at him, open-mouthed. He was aroused, she could see his stiff erection until his loin cloth, but he seemed completely disinterested in touching her.

"It's to get you ready for your customer," Dani said, coming up behind her. "If we let Kail finish the job, it would defeat the purpose."

"That's a dirty trick," Calla muttered, her face growing flushed. She felt so embarrassed. She'd almost come on the table, yet for Kail this was simply business.

"Don't worry, darling," Kail said, lifting her chin with one gentle finger. He smiled into her eyes. "It's all right to enjoy the massage. And it's all right to enjoy your client. You're going to have a wonderful time tonight, you just need to let yourself go."

Calla nodded, mesmerized by his soothing voice, and Dani held her robe out. The rough fabric rubbed her nipples, and she gasped at the sensation.

"Come along," Dani said with a wicked smile. "Let's get you some more wine and find you something to wear."

They walked slowly back to Dani's dressing room. Every move felt fluid, surreal, to Calla. Was it the wine? The massage? She didn't know, and she didn't care, she realized with a start. She simply liked it.

Dani spent the next hour and a half getting her ready. She created an artless, simple style for her hair, rubbed subtle creams and cosmetics on her face, and even gave her rouge for her nipples. Calla giggled at this, thinking Dani was joking at first. Dani just smiled and shook her head; her little Calla was a true innocent. She had no idea how wild Seth would be for her.

The final touch was a barely-there dress made entirely of floating, semi-transparent scarves. It covered her completely, yet with every step she took her legs were outlined or exposed between layers. The peaks of her breasts were outlined as well, and as Calla stood looking at herself in the mirror she was stunned. It was as if Calla the slave girl had disappeared. In her place was Devora, a pleasure worker whose face was flushed with arousal and anticipation. She licked her lips, then looked at Dani for her reaction.

"Oh, Seth will like that," Dani whispered.

"I'm ready for him," Calla replied in a throaty voice. She took a final swig of wine, then set down her glass and turned to the door, tossing her hair and laughing with happiness. She felt like she was just about ready for anything.

As they walked through the house toward the room Dani had reserved, Calla found it was getting harder and harder to stay focused on the task ahead of her. Each and every man she saw as she walked through the House of Lilies looked good enough to eat.

"I think you drank a little too much," Dani said with a wicked laugh, guiding Calla along a gallery that looked over the main performance area. Along the way were entrances to the small rooms used to entertain clients. Dani had introduced her to the other Guild workers as her cousin Devora, and explained she was setting up a private contract. The women had been polite, but distant, tolerating her presence because of Dani. The house manager had made it clear that "Devora" was only to visit with her proposed client, however, and just for one evening. She might have been Dani's cousin, but she was competition, and the Guild wouldn't allow her to stay for long.

They hadn't forbidden her to watch what was going on around her, though, and the sight was even more educational than the training vids. Dani had told her that most of the activity took place in the private rooms. It must have been some pretty spectacular stuff, because as far as Calla could tell just about every possible kind of sexual activity was already happening all around her–and the floor show hadn't even started yet.

A passionate female moan, followed by the sound of clapping, sounded through the room, startling Calla. Pulling away from Dani, she leaned over the edge of the gallery to see what had happened. Directly below her a threesome was underway, something she had only ever imagined. One man was sitting in on a bench. Straddling him was a woman, and behind her was another man!

"What are they doing?" Calla asked Dani, mesmerized. The sight made her insides twist and her nipples stiffen.

The man on the bottom had his face turned up toward them, his eyes closed. His expression was one of strain and intense lust; a bead of sweat ran down his forehead as he thrust up into the woman on his lap. She seemed hardly able to support her own weight, but all around her were the helpful hands of her audience. The man pounding into her from behind seemed almost in a frenzy, grunting and moaning each time he slammed into her ass. Her own cries answered each thrust.

"They're having sex, sweetie," Dani said with a laugh. "They're just doing it a little differently than you may be used to."

"But two men at once, isn't that hurting her?" Calla whispered. Without even realizing what she was doing, one hand dropped toward her own wet cunt. She caught herself and pulled the hand back quickly. What was wrong with her, she wondered?

"Does she look like she's in pain?" Dani asked. "Trust me, two men at once can be very … stimulating … under the right circumstances. Now I know you're enjoying the show, but we've got to get going. I don't want Seth showing up before you're completely ready for him."

Calla nodded, dragging her eyes from the scene below them. Who would have thought such a thing was possible? *Two men at once…*

Dani led her wide-eyed friend to one of the rooms, and palmed the door open. It was lushly decorated, strewn with pillows and hung with draperies. To Calla's surprise, there wasn't a bed. Instead, the entire floor was softly padded. With a reassuring wink, Dani told Calla she'd be back soon with Seth.

Calla settled herself down to wait against a pile of pillows. Soothing music was playing in the dimly-lit space. The drug had worked its way throughout her body, and every nerve cell tingled with sensation. Without thinking, Calla ran a finger gently around her right nipple, enjoying the pleasant, tightening sensation. Then she let the hand drop lower to her crotch, rubbing the same finger against her clit almost absently. The ceiling was hung with soft fabric, and if felt like room was completely separate from the real world. It was a sensual nest, so comfortable that she felt like rolling in sheer pleasure.

With a drug-induced giggle, she realized she could. Calla stretched herself out like a kitten, alternately rolling and clawing. It was the most wonderful, liberating sensation she'd ever felt. *Here I am*, she thought, *in a Guild-owned pleasure room. I'm free and I'm about to enter into a service contract where everything I earn will be all mine!* It was a glorious feeling.

A soft chime sounded through the room, and one of the drapes drifted to one side. The music in the room faded, and silence filled the room. Behind it was a full-size holo-screen, displaying the stage in the main room. The floor show was about to start, and thanks to the holo-cameras Calla was going to have a front-row view. Fascinated, she drew one of the pillows in front of her and settled down to watch.

After a few seconds, a stunningly-beautiful woman sauntered out on to the stage. Her skin was creamy brown, and a gorgeous mane of curly black hair fell down her back. She was dressed in a filmy, semi-transparent gown that draped gracefully, trailing to the floor. As she walked, a low, rhythmic beat started working its way through the air. The music paused dramatically when she reached the center of the stage.

Shrugging her shoulders proudly, the gown slipped down, baring her breasts. Like the rest of her, they were magnificent. A low, backless couch rose out of the floor directly behind her; she sat down and leaned back comfortably.

A man dressed in black leather pants followed her on to the stage. His chest was bare, and the slight swing of his arms as he walked caused his tight muscles to ripple. His skin was light, almost white, as was his spiky hair. His facial features were classic and sharply chiseled. The only spots of color were his lips and eyes, both pink in color. He strode purposefully toward the reclining woman, licking his lips slightly in anticipation.

Calla felt a tingle run through her at the sight.

The woman watched him dispassionately as he came to a stop before her. She pointed imperiously to the floor, and he dropped to his knees in front of her unhesitatingly. Flicking a finger at him, she directed his attention to her bare breasts before tossing her head back against the couch and closing her eyes.

The man leaned over the reclining woman, flicking first one and then the other nipple with his tongue, before settling his attention to one firm, dark breast. He laved it slowly, and while the woman remained almost motionless, she quivered slightly in pleasure from time to time.

After several long minutes, the man started working down her belly toward her waiting cunt, gently untying the sash that held her gown together. The gown fell in soft folds to either side of the woman's body, revealing long, slender legs. She lifted one knee and spread them slightly, allowing him greater access. He dropped his head between her legs and started working her clit with his tongue, every movement timed to echo the sensual beat of the music.

The sight was so erotic that Calla couldn't control her hand from sliding down toward her own nether lips, shivering with pleasure as she gently stimulated the swollen flesh. It felt almost as if she were on the stage with the performers. A small, distant part of her mind was aware that without the drug she probably wouldn't have felt so free to enjoy the show, but she didn't care. At that moment, anything was possible. The freedom was *delicious.*

The woman on stage was still lying with her head thrown back and her eyes closed, but she was visibly squirming from the intensity of her arousal. Both of her hands had worked their way down to the man's head, pressing him against her flesh.

Her body started jerking in response to the actions of the man between her spread thighs.

Calla's own self-ministrations moved more quickly at the sight. Waves of pleasure coursed through her body, centered not only between her legs, but her heart and mind as well. It was glorious to lie there among the cushions, watching the beautiful black woman take her pleasure. As the pleasure built in pitch through Calla's body, the joy was almost too much to bear. She was in control of her body, she was in control of her future and she was in control of her own sexuality. She felt like a magnificent goddess.

The woman on the stage seemed to feel the same way, because even as she approached her orgasm, she pulled the man's head away from the opening between her legs and sat up. Sliding sinuously off the couch, the woman dropped to the floor and knelt face-to-face with the man. Leaning forward, she gave him a deep kiss, then started pushing against his chest with the palms of her hands. The man allowed himself to be pressed to the floor, until he was lying prone on his back. The bulge straining against the front of his leather pants pulsed visibly, and from the tight look on his face Calla could see that he was not nearly as relaxed as his posture indicated.

The woman shifted herself until she was kneeling over his legs, then leaned down and gave him another long, slow kiss, rubbing her dark nipples against his own pale ones. Then she sat up slightly, slid her hands down his chest to the front of his pants, and slowly opened them. His large cock sprang free of its confinement, and she wrapped one hand around it and stroked up and down a few times. The added stimulation was almost too much for him, and he jerked from tension and pleasure. A knowing smile swept over her face, and for a second her eyes spoke to Calla through the holo-screen. She seemed to be saying, *He's mine to play with, and I love it.*

Calla started moving her hand more quickly, eyes glued to the screen.

The woman on the stage let go of the man's penis, then raised herself slightly and positioned it against her waiting pussy lips. Leaning against his chest with both hand, she impaled herself on it. A look of sublime pleasure came over her face, and she licked her lips in satisfaction.

The sight was too much for Calla. Working her clit furiously, she took her other hand and massaged her breast as she rolled back into the cushions. The dress Dani had given her, made of filmy scarves strung together, twisted up around her waist. The waves of orgasm were very close now, and Calla threw back her head, eyes closed, to revel in the twin glories of sex and freedom. The remembered sensation of Seth thrusting into her cunt flashed through her, and with a wail she exploded into a thousand stars, each a separate flashpoint of joy.

* * * * *

Seth's cock was rock hard from the minute he saw her. She was lying in the middle of the room, surrounded by soft pillows, clothing askew and moaning with pleasure. Dani, who had arranged for him to meet with her cousin, stood next to him with the contract. He'd told her several times that he didn't want a contractual relationship, but the sight of her cousin climaxing was eroding his certainty. There was something about her, he couldn't pin it down, but he wanted her. Immediately.

"Dani, I want to interview Devora privately," he said, not bothering to look at the woman next to him. He was accustomed to being obeyed, so he was surprised when she failed to leave immediately.

Instead, Dani strolled leisurely into the room ahead of him, taking up a stance between him and the lovely woman still shuddering against the floor. "Let me introduce you," Dani said, smiling at him placatingly. She turned to Devora, who had come out of her self-induced orgasm to find them watching her. Dani gave the young woman a hand up.

Seth watched with intense interest as Devora straightened her clothes slightly, then pushed her dark hair back with both hands to smile directly at him. She seemed completely unembarrassed by the fact that just seconds earlier she'd been twisting in ecstasy before him.

"You!" he said, shocked at the sight of her freckled face. It was Calla, the little slave who'd run away from the hostel. He'd bet his life on it. "You're Calla, from the hostel. I know you!"

Devora looked at him with surprise, and then a confused smile crept over her pretty features.

"I don't know what you're talking about, Commander," Dani said smoothly into the awkward silence that followed his accusation. "Devora is hardly some slave, she's my cousin. I don't think this is the way to start what we all hope will be a mutually beneficial relationship."

Seth glowered at Devora, yet she merely stared back at him with that slightly confused smile. He knew it was the slave girl. The inn-keeper, Mistress Jenner, had complained bitterly that she'd run off after some male slave had been sold, presumably her husband. The slave's presence here with Dani made no sense at all.

"Commander," Devora's soft voice broke his concentration. "I don't really know what you're talking about, but if you liked this slave girl, I'm sure I could pretend to be her for you." She smiled at him with seductive intent, eyes all but feasting on his face. She looked hungry.

Continuing to stare at her, Seth tried to decide whether he was imagining her resemblance to the slave girl. They both had the same build, with freckly skin and dark hair, but upon a closer examination, Devora did seem somewhat more lush in appearance. Her lips were full and moist, and even as he watched, her small, white teeth caught her lower lip winsomely. Unlike his little slave, this woman seemed self-confident and aware of her own charms. Their facial features were also similar, but with a start, Seth realized he didn't actually have a particularly clear image of the slave's face. He hadn't spent much time face to face with the girl...

"Commander, I can assure you that Devora is an experienced and professional pleasure-worker, although she isn't Guild-registered," Dani said, smiling at him serenely. "You've already seen her resume and references. Perhaps I should leave you for a private interview, then we can discuss a contract?"

Devora blew a small kiss toward Seth, then lifted her hands to cup her breasts lightly, playing with the nipples. They hardened immediately, and his cock twitched in response. Damn, he thought, his pants were too tight.

Seth hadn't seriously thought Dani's cousin would interest him enough to contract with her, but his body didn't seem to agree. This little vixen might be just what he needed to make his information-gathering mission through the asteroid fields tolerable.

"Commander?" Devora asked seductively.

"Yes," Seth said, and to his surprise the word came out rather hoarsely.

"I don't think you need me right now," Dani said with a laugh. "I'll just lock the door behind me."

Seth barely heard Dani leave; he was so intent on Devora.

She sauntered closer to him, then raised her arms above her head, stretching sinuously. The movement caused her pert breasts to lift enticingly, and emphasized the lean length of her stomach. She finished stretching and reached around Seth's neck, pulling him in for a kiss.

It started softly, but within seconds his arms were around her and their mouths became ravenous. His penis was rock hard against her body, and she wiggled against it in appreciation. Seth instantly wanted, needed, to thrust inside her body.

She seemed to want the same thing, because her arms tightened around his neck and, using him for support, she boosted herself up against his body. In seconds, both legs were wrapped around his waist and she was grinding her cunt against the powerful ridge of his cock. The sensation was exquisite, and for an instant she thought she might come right on the spot.

Holding her to him with one arm, his slid the other to cup and support her bottom. The new position gave him the leverage to thrust her against the length of his dick. Devora was moaning into his mouth, pulling herself even closer. Then she broke away from the kiss long enough to gasp out, "Fuck me."

Seth didn't need to be asked twice. Still supporting her weight with one arm, he reached the other between them to free his hard length from his pants. Without pausing, he slammed her down onto his cock, groaning at the hot, tight feel of her cunt closing around him. He needed better leverage…

Holding Devora impaled, Seth turned to the wall and pressed her against it. Then he started pounding in and out of her with a series of powerful strokes, leaving both of them gasping for breath. The pressure was almost unbearable now, and he could feel his orgasm building. He wanted her to come, too. Pulling her legs further apart, Seth surged into her moist opening, deliberately stroking against her clit each time.

Within less than a minute, she was panting loudly, and he could feel the spasms building around his dick. Then she came, squeezing him repeatedly with her inner muscles, milking him with her cunt.

He exploded with pleasure, shouting without words. Then his legs gave out and they ended up on the floor, nestled in the pillows.

They didn't speak immediately afterwards, they were both too exhausted. Instead, they laid back on the pillows and gasped for air. For one of the first times in his adult life, Seth didn't feel like the pressure was already building to fuck again. He was actually somewhat satisfied. He would have her again, he mused–he was definitely going to take the contract–but for the moment he was content to rest. The closest he'd ever come to such satisfaction before was with the little slave, Calla. She'd made him so angry, though, that as soon as she'd left he'd been frustrated and horny again. He'd wanted something, needed something after that, but Devora seemed to be enough for now.

A quiet sound caught his attention. Next to him, Devora had fallen asleep, and to his amusement she emitted a soft, snuffling snore. She looked younger, less sophisticated, asleep...adorable. He liked the idea of her sleeping at his side. He'd never been one to sleep with him women, preferring to take his pleasure then return to his own quarters; it was less complicated that way.

But this woman he wanted hold, to feel her skin next to his. With amusement, he realized that he had just had the most satisfying sexual experience of his life, yet he was still fully clothed. Gently disengaging himself from Devora's side, Seth quickly pulled his shirt over his head, then kicked off his shoes and pants as quietly as possible. He would have liked to undress Devora, too, but she was so peaceful and comfortable looking that he couldn't bear to disturb her. Instead, he settled down on the pillows next to her, and she cuddled into the curve of his body instinctively. Pulling her close, he contented himself to smell her hair and reach each hand down between the filmy layers of her dress until he reached bare skin. One hand moved to her breast, clasping it possessively while the other drifted between her legs. Soft curls wrapped around his fingers and Devora gave a contented murmur. A smile came over his face. Even in her sleep she was responsive to him.

Holding her was so comforting, so right that within minutes he was on the verge of sleep. Devora was the best discovery he'd made in a long time. Of course it wouldn't last, relationships with women who were non-Saurellian never could, but keeping Devora around for a while would be well worth the money. With that thought, Seth drifted into a contented sleep.

Chapter 4

"I'm glad you and Devora find yourselves compatible," Dani said, smiling broadly at Seth. She sat behind an elegant little desk in the House of Lilies' small business office. "She tells me you're interested in a contract after all. Shall we go over the details?"

Seth sat across from her, less concerned with the contract than getting his hands back on Devora. He'd awakened to find her gone. Dani had been waiting instead, contract in hand. She seemed to know that things had gone well. Hell, for all he knew she'd watched. The idea didn't appeal to him; next time he and Devora met, it would be in a more private setting.

"Now, I've set this up as a standard personal contract, but there are some special conditions due to conflicts with Devora's schedule. It's my understanding that you plan to leave the station at the end of the week?" Dani asked, one eyebrow cocked questioningly.

"Yes," he said shortly. He wished Dani would stop talking and just hand over the paperwork. He didn't have time for this.

"That's perfect," Dani replied with a serene smile. "Devora finishes her current contract in six days. The timing couldn't be better."

Her words hit like a punch to the stomach. Devora's *current* contract? An icy rage washed over him. Devora was *his*. He couldn't stand the thought of her having previous clients, but for all he knew she was fucking some man at this very minute. It was intolerable. He couldn't allow this to happen–he wasn't going to let another man touch her. Ever.

The ferocity of his thoughts startled him. Why should he care if she slept with another man? After all, she was a pleasure worker; it was her job to give pleasure to whoever paid for her services.

The very idea made him cold.

"Unacceptable," he told Dani in a grim voice. "Her other contract must be terminated immediately. When I leave today I'm taking her with me."

His answer seemed to startle Dani, who frowned at him.

"Seth, I can tell you're very interested in Devora, but she has obligations. She simply isn't available to start her contract until you leave the station," she said.

"I want her now," he replied, eyes hardening. "She's coming back to the hostel with me tonight. This is not negotiable."

"Seth, I'm so very sorry, but Devora is not available to return to the hostel with you this evening," she said unblinkingly. The grim countenance that had frightened a thousand imperial soldiers was having no effect on her. "Devora is extremely interested in making this contract with you work, but she isn't going to be able to join you until you start your trip. If you can't agree to this, then I'm afraid Devora will need to break off contract negotiations."

Seth had always liked Dani, but the time had come to put her in her place. He was commander of Discovery station, and he would be taking Devora home with him.

"I do not wish to do this to you, Dani," he said tightly. "But I am the military ruler of this station. My forces occupy every corridor, and I am ordering you to hand over Devora or face the consequences. They will not be pleasant."

Dani stiffened, placing the contract carefully on the table. She didn't reply for moment. Then, carefully folding her hands neatly on the desk in front of her, she said, "Seth, I feel it is my duty to remind you that not only am I pleasure worker negotiating a contract for Devora, I am a fully licensed member of the Pleasure Guild. You may not realize this, but Guild Houses such as this one are not merely places of business. They are sovereign Guild territory, and enjoy full diplomatic immunity. At this point in time, the Guild and the Saurellian Federation enjoy a relationship based on mutual respect and understanding. This relationship may be jeopardized if you choose to forcefully remove a woman from Guild premises without Guild support. Is this something you really wish to do?"

Her expression didn't change, but her eyes had become as hard as his had. Seth was livid.

"Don't play these games with me, Dani," he said coldly. "I'm better at them than you are, and you could get hurt."

"It's not about me, anymore," Dani said tightly. "This is about diplomatic immunity and Guild sovereignty. To date, the Guild has not opted to take sides in your little conflict with the Empire. We find that neutrality is better for business. Once you breach that neutrality, we could change our minds. I think you're too good a commander to allow that to happen over something as unimportant as a *personal* pleasure contract."

She had him, Seth realized. He could easily tear apart the house to find Devora, but doing so would be criminally irresponsible if it drove a wedge between the Saurellian High Council and the Guild. There was no justification for allowing his private battle to hurt his people.

Nodding tightly in agreement, Seth stood up so abruptly that his chair fell back. Dani wasn't as cool as she pretended, he noticed with dark satisfaction. The sound made her jump; her folded hands clenched in tension.

"I'll leave, but I'm warning you that if I find Devora off Guild property I'm taking her," he said. "And you might want to warn her other client that if I find out who he is, he's mine. Tell him it's in his best interests to stay away from her. Send the contract to my office. I'll want full control of her when I leave at the end of the week—there won't be any vacation and there won't be any time off. Money is not an issue."

With that, he turned and stalked out of the office, slamming the door behind him. Dani let out the breath she held with a mixture of relief and trepidation. Seth was taking the contract far more seriously than she ever imagined. Calla might be in trouble.

* * * * *

Seth kept his promise.

Within an hour of his leaving, guards were posted at every door of the House of Lilies. Every visitor was scrutinized carefully, his entry and exits recorded in a log.

With Dani's assistance, Devora made a formal request for temporary asylum to the House manager and governing council, which was approved on the understanding that she would leave within a week. Seth struck back. He made a formal request that she be held under house arrest, and barred from receiving any guests or visitors who were not Guild members.

It was a condition that Calla and Dani agreed to readily. The last thing Calla wanted was more attention, and her little room in the House of Lilies provided far more comfort than she'd ever experienced during her life as a slave. At Dani's suggestion, she spent her time preparing for her trip, compiling data on everything from Imperial legal codes to star maps and cultural histories of a thousand planets on a small computer tablet. She and Jess would need the information to plan their new lives, assuming she ever found him.

She also shopped using the terminal in her room. It was a difficult process, because Dani was almost completely out of funds by then. Fortunately, she had the credits Jess had been hiding in the storeroom. It wasn't much money, and she had to be careful to select clothes costly enough to keep Seth from becoming suspicious about her origins. Dani had a few things that might work but she was bigger than Calla, and neither woman was skilled enough to make alterations. Calla finally decided on a mix-and-match wardrobe of attractively-cut yet sturdy tunics, pants and skirts. They flattered her figure without being too overtly sexual–the mark of an amateur, according to Dani.

To add a little spice, Dani selected a variety of lingerie that made Calla blush. Everything from a silken, white dressing gown that covered her fully to tiny black and lace garments that left nothing to the imagination.

"Remember," Dani told her during one shopping session. "The key is to keep him guessing. Every time he sees you, he should be wondering what he'll find under your clothes. Are you the virgin or the whore? Are you ready and naked or will he have to unwrap you slowly? It's a game to heighten the pleasure–make the most of it. Six months is a long time to entertain a man like that, so make your clothing work for you."

In the end, the week went by far too quickly for Calla. She had watched the recording of Dani's meeting with Seth, and she was nervous about seeing him again. He'd said "full control," something that had been emphasized in the contract negotiations that followed. Each time Dani sent over a contract, he'd send back revisions. "Devora" would be under contract for six, not three, months. She would have no personal leave during that time. She would be available to Seth all day, every day. She would be required to participate in any and all sexual acts he requested, no exceptions.

It was hardly standard, but he had all the power. Calla's Guild asylum would end in a week, and then he would take her whether she had the protection of a contract or not. At least with a contract there would be a substantial sum of money waiting for her in a Guild escrow account in six months. She'd be off station, she'd be free and she'd have enough money to set herself up somewhere. Calla figured that whatever those six months held would be worth it, especially if she could find Jess.

Dani was less comfortable with the situation. Seth had her followed day and night. Her apartment had been seized and searched twice, and her Saurellian customers were avoiding her. She was used to being appreciated by men, not punished.

* * * * *

On the day Seth was supposed to come and pick up Calla, Dani felt like a mother hen losing her chick. Despite Calla's reassurances, she paced back and forth in the small House of Lilies parlor where they sat. Finally Calla actually grasped her by the shoulders, forced her to sit down and brought her a glass of fortified wine.

"Dani, I can never thank you for all you've done for me," Calla said, gazing into her friend's eyes with affection. She hated the thought of Dani worrying about her. "You've risked so much to help me, and I'm ready for whatever happens on this trip."

"But honey, you need to understand this isn't a normal contract," Dani burst out, momentarily losing her composure. "You're going to have to protect yourself. This man is obsessed with you, far beyond what's normal! You've got to be careful, because this kind of thing can get ugly. Do you understand what I'm telling you?"

"I'm not sure that I do," Calla said carefully, trying to gage Dani's meaning. "But whatever it is, I can handle it."

"Really?" Dani asked spiritedly. "Do you realize that men sometimes beat private contractors? There have even been murders! Usually you're pretty safe going through the Guild, because we take contract violations very seriously. If this guy hurts you, we'll find him and make him pay, that's just good business. But that won't bring you back. You've got to be careful."

"Dani, I understand that there are risks, and I also understand that this isn't the kind of contract we'd hoped it would be," Calla replied with feeling. "This would be a terrible contract for you, but it's more than I'd ever dreamed could happen to me. You need to understand that.

"Remember, I was born on an imperial slave farm. It's not like I lost my mother. I never had one. I'm the product of synthetically created human egg cells. Do you understand what that means? Do you understand how many religions don't even consider me to be human? When I was at the hostel, Jenner could beat me any time she wanted. She could sell me to whoever she wanted, whenever she wanted. She could even kill me and no one could complain!

"I lost my crèche-brother because he was a slave. Do you know what it means to be raised in the same crèche?" Calla continued bitterly. "Fifty infants were born–expelled–from incubators on the same day. We were placed in one room, tended by two slave nurses who had raised a thousand others like us. Thirty-five of us survived the first year... it was a higher survival rate than usual. They were very pleased with us."

"Oh, Calla," Dani said. She was at a loss for words–she had never heard Calla's story before, had no idea where slaves came from. She had always just assumed they were born to slave parents and were raised like other children. It was an ugly truth to confront .

"The nurses left when we were five, and we started our training," Calla continued, her face wooden. "We were moved into a training camp. We spent all day, every day learning to be excellent slaves. We learned how to work, we had obedience conditioning–I wouldn't have been able to even *think* about escaping if Jenner had been more regular about keeping up the conditioning sessions–and we learned not to care about each other. At night we were at the mercy of the older slaves... the oldest were only ten-year-olds, but they were twice our size, and they were hard from living in the camp for five years.

"Jess protected me," Calla said, the pitch of her voice raising slightly. "I was small for my age, a natural target. Somehow he was always there, always taking care of me when things got rough. Sometimes he got in trouble for it, but he managed not to get in enough trouble to make the termination list..."

"T-t-termination list?" Dani asked in a horrified whisper.

"Well," Calla said in a matter-of-fact voice, "If a child caused a problem, they would cull them out and terminate them whether it was that child's fault or not. If you complained, that was causing a problem. Trust me, it's an extremely efficient way to keep the peace. Those kids were willing to do a lot to keep someone like Jess from bringing trouble down on them. He did terrible things to keep us alive."

"I had no idea," Dani said, tears building in her eyes. No wonder the Guild wouldn't allow members to own slaves.

"When we were ten, our entire crèche was sold in one lot to a broker," Calla continued. "He had been taking orders throughout the mining field, and since Jess and I were born in incubators next to each other, we had sequential identification numbers. That's the only reason we ended up together at Jenner's."

Calla looked up at Dani with a soft, mocking smile.

"It was easier for the accountant to give us to her, it made the books look tidy. That's all we were, numbers in a book."

"Calla, I don't know what to say," Dani whispered after a second. "I didn't realize…"

"Few people do realize," Calla said harshly. "Besides, I wasn't even conceived. I'm not even human. Why should it matter?"

Dani just sat there, trying to digest what she'd heard. She had known there were slave farms, had guessed they were awful places. She never approved of slavery, never owned slaves… but she had friends who did. With horror, Dani thought of the times she'd been served by a slave in a restaurant. How many of her clothes had been made by slaves? Public slaves cleaned the streets and corridors of most communities where she'd lived. How many times had she carelessly dropped a food wrapper? Not often, but enough.

"So you see," Calla continued. "I'm not actually that afraid any more of what Seth might do to me. I am afraid of things. I'm afraid of the asteroid field, I'm afraid I'll get caught, and I'm afraid that I'll never find Jess. I'm even afraid of Seth. But I'm tired of living in fear. I got soft at Jenner's hostel–she was actually a pretty good mistress. She fed us and she was too cheap to pay for obedience conditioning. In fact, she was so good to us that we forgot she could get rid of us. Jess wanted to escape but I talked him out of it. I was wrong, Dani. We should have gone while we could. If I can't find Jess, I'll never forgive myself."

Tears were pouring out of Dani's eyes, running down her cheeks and even dripping on her beautiful silk tunic. She dropped her head in her hands, overwhelmed by Calla's story. Calla seemed unmoved, carefully picking a small piece of lint off the elegant yet practical traveling outfit she wore. Her hand shook, though, and Dani realized she was not as calm as she appeared.

"Dani," Calla said after a second. "It's almost time for me to go. I don't want our last moments together to be sad. I don't know if I'll ever see you again, but if I make it I'll send you a letter to let you know."

Dani pulled herself together. Calla was right. This was no way to say goodbye; realistically, they might never see each other again.

"I can never thank you enough for what you've done for me," Calla said, then stood and held her arms out to her friend. The two women embraced for several minutes without talking. Dani, the taller, rested her head against Calla's, wishing they had more time. Calla had become far more than a friend, she realized. This was like losing a family member. The past few weeks had brought them closer than many people would get in a lifetime. There was a soft knock at the door, and the house manager stuck her head in.

"Your client is here, Devora," she said, looking at the younger woman with sympathy. Devora had made friends during her brief stay at the house; they were all concerned about her.

Dani put both her hands on Calla's shoulders and looked deeply into her eyes. Then, her voice breaking, she whispered, "Whatever anyone ever tells you, you're just as much a beautiful, strong and fully human person as anyone else–I've known that from the day I met you. Don't believe what Jenner told you, and don't be afraid to go out and take what you deserve."

Calla pulled away from Dani's embrace, and wiped her eyes. Then she straightened herself resolutely and pulled a light veil down over her face. Dani handed Calla a satchel. A larger trunk–filled with her new clothing–had already been sent ahead to Seth's ship.

"Goodbye," she said briefly, then turned away from Dani. She stepped out of the room and walked over to where Seth stood, glowering at her. His face was grim, and he had several armed guards with him. He watched Calla, fingers flexing with anger, then turned his attention to Dani.

"I won't forget this," he said, flaying her with his eyes. His hands clenched again, and for a second Dani was worried he might break into violence right then and there. Poor Calla deserved better than this, she thought. She'd failed her friend with this contract–Seth was a madman.

When Calla reached his side, he reached out for her satchel. After a second's consideration, she handed it to him. He passed it to one of his men, then placed one hand at the small of Calla's back to guide her. The implication was clear–'Devora' was his. As they left the House of Lilies, the only thing giving Dani any hope for Calla was the fact that his touch had seemed gentle.

With a sigh, Dani allowed herself to sink into a chair and dropped her head back. It was over; there was nothing more she could do. Tension flowed out of her, and she realized she was shaking. It was time for a vacation, she though wearily. And then perhaps a new work placement. She was sick and tired of Discovery station.

* * * * *

Calla's last trip through the station was a blur of excitement and trepidation. After seventeen years of slavery, she was finally free. All she had to do was make it out of the station unrecognized. Given the contingent of warriors surrounding her, that probably wouldn't be a problem.

Seth had a transport waiting, which deposited them at his ship within five minutes of leaving the House of Lilies. The ship–only briefly visible to Calla through a porthole in the station's bulkhead–was small and light. The kind used by smugglers. There wouldn't be much room on board, she realized. His men must not be going with them. That was all right with her. The last thing she wanted was to have to service another man if Seth got tired of her.

"Your things are already in the sleeping room," he said, firmly guiding her into the ship. She could feel the tension in his arm, though he remained gentle. "As you can see, it's small. There's the cockpit, an all-purpose room and galley, the sleeping chamber and some cargo space. Stay out of the cockpit unless I tell you otherwise."

With that, Seth turned away from her and entered some numbers in the portal control panel. The little light over the door went from green to red, and Calla could hear internal pumps clearing the air out of the airlock. They were really leaving the station. She could hardly believe it!

"Can I watch as we leave?" she asked excitedly. She had all but forgotten he was angry with her. Seth looked at her with surprise; such enthusiasm wasn't something he'd expected.

"Very well," he said after a second. It wouldn't harm anything, and while he was still upset with her for refusing to come with him earlier, she was his now. He could afford to give her this. "The cockpit is up the ladder. Go stow your things in the sleeping room, then join me there."

Nodding, Calla all but ran through the all-purpose room toward two small doors on the other side. She looked back at him questioningly, wondering which one she should use. With a gesture, he indicated the door on the left. The other must lead to the cargo area, she concluded.

The sleeping area was not what she'd expected, since at the hostel she had cleaned his room many times. There had been nothing personal there, but this was different. Clearly he had lived on this ship for a long time, because there were pictures littering the walls. Setting down her satchel, Calla examined one closely. There was a man who looked somewhat like Seth, with a woman and three little boys. Seth's brother? She wondered.

There were quite a few pictures of children in the room, she realized, looking around more carefully. Several were of the boys in various stages of growth. There were also colorful drawings, clearly the work of a child. One showed a large house, with two suns shining down on it. Another was a picture of a woman holding a baby. In large, scrawling print across the bottom was the name "Tasha." Next to the drawing was a photo of the little girl. She looked about six months old, and she was smiling beautifully for the holo-cam. The fearless warrior had a loving family back home, Calla thought. Somehow it made him seem more human.

A vibration went through the floor beneath her feet. Seth was powering up the drive; it was time to get up to the cockpit.

Calla made her way back through the main room then pulled herself up the ladder to the cockpit. She noticed a series of handholds along the way, and wondered if the ship was big enough to have artificial gravity generators. The only other time she'd been in space was when she'd come from the slave farm. There was no gravity for that flight, and the experience had been hideous. She'd never forget the sounds and smells of thirty children vomiting for days.

Pulling herself into the cockpit, Calla gazed around in excitement. Seth was seated in a comfortable-looking chair in front of the main computer. There was a large view screen in front of him, but it was covered by a set of metal plates for the moment. Turning briefly, he gestured to the chair beside him.

"You'll want to strap yourself in," he said without looking at her. "It shouldn't be rough, but it's usually about five minutes before the internal gravity comes on line."

He was being extremely civilized about things, Calla thought as she strapped herself in. Dani had overreacted. She wasn't in any danger from Seth.

It took him several minutes to run through his pre-flight checkout. Once it was completed, he tabbed the com panel and asked the station's flight control for clearance. The flight controller gave it to him and with a flick of a finger he pressed a button to open the panels covering the screen.

Calla gasped with surprise and pleasure at the vista unfolding before her.

It wasn't a view screen after all, she realized, it was actually a window onto space. To one side she could see the mass of the station's exterior bulkheads stretching away from them. All around were ships, and in the distance she could the faint outline of an enormous ore-transport at one of the free-floating processing plants. She had lived on the station most of her life, but she'd never personally seen the commerce that gave it life. Vid screens weren't the same, she realized. What else would she see on this trip?

Trying to act casual, as if this was nothing new to her, Calla asked Seth, "Are we going to light speed, or are you planning to use the standard drive for now?"

Seth looked at her curiously. He thought everyone knew you couldn't use a warp drive in an asteroid field; it was simply too dangerous, not to mention overkill. But then again, she was a pampered pleasure contractor who probably never had to worry about transportation. She had clients to take care of that for her, he thought with a spark of disgust.

"We'll be using the standard drive," he said curtly.

Okay, he doesn't want to talk to me right now, Calla thought. That was fine–he might still be angry, but she wasn't going to let it get in the way of enjoying this experience.

The vibrations running through the hull increased in pitch, then with a click they broke free of the station and the vibrations eased. Seth eased forward with a small control stick.

Calla realized he was manually guiding them. She'd thought computers would do all that.

As if reading her thoughts, Seth spoke. "I like the feel of the ship under me," he said softly. "She's small enough that I can feel every motion, every change in tempo. Sometimes she's touchy, and I can handle her better than any computer program."

The sound of his voice, low and smooth, sent a chill through Calla's spine. He spoke like the ship was his lover. She wondered if he would ever speak about her that way, then mentally kicked herself for the thought. She had to keep her priorities straight: Seth was a Saurellian. He wouldn't stay interested in her for any length of time. Dani had told her time and again not to allow herself to get attached to him. Their futures were too far apart for anything other than sex.

The ship was moving through the traffic now, joining a ragged line of other ships, transports, and even the occasional cruiser headed toward the belt. After about half an hour they had cleared the worst of the traffic. Seth switched on the autopilot, then pulled up a course-plot on the holo-projector.

"We're headed to mining outpost 12563 first," he said, pointing to a small dot on the chart. "It's here, in the alpha quadrant of the field. It should take us about three days to get there."

Turning the projector off with a click, he turned to face her.

"So, how are we going to pass the time, Devora?" he asked, inspecting her slowly from the tips of her small feet to her carefully groomed hair. His voice was low and smooth, and his eyes flashed with desire. He licked his lips, and smiled as Calla shivered in response. He was a predator, and she knew instinctively that she was the prey. "Any suggestions?"

Chapter 5

The question hung in the air between them.

"Well, I suppose there are a number of things we could do," Calla finally said, unable to bear the silence any longer. "I'm here to serve you. What would you like?"

"Why don't you show me what you have to offer?" he said, gesturing languidly toward her small frame. His gaze moved across her body in a mixture of lust and something else, making her feel naked under his stare. "Unless you want to talk? We could discuss your refusal to start your contract until now."

The *something else* was definitely anger, Calla realized. She had to distract him quickly, before things got out of control.

"I'd rather show you what I have to offer," she said, purring sensuously. Turning her chair to face him, she pulled off her veil and shook out her long, brown hair. It was nothing special, but with Dani's help she'd put in some soft highlights. Seth failed to respond, but Calla decided she just needed to take things a little further. Kicking off her shoes, Calla raised one foot delicately and rested it on his lap. Then she leaned back in her chair and started unbuttoning her dress slowly.

Seth still wasn't giving her any kind of reaction, but as she reached the buttons over her breasts she felt a stirring against her foot. She continued unbuttoning, allowing the dress to gape open nearly to her waist. The movement exposed the silken black undergarments she'd put on that morning, another gift from Dani. The bulge of Seth's manhood against her foot was growing as she rubbed it with her toes. Then she reached down inside her dress to her clit, rubbing herself sensuously with one hand. The other cupped a breast through the black fabric of her lacy camisole.

Calla saw the pained look Seth had on his face, but she couldn't get him to say anything. Apparently he had decided to make her life difficult because she'd held out on the contract, Calla thought. She knew he was aroused. She could feel the evidence against her foot. She was just going to have to work for her money; that was all right, she was grateful for the opportunity. She'd make sure he got what he paid for.

She gave one last sinuous stroke to his hard length, then removed her foot slowly and stood in front of him. Slipping her dress off her shoulders, she allowed it to fall to the floor. Kicking it away, she deliberately squeezed her breasts before running her hands down the length of her body to her clit. Working her swelling flesh gently through the fabric, she leaned over and kissed his mouth with closed lips.

Dropping slowly to her knees, Calla ran her hands lightly from his shoulders across his chest, enjoying the tight sensation of his clenching muscles. He was far from unaffected, she thought with satisfaction. He wanted her, regardless of how angry he might be.

His stomach was hard and muscular under her hands, and the bulge in his pants leapt in response to her touch. Leaning over, she started giving his belly delicate kisses through the light fabric. His thighs clenched, and almost involuntarily his hand reached down to grasp the back of her head. He pressed her down further. With a knowing smile, she complied.

His cock was rigid under the fabric of his pants, straining desperately for freedom. Resting either arm on his thighs, Calla sat back on her legs and gave it a light kiss through his pants. His entire body jerked at the sensation, and his hand pressed her closer. Molding her mouth around the fabric, Calla gently engulfed as much of the head as she could. She could feel it pulse against her as she started softly sucking. Then she grasped the rest of his length with her hand, massaging it in time with her mouth.

Seth strained against her, as if he would shove his penis directly through the fabric and into her mouth. The cloth of the pants was too strong for him, though. Calla increased the tempo of her motions, sucking and working him harder with her hand. He started moving against her rhythmically. His breath was coming quickly now; his thighs had turned to steel under the strain of his arousal. Calla paused for a moment, thinking to open his pants and pull out his erection, but the cessation of movement was too much for him.

He pulled her mouth back down over the now-damp fabric roughly, straining himself up at her. The hand at the back of her head kept the rhythm with her as his hips thrust against her warm opening.

Following his direction, Calla kept moving and he started moaning. She could tell he was close to coming despite the fact that she had yet to touch his bare flesh. The realization was empowering–as long as she could give him this kind of pleasure her position would be secure. She redoubled her efforts.

Seth groaned loudly in response, bucking his hips. He ground Calla's face against his cock, and his cock jerked beneath her mouth. Then he crushed her against him so tightly she could barely breath, and a warm liquid started soaking through the cloth; Seth had come without even removing his pants.

A heady combination of satisfaction and arousal coursed through her at the realization.

Dropping his head back for a moment, Seth cradled her head against his still hard cock. He encouraged her to continue her ministrations for a few seconds, then watched as she raised herself slightly to rest her cheek against his stomach. His hands held her gently to him. His release had helped with his anger.

"I'm sorry about that," he said, rubbing his fingers against her scalp absently. "I haven't come in my pants since I was 13 years old. I don't know what came over me. Next time it will be better."

"It's fine," Calla said softly. "We've got plenty of time, remember? Just a few minutes ago you asked me what we should be doing with all that time." She dropped one hand to his penis, which still bulged noticeably. Rubbing it softly, she felt it harden. She watched Seth shift, allowing her more access.

After a second, he said, "Let's go down where there's more room. I think we need to finish this."

Rising to her feet, Calla picked up her clothing and started to put it on.

"Don't worry about that," he said quietly. His voice was low and smooth, dancing across her spine. Calla shivered in anticipation. He may have reached satisfaction, but she was still restless with arousal. The molten look in his dark eyes promised she would have her own release before long.

Dressed only in the black silk, she made her way down the ladder. Seth followed her, and they walked slowly across to the sleeping chamber. Once inside, Calla turned to him for direction, uncertain what he expected from her.

He stood there, gazing up at her for several seconds. It was nerve-wracking. Finally he spoke. "This time is for you, Devora," he said. "We'll go slow, because I want to give you as much pleasure as you just gave me."

The thought of him giving her pleasure was delicious. Calla smiled at him tentatively, waiting.

Seth walked up to her and reached both arms around her. Pulling her into the circle of his embrace, he dropped his head and gave her a soft, slow kiss. His lips felt like little butterflies dancing over hers, gentle and light. She leaned into him, looking to deepen the kiss, but he pulled back. "Slow..." he reminded her. "Let's make it last this time." Dropping his head again, he gave her another long kiss, then moved his lips across her cheek to her ear. He could tell that the little nibbles that followed tickled as he felt her giggle. Sensing a vulnerability, he quickly moved his fingers against her sides, and she squirmed, laughing.

"Ticklish, are we?" he asked, burrowing his mouth against her neck. "I'll have to remember that." His hands stilled as he started kissing her again. First her neck, then down to her shoulder, dropping small caresses along her shoulder. His hot breath against her skin made her shiver, and he gave a quiet chuckle of pleasure at her response to his touch.

Calla's breath quickened as he continued his slow journey downwards. His mouth reached her breast, and then he started suckling her nipple through the silk. Tendrils of sensation ran through her, and she felt a tightening between her legs. Shifting herself restlessly, she pressed against his mouth.

Seth moved his tongue to the other breast, laving it for nearly a minute before working down toward her belly. Somewhere along the way he had dropped to his knees, although both arms were still wrapped around her waist, loosely holding her prisoner.

The feel of his lips against her belly button caused her to stiffen, as he lightly flicked his tongue into it. The sensation made her laugh, and she twisted against him, trying half-heartedly to get away. He grinned up at her, and she was struck by how boyish he appeared. She had never seen him look anything but harsh, or angry. Now it was as if a weight had been lifted off his shoulders; his mood was lighter, more playful. She liked this new version of Seth. Unable to help herself, she dropped a quick kiss on his nose. It startled him, but she could tell he liked it.

Seth gave her a funny little smile, then started working down her stomach again.

As he approached the cleft of her legs, Calla felt her knees growing unsteady. He'd never touched her like this; she liked it, but it also made her feel tense and restless. The feeling grew as his tongue found her clit, lapping at the small nub through the black fabric. Calla twisted against him as the feeling grew. She could feel herself becoming wetter in anticipation. He was torturing her–she needed more. Moaning pleadingly, she reached into his thick hair with both hands, trying to drag his head back up. Either that, or make his tongue move faster…

Seth resisted her touch, continuing his slow stimulation of her most sensitive spot.

The pressure rose in her, and she shifted from foot to foot, holding on to Seth tightly for balance. "Oh, that's too much," she gasped out faintly. "Seth, I can't take this anymore. I need you now."

His only answer was to quicken his pace. Both of his hands dropped from her waist, pulling her more firmly against him as his palms rested on the smooth curves of her bottom. His tongue delved deeply into her folds, the soft silk of her undergarment easily conforming to his motions.

Calla's legs sagged slightly, and she was leaning heavily on his shoulders for support. It had to be uncomfortable for him but he never paused in his attack on her clit.

The pressure was building. Waves of need and lust coursed through her, and she bit her lip to keep from screaming at him to do something to make it end. She was going to explode from the pressure. Each time her orgasm almost hit, his tongue would slow ever so slightly until she started panting heavily. Eventually, he seemed to decide she'd had enough, and started moving his tongue more quickly. Alternating between suction and motion, he all but commanded her to come under the caress of his tongue and lips. Just when she thought she would die from need, pleasure rushed through her and she stiffened in the throes of her climax. Her body seemed to dissolve, and the room darkened around the corners of her vision.

She came back to reality to find herself sagging in Seth's arms. He was standing again, supporting her weight easily. His look was one of smug satisfaction, although she could tell from the bulge of his erection against her stomach that he was painfully aroused.

"That was fantastic," she said softly, wrapping her arms around him. His body, solid and warm, seemed to stabilize her. After a second, she rubbed experimentally against his hips. He responded in kind.

"Shall we move to the bed?" he asked after a moment's silence. "We still haven't done this the traditional way, you know."

Calla laughed at the strained tone in his voice.

"That sounds like a wonderful idea," she said, gazing up at him with joy. They exchanged another long kiss.

"Devora, you're so beautiful," he said, eyes tracing the contours of her face.

"So are you," she answered, holding out both arms. He laughed at her response, then caught her up in his arms and carried her over to his bed. Cradled against his body, Calla wrapped her arms tightly around his neck. When he tried to lay her down on the bed, she refused to let him go, preferring to pull him down on top of her. With a smile, he complied, sprawling across her small form before taking her mouth in a series of kisses that drove everything else from her mind.

His mouth was powerful, his tongue thrusting intimately into the recesses of her mouth possessively. He was careful to balance the bulk of his weight on his arms, yet his sheer size pinned her down into the bed.

She realized at that moment that she was completely in Seth's power, yet she wasn't afraid. He had been angry and frustrated earlier, but even then he hadn't taken it out on her. Being with him was a beautiful, wonderful thing, she thought. She wouldn't have him forever, but he was hers, right this minute. The sensation was heady and beautiful. This magnificent man–hers, however temporarily–was on top of her, and he wanted her body.

She could feel his aroused length pulsing with need as Seth shifted against her, pressing his hips against hers. An answering, agonizing twinge leapt through her as he pushed her legs apart with one knee, settling himself between them. They kissed deep, and Calla arched her body against his, grinding her aching cunt against his hard cock.

"We have on too many clothes," Seth gasped out, wrenching his mouth away from hers. "I want to feel your skin against mine."

Together they stood, each ripping their clothes off as quickly as possible. Even those few seconds apart from Seth's body were too much for Calla. As soon as he was nude, she threw herself at him, knocking him back on the bed. He landed with a grunt, and for one second she thought she'd hurt him. Then he gave a growl of hunger, and rolled her beneath him so quickly it took her breath away.

Within seconds he was poised at her hot entrance, and she squirmed against him, ready for penetration. Then he paused, staring down in to her face. He heard her moan in protest, but he refused to move. The effort cost him greatly, the muscle in his jaw twitched with strain, but he didn't move. Finally, he spoke.

"Devora, I want to see the look on your face as you come," he whispered harshly. "I want you to forget all your other clients, every other man in your life, and think only of me. You're mine, and at this moment I want to be in you more than I've ever wanted anything in my entire life. Do you want me?"

"Yes," Devora gasped. "Please, come into me. I want you, Seth, I need you right now."

With a cry of triumph, Seth surged into her, slamming his entire length into her waiting channel.

The movement was so hard it felt as if he might come right up through her throat. Calla screamed as sensation surged through her, orgasming wildly around him. Her legs gripped his waist with all her strength, and she held tightly to his massive frame as he pounded into her.

Seth's movements gained speed as he approached his own pleasure. He captured her mouth with his, plundering her depths with his tongue even as he thrust, as he forced her to feel another orgasm building. He shifted his weight slightly, allowing his penis to scrape along her clit more fully each time he came into her. He could feel her entire body jerk in response.

The sensation was unbearable. For one horrible minute she thought she'd die from the pressure. Then she exploded again, and he came with her. Locked together in each other's arms, they shared their pleasure, hearts pounding.

After several minutes, Seth rolled to his back, carrying her with him. They were still joined, although he had softened somewhat. With a sigh, she nestled her head against his neck. One of his hands cradled her, fingers running through her hair, and Calla slept.

Twice more in the night he awakened her, each time already hard within her channel. Barely moving, they made love sleepily. By the second time, neither of them came. Instead, they cuddled together while joined at the sex, and kissed languidly.

The sensation of his hands massaging her back gently eventually lulled Calla back to sleep, where she dreamt of being safe and warm for the first time in her life.

* * * * *

Seth awoke well-rested.

A movement against his side startled him, and for a moment he tensed, automatically preparing himself for battle. Then memory came back. Devora was with him in bed, the woman he'd hired to travel with him. A brief flash of anger threatened his composure as he wondered how many other men she'd traveled with, but he tamped it back down. It wasn't as if she'd lied to him about her profession, and he certainly hadn't come into their contract a virgin. He needed to focus on enjoying her, he told himself firmly.

And he *was* enjoying her. She was nestled trustingly into the crook of his arm, exhausted from their workout. Seth smiled at the memory–by their final encounter both had been too exhausted to orgasm, something he'd never experienced before. Instead he'd simply held her in his arms for hours, content to luxuriate in the bond that seemed to be between them. She felt so *right* in his arms...

That bond puzzled Seth, though. He'd never felt as close to a woman as Devora. He'd certainly never had such amazing sex, but it was more than that. With a sense of disbelief, he acknowledged to himself that she seemed to fill the hunger within him that was always present; the same hunger that had driven him from his Saurellian homeworld.

Like every young man of his people, he'd searched for his life mate back home. Once it became clear he wasn't one of the lucky few to have one, he'd left. It was too painful to watch other men with their women, their families. He hadn't even been able to stand his own brother's company, although he enjoyed the pictures the family sent him. Nothing had been able to touch the ache inside of him until Devora, he realized. For one second his heart leapt in hope–could she be his lifemate? Was she actually Saurellian?

Seth turned her head to his, studying her features carefully. His heart fell, and a small, mocking part of his brain chided him for his foolishness. Devora couldn't be Saurellian. No Saurellian woman had ever been as short as she was, let alone freckled with brown hair. The women of his race were tall, with translucent skin and dark hair. They bred true, generation after generation, sharing common features and an uncanny ability to communicate with the Goddess. Legend held that they had been created in Her form to serve as Her priestesses.

No, he thought sadly, his relationship with little Devora couldn't last. The troubling image of the slave, Calla, rose again in his head. She had made him feel this way, too. When he'd heard that her tracer had been found in the recycling pit, he'd felt a sadness that went beyond compassion for the death of a young woman. Two women had touched him within a span of weeks. Perhaps he was losing his mind, he mused.

Devora snuggled more closely against him, snuffling softly in her sleep and interrupting his thoughts. He loved the feeling of her lying there, he realized. It felt right to hold her in his arms–almost as if he was complete. She assuaged his gnawing, restless hunger.

Devora opened her eyes, lifting her head to gaze at him. Giving him a sleepy smile, she said, "Hmmmm... maybe you could set the autopilot so the trip takes more than three days? I think I could get used to this."

"Sounds good to me," he said, chuckling at her. Her brown hair hung around her face in un-kept curls. Her almond-shaped eyes laughed back at him, and on an impulse he pulled her up onto his chest for a kiss. Their lips met for a long moment, and then she started rubbing herself sensuously against his morning erection. It was enough to make him gasp.

Allowing her knees to drop to either side of him, Calla reached down with one hand to guide his penis to her opening, sliding slowly down on him.

They kissed again, and his hands rose to her hips to guide her motions. The warm, slippery feel of her cunt enveloping his cock made him groan with pleasure. He couldn't get enough of her.

"I'll definitely have to reprogram our course," he said, grunting in time with her movements. "I think we should try to focus on doing this for a while. The miners can wait."

Part II: The Rock
Four Months Later

Chapter Six

There were butterflies all around her.

Calla lay in a field of green grass, warm and content. The sky above her was filled with bright, yellow sunlight, and in the distance she could hear the tinkling of a stream. Birds were singing and the butterflies seemed to dance in time to their song. Then birdsong gave way to the soft hum of the ship. Something delicate touched her–a butterfly? No, a finger traced her spine sensuously, and a voice spoke in her ear...

"Wake up, sleepy," the voice said. It was Seth whispering to her, his voice cool and dark. Calla stretched, enjoying the feel of his fingers running across her body. "Wake up, Devora. We'll be arriving soon."

Realizing the field was only a dream, Calla opened her eyes reluctantly. Seth was right, it was time to wake up. But her dream had been so pleasant–were planets really as beautiful as she imagined? Perhaps she would find out some day, she thought with a smile.

"What are you smiling about?" Seth asked huskily. He was lying beside her, running his hand up and down her back.

"I was having a lovely dream," Calla whispered, turning her face toward his.

"Mmmmm?" Seth replied, dropping little kisses along her shoulder.

"I was in a field, on a planet, and there were birds and butterflies all around," she explained. "In fact, when you first touched me, I thought you were a butterfly."

Seth gave her an indignant look.

"I was a butterfly?" he asked. "I don't think so."

"Oh, but you were," Calla replied, grinning at him wickedly. "Your fingers felt just like butterflies. Or at least they felt like I imagine butterflies would feel. I don't know that I've ever actually seen one in real life."

"I have," Seth said with amusement. "And I assure you, nothing about me could ever be mistaken for a butterfly. They're small, weak things. If you even touch their wings, they can't fly any more. I'd say you're more like a butterfly than I am," he added thoughtfully, eyeing her delicate bone structure in the cabin's dim light.

"Oh, really?" Calla replied with spirit. "I think you might be surprised by how strong I can be."

"I doubt it," Seth said, a grin playing around the corners of his mouth.

"Is that a challenge?" Calla asked.

"Maybe," Seth replied. "What are you suggesting?"

"Well, perhaps we should have a contest," she said. "A contest of strength and weakness...Winner takes all!"

Seth looked at her askance.

"Are you sure you want to do that?" he asked. "I hate to sound too confident, but I'm pretty sure I can beat you in a contest of strength."

"Not that kind of strength," Calla replied smartly. "I was thinking more about strength of will."

Seth cocked an eyebrow at her questioningly.

"And just how do you propose this contest of wills should take place?"

"Well," Calla said with a giggle. "I was thinking that maybe we could take turns tempting each other. Whoever gives in to temptation first wins."

"And you think you'll win this little game of temptation?" Seth asked, laughing back at her. "I'll have you know I'm a Saurellian warrior, not some sex-starved boy. You'll be begging me for release by the time I'm done."

"Will I?" Calla asked archly. "We'll just have to see. I'll start. Sit back on the bed and watch."

Seth followed her instructions, leaning back against the head-board. He had a smug look on his face, and for a moment Calla questioned whether her challenge had been a good idea. He had been acting so cocky she hadn't been able to resist, though. Taking a deep breath, she stood up and looked him in the eyes.

While he was fully clothed, she had been sleeping in the nude which proved a distinct disadvantage. It would be nice to start with a strip-tease, but that wouldn't be possible. She'd have to bring out the heavy artillery right away...

"Computer, turn the lights up by 50 percent," she said softly. "And soft music, something classical."

Gazing at him with all the longing she felt in his presence, she slowly lifted her hands and ran them loosely, through her hair. The curly locks fell around her body, partially obscuring her breasts. Then she stretched in slow pleasure, allowing herself to revel in the sensation of every muscle pulling and relaxing. Seth continued to watch her with amusement, although she detected a slight tightening of his features...

Turning away from him, Calla faced the mirror on the bedroom wall. He was clearly visible in it, just as her reflection was visible to him. Perfect, she thought. Reaching both hands up to her breasts, she started to massage them slowly, paying special attention to the stiffening peaks. She knew how much he loved the sight of her breasts, loved the feeling of those tight nubs against his chest. Now he could see them in the mirror, but just barely. Her hair provided a protective veil, and she shivered as a strand of hair grazed her nipple.

In the background, Seth shifted, raising one knee. Calla fought to hide her smile, then leaned her head back and shook out her hair. The reflection of her aroused breasts was now fully visible to him. She stretched once again, both arms over her head. Her breasts quivered at the movement. Still stretching, she leaned to one side and then the other, before allowing her body to drape forward from the waist. Resting both hands flat on the floor, she spread her legs slightly. The movement opened them to Seth's gaze, and she thought she heard his breath catch. She could feel his gaze on her exposed cunt.

"I find that stretching is important before any physical exertion," she said. "What do you think?"

"You're right," Seth said in a strained voice. "Stretching is important."

"I'm so glad we can agree," she replied. Then she moved one hand from its position on the floor and ran it up the inside of her leg experimentally. "That feels good," she whispered. "Does it look good, too?"

Seth didn't answer, so she ran the other hand up her leg, allowing her fingers to drift delicately over her flesh. A tingle of sensation followed each finger, and little trails of sparkling desire ran through her. Moisture gathered between her legs.

"This feels so good, I could just do it forever," she finally said. "But I think you probably need more of a show than that."

Seth watched with gritted teeth as Devora stood up, turning to face him. He was rock-hard in the flimsy jumpsuit he wore, although he had raised one knee to hide the evidence. Despite his confident words, he wanted her so badly that it took every ounce of strength to keep from grabbing her and rolling her body under his. Just the thought of thrusting into her hot, wet flesh made his cock leap, and he bit down a moan. Against his will, one hand drifted between his legs, grasping his hard length. It was exquisite, but nowhere near as good as Devora's flesh would feel.

She smiled broadly at him, then gently rested a finger on her mouth. Her lips were closed, but the finger pressed against them and after a second disappeared into the warm, wet opening. She drew it out again slowly, then opened her mouth and ran her tongue around the finger.

The night before she had done the same thing to his cock, licking and sucking at it like it was candy until he'd exploded like a rocket. His fingers squeezed his hard length restlessly in memory. Nothing was as hot as Devora's mouth, unless it was her cunt...

She seemed to read his mind, because her other hand dropped to the moist spot between her legs. One finger rubbed gently against her clit, and she shivered. Continuing to suck her finger, she pulled it deeply into her mouth, then allowed her cheeks to hollow with the suction as she slowly pulled it out again. All the while she worked her clit, shivering as the delicate skin swelled under her fingers, gazing deeply into his eyes.

His pulse pounded in his ears, and he could feel blood rushing to his face. He felt hot, and he knew he had to have her.

She suddenly dropped her hands and smiled at him.

"So, how are you feeling, Seth?" she asked sweetly, innocence written all over her face. "Feel like doing anything? Or are you too much of a warrior to give in to your desire? I'm willing to be a gracious winner."

"Fuck," Seth said, dropping his head back against the wall. She had him by the balls. His cock was poised to go off in his pants like a boy's, yet she stood before him with laughter in her eyes. It was time for payback.

"Sit down, it's my turn," he said darkly, rolling to his feet.

Calla forced her expression to remain nonchalant, and sat down on the bed. It had taken every ounce of self control to keep herself from jumping on him, yet she'd be damned if she would let him win that easily. If he had any idea how hungry she was for his touch...

Seth stood before her, one hand wrapped around the long, hard bulge at his groin. He was heavily aroused, yet he massaged himself almost absently.

If she hadn't seen the glint of desire in his eyes, she would never have guessed how much he wanted her. His eyes, though, were hard with a need that couldn't be denied.

He grasped the zipper of his coverall, pulling it down slowly to his waist.

The beauty of his dark chest, sprinkled with hair, made her breath catch. He was the most magnificent man she'd ever seen. A twist of desire caught her off-guard, and she moaned. She watched his face light up in triumph, and she scowled in response. He was so sure of himself, it wasn't fair, she thought to herself.

He shrugged one shoulder out of the suit, exposing his muscular arm and shoulder.

Those arms had held her so many times, imprisoning her as he pleasured her, cradling her as she returned the favor. She felt so safe when they held her close, like nothing could ever hurt her. She caught herself leaning toward him, ready to accept his embrace.

He raised one finger and twitched it in reproof.

"Ready to give in so soon, Devora?" he asked in a silky voice. "I know I'll win, but I thought you'd last a little longer than this..."

Calla scowled at him, disgusted at her own weakness. It was time to fight fire with fire, she decided. Scooting down the bed, she stretched out comfortably, head propped up on a pillow so she could continue to watch him easily. Then she started massaging her clit with one hand, legs spread wide open.

"Oh, I'm not ready to give in," she said huskily. "I'm just settling in to enjoy the show."

She noted with satisfaction that the sight made him gulp, but he quickly shrugged off his suit, exposing the proud jut of his cock. Then it was her turn to gulp.

He was long and hard, and the smooth, helmet-like head flushed red with arousal. One hand continued to stroke slowly up and down, and he flinched slightly as he grazed the sensitive notch on the under-side.

Calla closed her eyes, it was too much.

"Oh, no you don't," Seth said huskily. "You watch me every second, just like I had to watch you."

Calla forced her eyes open, and another shock of arousal struck her at the sight of him standing there, a drop of pearly moisture hanging on the end of his proud length. Her body convulsed in response and her fingers moved more frantically between her legs, the familiar pressure building.

"Ah..." Seth said, continuing his own long, slow strokes. His face was tight and his breathing harsh, but every movement was tightly controlled. "If you come, first, that means I win. Are you ready to give up?"

Calla shook her head furiously, but her hand refused to stop moving. Seth moved closer to the bed, standing over her as he worked his own sensitive flesh. The veins on his neck stood out with tension.

"When I do this," Seth whispered. "I'm thinking about what it would be like to thrust into you. I'm thinking about how hot and tight you are, about shooting into you and exploding over and over until neither of us can move. That's what I want to do to you right now."

"I'm thinking about it, too," Calla said, mesmerized. She couldn't quite remember why they weren't already doing that... What was she trying to prove anyway?

Seth seemed to read her thoughts, because his eyes lit with triumph.

"Tell me to come to you, Devora," he said. His soft, smooth request wove through her consciousness, and he watched with anticipation as she twisted in desire. "Tell me you want me inside of you. Tell me there aren't any others who can fill you like I do."

"Oh, Seth," she moaned. "Oh, Goddess, I'm so close."

"That's good enough for me," Seth muttered. He fell on her like a man starved, his mouth crushing against hers. One strong arm was braced above her head, and the other worked its way underneath her body. Then he was pulling her to him and thrusting into her flesh.

The shock of contact swept through her, and she came in a burst of pleasure so intense she screamed against his mouth.

As Devora convulsed around his taut flesh, Seth surged forward in search of his own pleasure. The feel of her tight body gloving his was like hot silk, and every stroke brought him closer to the ecstasy he knew was waiting for him. Then he pressed home one last time and orgasm ripped through him. He cried out, then collapsed against her. She held him tightly, wrapping his body with her arms and legs.

After a minute, she asked him quietly, "So, who won the contest?"

Seth laughed, amazed at the feeling of contentment and joy that filled him.

"I think we both won," he said finally, kissing her soft, swollen lips gently. "Or at the very least, we both got the prize."

* * * * *

Later that day, as she was preparing their evening meal, Calla reflected on how much her life had changed since she'd joined Seth. Four months had passed since they'd left the mining station. They were the best months of Calla's life, so pleasant that she felt guilty at times. Jess' survival was hanging in the balance and what was she doing? Falling in love. And it was love–she had resigned herself to it by now.

Travelling with Seth from outpost to outpost might have seemed tedious to a more experienced woman, but to Calla each day was a new adventure. They'd visited twelve groups of miners so far, their homes ranging from one-man operations to a corporate mine employing more than 100 managers and a thousand slaves.

The corporate outpost had been the hardest stop for Calla, both logistically and emotionally. Each time they arrived at a station, she anxiously scanned the faces of those around her, seeking Jess. Several times she'd shown his picture to groups of slaves, always careful to keep her activities a secret from Seth. So far he suspected nothing, but she couldn't afford to take anything for granted.

The corporate mine had been too large for her to question the slaves; even if she'd had the time to talk to all of them, the security was too tight. She'd taken another route instead, cozying up to the personnel manager while Seth was taking a tour. She'd created a cover story, telling the manager that the slave, Jess, had been sold by accident. According to her story, Mistress Jenner had regretted selling him within days of his departure. Devora, as Mistress Jenner's friend, had agreed to keep an eye out for the young man during her tour of the asteroid field. She would, of course, offer generous compensation for Jess' return.

The manager had looked through his books, scanning the transactions to see if he had any workers who fit Jess' description. He even had a series of holos of each "unit," as he called the slaves. Calla scanned the most recent purchases carefully, but none looked like Jess.

"I didn't think we'd have the unit you're looking for," he told her after she'd examined the last of the holos. "We buy most of our units in lots, so unless it'd been resold to a wholesaler, odds are we wouldn't see it. I think you'll have better luck checking with smaller operations."

His callous attitude toward the men who lived and died under his care horrified Calla, but she was careful to keep a casual smile on her face. The last thing she wanted to do was arouse suspicion by betraying her emotions. *You're a free woman now,* she reminded herself. *The fate of slaves is unimportant to you.*

But the faces of the captive men, filled with fear and trepidation, haunted her. Most of them would be dead within a year, none would ever leave the asteroid belt. Death, Calla thought sadly, would be merciful for these men.

And now Jess was one of them.

* * * * *

Seth gently guided the sleek ship toward the remote asteroid, eyes scanning its surface for a place to land. He'd heard from some miners at his last stop that there was an encampment here, although no mining claim had ever been registered. They'd warned him not to go there because the miners were crazy. According to Seth's sources, they'd spent too much time in the middle of nowhere; they were paranoid. Once they'd even fired on one of the harmless peddlers who worked the asteroid fields, carrying supplies and trading among the camps and stations.

To Seth's mind, it sounded like they might be exactly who he was searching for. Intelligence reports indicated that a group of extremists was hoarding weapons in preparation for some kind of holy war against the Saurellians. The whole thing sounded ridiculous to him, but his source insisted that the threat was real. The whole purpose of his mission was to find these people, and return to his superiors with a report on how to control the threat they represented to the Saurellian occupation.

As he approached the asteroid, however, he felt a twinge of unease. He didn't like the idea of bringing Devora to a potentially dangerous place. Having a willing woman with him seemed like a good idea when they'd left Discovery station, but now he was less sure of his decision. He had long since realized she was the best thing that had ever happened to him; he was happier with her than he'd been since he was a child. He didn't understand why, but even the thought of her in danger was enough bring cold sweat to his skin.

He didn't have any other option, though. He'd seen the way men's eyes followed her at their stops so far. Women were hard to come by in the mining fields; he had little doubt that if he dropped her off at even the most civilized of posts she wouldn't be safe. He'd allowed her to move about freely at their previous destinations, but this time he was going to have to keep her on a short leash. Otherwise he could lose her, and that simply wasn't an option.

"Are we almost there?" Devora called up to him from the base of the ladder. "Do you mind if I come up? I'd like to watch as we approach."

"That's fine," he said lightly. "Make sure you stow everything first. I don't know what the gravity will be like on this thing, so we could get bumped around a bit until the ship compensates for it."

She still always asked permission to come up into the cockpit, although he'd long since stopped worrying about her moving or damaging anything. She was a puzzle, Seth mused. Half the time she was a self-confident seductress; the rest of the time she was almost pathetically eager to please. She took care not to intrude on his space and was constantly doing little things to make him more comfortable. Most of the pleasure workers he'd known in his life were prima donnas. They might do almost anything to bring physical pleasure to their clients, but they wouldn't dream of cleaning. At times he had to force Devora to stop working. It was strange… it wasn't that he didn't enjoy being cared for, but she did more than her fair share. It wasn't right, and it wasn't part of their contract.

The thought of that damned contract made him wince. He didn't like the idea that Devora was only with him for his money. Not that she didn't enjoy his company. He could tell she genuinely liked being with him, and not just because they had great sex. They'd spent countless hours studying the holo-maps together, discussing politics and swapping stories. She had remarkably little understanding of the war between the Empire and the Federation, but she was eager to learn. In the evenings they would play card games and even read books to each other. One night they got drunk on *bakrah* and chased each other around the ship like wild children. Seth had never spent time doing such mundane things with a woman, yet he was never bored. Sometimes they didn't even have sex. His friends wouldn't believe him if he told them that, he realized with amusement.

"All right, everything is stowed," Devora yelled from below, then he could hear her climbing the ladder. She sat down beside him, looking eagerly out the window. "So, who are we visiting here? Is it another corporate mine, or something smaller?"

"I don't really know what we're going to find here," he replied after a brief pause. They were getting closer, and he could see what might have been a habitation bubble on the surface, but it was hard to tell. "This one isn't actually on the charts, and there's no official claim filed. I think they might be members of a survivalist group."

His words sent a shiver through Calla. What kind of survivalist group, she wondered. Were they Pilgrims, like Jenner? If so, this stop might lead her to Jess. But she'd have to watch her step. She had met hundreds of Pilgrims at the hostel—they came for meetings once or twice a year, although she'd never learned what they were meeting about. They were extremely private, and didn't even allow the slaves in to serve them food.

"What kind of survivalists?" she asked, trying not to sound too interested in his answer.

"Well, I'm not sure," he said after a second. They were getting closer to the asteroid, and his maneuvering was becoming more complicated as several smaller asteroids brushed by their path. "I think they might be part of a group called the "Pilgrims of the Apocalypse,' ever heard of them?"

"Um, no," Calla replied, nervously crossing her fingers. She was so tired of lying to Seth. If only she could be sure he'd understand, she would tell him the truth. If it was just her life at stake, she probably would have. She had Jess to worry about, however.

"I guess it's kind of a strange group," he said. "I don't know too much about them, because we've never had them in the Federation before now. That's partly why I decided to take this trip. I'm curious about them."

"Oh," she said, unsure of how to answer. She was surprised he hadn't realized Jenner was a Pilgrim after staying at the hostel for so long, but after a bit of reflection she realized it wasn't really that strange. Jenner hadn't held any meetings while the Saurellians were in residence, and there hadn't been any other guests. In fact, there was no reason to think he would know Jenner was a Pilgrim. The old bitch certainly hadn't gone out of her way to advertise the fact to the Saurellians, which was strange in and of itself. Usually if they had a guest who wasn't a Pilgrim, Jenner would corner them to try and discuss religion.

"So, I take it they aren't very friendly?" she asked finally.

"That's their reputation," he replied. "We know they're opposed to the government, and the Saurellian government in particular, but we don't know why. I'm not going to tell them that I was provisional commander of the system until recently, and I want you to stick close to me the whole time. I just don't feel entirely comfortable about this visit. Maybe it would be better if you stayed on the ship," he added, looking over at her with concern.

That wouldn't work, Calla thought in panic. She had to do something, or she'd never find Jess.

"That's not fair," she said in a pouty voice. She didn't want to overdo it, but she had to convince him to let her leave the ship. If he didn't want her leaving, she had no doubt that he'd find a way to keep her on board. "I've been trapped on this ship every bit as long as you have. I have every right to see some new people, even if they are some kind of strange Pilgrim." She glanced at him under her eyelashes, trying to see his reaction to this new ploy. He looked somewhat startled.

"I didn't realize you were feeling trapped," he said after a brief pause.

"Well I am," she said, tossing her hair a bit for effect. "I mean, I'm enjoying the trip, but I've been looking forward to each stop. I like meeting new people and going new places."

"I'm just not comfortable with you leaving the ship here," he said. "It may not be safe."

"You know," she said, adding a bit of pique to her tone. "I've traveled all over the Empire and managed to take care of myself. We have these 'Pilgrims' there, you know."

"Would those be the travels with your former clients?" he asked tightly.

"Yes," Calla said breezily. "And I've always managed to take care of myself. I want to go down on that asteroid. It's ridiculous of you to tell me I shouldn't."

Seth stared at the asteroid looming ahead of them, a muscle in his jaw twitching. Calla suddenly realized she might have spread it on a little too thick.

"I mean—" she started to say, but he cut her off.

"I think you made your meaning clear," he said tersely. "You're tired of being trapped with me on this ship, and you're perfectly capable of taking care of yourself. Quite clear."

"That's not what I meant at all," she said. She could feel the intimacy they'd built between them slipping away. This wasn't what she'd been trying to do. A panicky feeling came over her.

"Don't worry, I won't make you stay here on the ship," he said, not bothering to look at her. "But I want you to keep close to me out there. Now why don't you go down to the main room and strap yourself in. Like I said, this could be a bumpy landing, and I don't want to have to worry about you getting injured."

"I'd rather stay up here with you," she replied in a small voice. She'd hurt him, and she didn't know how to fix it.

"I don't think that's a good idea," he answered. "I need to focus on this landing, and it will be easier if you're not around."

"I see," she said quietly. "Seth, I didn't mean to hurt your feelings. I know you're just trying to protect me."

Seth finally turned to look at her, the asteroid momentarily forgotten. His expression was one of incredulity.

"Hurt me?" he said. "Don't be ridiculous. I think you're forgetting what we have here. I'm a Saurellian warrior, and I've hired you–a pleasure worker–to give me physical release on this trip. Nothing more. A woman like you could never hurt me."

The cruel words hit Calla in the pit of her stomach. Abruptly, reality sank in. She was a slave on the run. She'd allowed herself to develop feelings for this man, but slaves couldn't afford to have feelings. It was a weakness and it had to be covered up before someone took advantage of it.

Pasting a bright smile on her face, Calla replied smoothly, "Oh, don't worry Seth. I know exactly what we have here." Then she turned away from him and walked carefully to the ladder. She'd be damned if she'd let him know how much his words had hurt her.

* * * * *

The landing on the asteroid was every bit as rough as Seth predicted. Usually he was able to program the computer to adjust the gravity stabilizers, but he simply didn't have enough information on this place. No one had answered his com hails, but at least they hadn't attacked him. That was something.

He put the ship down on a flat area about a quarter mile from the habitation dome. Another ship was already parked to one side of the field, a decrepit-looking junker that should have been scrapped decades ago.

He and Devora donned their pressure suits without speaking. He was still angry, although he wasn't quite sure why. Pushing his feelings down, he tried to focus instead on the task at hand.

As they finished, the computer chirped a warning. Someone was approaching the ship.

Seth and Devora stepped into the airlock, closing the door tightly behind them. With a whooshing sound, the ship started pumping air out of the small chamber. As Seth waited for the cycle to complete, he watched the figure coming toward them. By his size, Seth figured he was male. He was carrying a gun, although it wasn't held in a threatening position. Not the most promising of situations, but at he least hadn't come out shooting.

The light above the door flashed, and the outer portal slid open. Bouncing slightly from the low gravity, Seth made his way down the landing ladder. Normally he would turn to assist Devora, but this time he stayed focused on the man, keeping a hand on his blaster. He had a bad feeling about this stop; he should have made Devora stay on the ship despite her protestations and pouting.

They walked toward the man, Seth trying to raise him on the com. As they got closer, the man tapped the side of his helmet with one hand, indicating his radio wasn't working. He gestured to them to follow, and started walking back toward the habitation bubble.

The bubble itself looked every bit as old and unsteady as the decrepit ship on the landing field. Even after the airlock was fully cycled and the light turned green, Seth took care to check the instruments on his own suit before removing his helmet. He didn't want to take any chances. A stench, like rotting cheese, hit him as he pulled off the helmet. The inhabitants of the bubble didn't clean themselves very often, he realized. Devora must have come to the same conclusion, because she gasped as the odor hit her.

"It's a might close in here," the miner said in profound understatement. He had pulled off his helmet before either of them, but had kept busy fiddling with the airlock controls while they removed their own helmets. Now he turned to face them, and Seth fought to control his reaction.

The man was filthy. Black mining dust covered his face, hands and neck. He had the look of someone who'd been dirty for so long that the dirt was under the skin. His hair was lank and greasy, hanging from his balding head in stringy locks. Devora gasped in shock beside him.

"I'm Calvin," the man said, exposing rotten teeth. "This is my rock. I'll expect you'll be wantin' to trade before you leave."

That hadn't been Seth's plan, but Calvin didn't strike him as the kind of man who would make time for casual visitors.

"We might have something to trade," he said lightly. "We'll have to see."

Calvin grunted, then opened the airlock portal into the main bubble. The mechanism scraped from its coating of grime. Calvin strode into the room ahead of them, and Seth saw a woman and two children waiting for them silently. They were thin, pale and dirty, like Calvin.

"This is my wife, Sarai," he said. "And this is my son, Able." He didn't bother to introduce the girl.

They were the most pathetic people he'd ever seen. Sarai stood silently, not meeting his eyes. She looked to be in her mid-twenties, but it was hard to tell under all the dirt. He was gradually getting used to the smell, although every once in a while he had to fight off the urge to gag. Looking the woman up and down, he realized that she had made some attempt to straighten herself. Her oily hair had been freshly combed, as had that of the little girl. The little boy was the spitting image of his father, right down to his rotten teeth. All three seemed to be standing as far from Calvin as they possibly could.

"I would imagine your woman will want to help mine fix some food," Calvin said after a minute, giving his wife a pointed glare. She glanced furtively at Devora, smiling shyly, and then gestured toward the other side of the bubble. There seemed to be just the one room, serving as living area, kitchen and bedroom.

Devora gave the woman a sweet smile in return, and the two made their way across the room with the little girl trailing after them. Seth noticed with some disgust that Devora had to pick her way carefully to avoid piles of debris littering the floor.

"Now that we've got rid of them, I think we should talk business," Calvin said. He gestured Seth to a small, round table. "Have a seat. Able! Clear off a seat for the man."

Able leapt into action, scuttling around his father to pull out a chair. Whipping a piece of torn fabric out of his pocket, the grubby child made an effort to wipe off some of the grime before Seth sat down.

"Damn woman don't do jack shit around here," Calvin grumbled as he pulled out his own chair. "I don't know why the hell I don't push her outta the airlock. Oh shut up, Able, I'm just funnin'," he said as the boy snuffled in protest.

"Damn kid's got no sense of humor," Calvin said, spitting on the floor for emphasis. "Now go get us some *bakrah*. I don't believe in beatin' around the bush, so let's have this out."

Seth cocked an eyebrow at Calvin questioningly. He had no idea what the man was talking about.

"I'm assuming you're here to trade, and that's a good thing," Calvin said bluntly. "I don't hold with traders, we're Pilgrims here and we usually take care of our own. But something's gone wrong up at Bethesda base and I ain't seen no one for a coupla months. Radio's been out for two weeks now. I'm wonderin' if you got news for me."

"What kind of news are you looking for?" Seth asked cautiously.

"News 'bout them damn Sarlins what took over the sector, o' course," Calvin said, spitting again. Able, who was approaching with two grimy cups on a tray, ducked to miss the wad of dirty phlegm. The boy slid between them to set the tray on the table. Calvin swatted at him, and he jumped back just as quickly. Apparently he'd had practice avoiding his father's fists, Seth thought with distaste.

"Do you mean the Saurellians?" Seth asked, trying to lead Calvin on.

"That's what I said," Calvin replied, eyeing Seth suspiciously. "Them's what been fightin' the emperor. I'm thinkin' they may've took out Bethesda."

"I don't know about Bethesda," Seth said, choosing his words carefully. "I'm relatively new to this trade route. But I haven't heard about the Saurellians coming out in this sector. Are you sure it's them?"

"Course it's them, who else would it be?" Calvin said. He grabbed one of the cups from the tray and handed it to Seth. "Have some *bakrah*. Make it myself."

Seth took the cup and sniffed at the contents. The fumes alone were enough to singe the tiny hairs in his nose, but he took a sip to be polite. At least it drowned out some of Calvin's smell, and the alcohol would probably be enough to kill whatever microorganisms were living in the cup. It was a comforting thought. The *bakrah* burned down his throat, and it took all he had in him not to cough. Calvin drank from his own cup deeply, then peered around the room myopically for Able.

"Bring the damn bottle, ya little shit!" he bellowed. "Now, back to business. I don't usually trade with your kind, but to be honest we're running a little short of supplies here. I usually gets all I need from Bethesda, but like I said, I ain't seen 'em for a while. Now, what's the news?"

"Well, the Saurellians are occupying the main access station, and have entered peace talks with the Empire," Seth said, unsure of where to begin.

"Bastards!" Calvin exclaimed with feeling, taking another deep swig. "I can't believe we have them bastards in charge of us. It ain't right."

"Have you ever met a Saurellian?" Seth asked, too intrigued by the man's attitude to resist. Calvin looked at him in horror.

"Hell, no," he said. "I don't take my family where we might run into those things. What kind of man would expose his children to that?"

"Those things?" Seth asked quietly. "I'm afraid I don't understand."

"Damn, you don't know much, do you," Calvin said in disgust. "Them Sarelins ain't no more human than a goat or a slave. They're monsters, that's what. That's why we ain't gonna tolerate them in our sector!"

"We?" Seth asked, but Calvin just glared at him suspiciously.

"I don't see no reason to talk 'bout this no more," he said after a long pause. "You wanna trade or not? I ain't got all day, I got things to do."

As far as Seth could tell, it had been a very long time since Calvin had "done" anything. "What kinds of things do you need?" he asked.

"Well, we're low on filters for the oxygen generator, and I ain't got much in the way of food packs," Calvin said, becoming suddenly fascinated with his *bakrah*. "We also need some parts for the radio. And some water."

Seth listened as Calvin's list continued, growing more horrified by the minute. The family had virtually nothing left–it sounded like their air would only hold out for a matter of weeks. He would have to evacuate them from the asteroid. Otherwise they would probably die.

"Well, I have a few of those things, but not all," he said when Calvin finally stopped grunting out his requests. "I saw your ship out there–any chance you could make a supply run?"

Calvin turned to stare at the wall, not speaking for several minutes.

"My ship don't work."

"I see," Seth said. With a sigh, he realized there was no way out of this one; even if he could justify leaving Calvin to die, he couldn't leave Sarai and the children. "Well, here's the thing. I can give you a few supplies, but not enough to last you for any length of time. From what I've heard, you scared off most of the traders a while back. That pretty much only leaves us with one option. I can take you and your family to a base nearby, where you'll be safe."

"We ain't leavin' our rock!" Calvin said indignantly. He glared at Seth with hostile, beady eyes. "You just want us to leave so you can jack our claim–I know your type, I know what you're like."

Impatience, tempered with disgust, welled up in Seth. It would be so easy to leave the man to die on his stupid rock. It might even be a service to the Federation, he mused. One less armed lunatic to deal with.

"Papa, dinner is ready," a small, frail voice broke through his thoughts. It was the little girl. She was like a skinny blond ghost, with pale, hollow cheeks and enormous eyes. Dressed in a dingy little dress that was clearly too small for her, she looked like she might collapse at any moment.

"Mali, you're a stupid little bitch–never interrupt me when I'm talkin' business!" Calvin snarled, rising as if to hit the girl. Seth reached out one hand and caught his arm, pinning it against the table.

"Don't," he said, his voice cold and hard. Calvin glared at him, then lowered himself back in his chair. The look he shot his daughter, however, promised retribution. Seth silently swore; even if he had enough supplies for the family he couldn't leave them behind. Calvin would kill them.

"Calvin, I speak as a friend," Seth said, choosing his words carefully. "You and your family will die here if you don't come with me. You've shot at other traders. Your base station isn't responding. For love of the Goddess, man, look at your children! They're starving."

"I don't believe in no charity," Calvin said harshly, glaring at him.

"You offered to trade," Seth said soothingly. "It doesn't have to be charity. Why don't you make me an offer? I'm sure we can work out something fair."

"Let's eat while I think about this," Calvin finally replied. "Sarai, bring the food over."

His wife and daughter came forward at the command, carrying plates covered with a dark, gruel-like substance. Seth noticed how careful they were to stay out of Calvin's reach. Devora hovered in the background, watching anxiously. Their eyes met briefly, and Seth could see the pain and compassion in her face. He knew she wouldn't object to taking the family along with them.

"I know it ain't great, but it's food," Calvin said. Then he started shoving spoonfuls of the dark, watery substance into his mouth. Trying not to grimace, Seth took a spoonful and ate it cautiously. It wasn't as bad as it looked–it reminded him of the basic survival rations every Saurellian warrior carried during battle - nutritious, and thankfully tasteless, powder that could be eaten with or without water.

As Seth ate, he noticed that neither Sarai nor Devora and the children were eating with them.

"Where's their food?" he asked, gesturing to the others with his spoon. He was sure Devora wouldn't mind missing out on her serving of the disgusting paste, but he was concerned about the children. They watched every spoonful with hungry eyes.

"They eat too damn much already," Calvin said. "The Book tells us that a woman and children exist to serve their master. They'll eat what's left over, and be grateful for it."

Seth all but choked. The little girl, Mali, was so pale he could see the faint line of a blood vessel in her forehead. The child needed food.

"Calvin, we both know you need to come with us," Seth said, losing his patience. Calvin started to protest, but Seth held up his hand before the man could speak. "Let's not argue about this. Now, what do you have to trade? I haven't seen much sign of mining activity, and this doesn't look like an ore-producing outfit. What do you do here?"

"Papa is a guard for the Movement," Able said proudly into the silence. He puffed out his chest slightly, and looked to his father for approval. Calvin glared at the boy, whose chest instantly collapsed. A wave of fear came over his face. "I-I-I'm s-s-s-sorry, Papa," he whispered, wincing under his father's gaze. "I didn't realize I wasn't s'posed to tell. Honest!"

"That's all right, boy," Calvin smoothly. Able blinked at him in confusion, but Sarai's face blanched in terror. Calvin turned back to Seth, his expression crafty.

"What he means is I sometimes work guarding ore shipments for the miners at Bethesda," he said. "But like I said, they ain't been by for a while. I gots some raw materials, though. Jansenite, about fifteen kilos of it. Should bring in a pretty penny with the right buyers, if you catch my meaning..."

Seth caught his breath. Jansenite was rare, one of the most powerfully explosive elements known. What the hell was Calvin doing with Jansenite? He was almost afraid to know the answer.

"That's a pretty specialized commodity," Seth said slowly. "Mind if I ask how you happened to come across it?"

"Now that ain't none of your business," Calvin said, taking another long pull of his *bakrah*. Seth estimated the man had drunk almost half the bottle in the short time they'd been talking. "Do you want it or not? If you take us outta here, we'll split the profits, fifty-fifty."

Seth nodded slowly, calculating the best way to transport the volatile material. As if reading his mind, Calvin said, "It's in block form, sealed in boxes in a viscous polymer. Shouldn't give us no problems."

Seth wondered if Calvin had any idea how ridiculously inadequate such packing was for Jansenite. Probably not–the man was a fool. The Jansenite had to belong to someone else. That person was probably the cause of the rumors. If he could get enough information out of Calvin, he'd be able to make his report to the High Council.

"We've got a deal," Seth said, setting down his spoon. "Devora, you help Sarai pack things up. Calvin and I will see to loading the Jansenite."

Calvin grinned darkly at him in response.

Watch your back, Seth told himself, because this guy is going to be trouble.

Chapter 7

"Seth?" Calla called cautiously, looking up into the cockpit. She hadn't had a chance to talk to him since that morning, when they'd said such hurtful things to each other. The enormity of the family's situation had overwhelmed her; she'd been working non-stop to help Sarai and her children get clean and settled in.

Calvin had been more difficult. He refused to wash, although, fortunately, the ship's air filters were powerful enough to counteract the worst of the odor. As long as she stayed away from him it wasn't that bad.

"Seth, can I come up?" she asked.

After a moment's hesitation, he replied. "Yes."

Calla pulled herself up next to him, settling in the co-pilot's seat. He was studying a star chart intensely, punching numbers into the navigation panel by hand. She widened her eyes in surprise. Usually the computer took care of that.

"I have to do this because where we're going isn't mapped," he said in response to her quizzical look. "Calvin wants to go to Bethesda station. He's worried about his people there. That's where we're going to sell the Jansenite and drop the family off."

"Seth, do you think Sarai and the children will be safe with him?"

Seth glanced over at her briefly, eyes shuttered. She could tell he hadn't forgotten their conversation that morning. He had cut himself off from her.

"What a man does with his family is his own business," Seth said tightly. "I won't let him hurt her on this ship, but I'm not going to stand between them."

Calla stared at him, aghast. She'd thought he'd have more compassion than that.

"I can't believe you don't want to help them," she finally whispered. "I really think we have to do something about their situation."

Seth swiveled his chair to face her, his face dark.

"I think you need to be quiet and remember your place here," he said finally. "You are here to take care of my needs. Calvin and I have a business arrangement. Don't try to interfere in things you don't understand. I need you to just have some faith that I know what I'm doing."

"I think I understand perfectly," Calla said in a small voice.

"Good," Seth said, his voice harsh. He stared at his charts a little more. "Come here."

"Why?" Calla asked cautiously. She didn't like the look on his face.

"Why?" he replied in a smooth voice. "Because I said so. Because I hired you to serve me whenever I want, and I want you now."

"But Calvin and Sarai are right downstairs," she whispered. "Besides, I don't want to right now."

Seth glared at her.

"You work for me, remember?" he snarled. "You signed the contract, I'm paying you good money to be here. Come over here and service me."

Miserably, Calla did as he said. He was correct, she signed the contract and had no right to complain. It hurt, though. She hadn't thought Seth was the kind of man to force a woman.

"On your knees," Seth said tightly. Resigned, Calla dropped before him. Seth leaned back in his chair, watching her coldly. She reached over to the front of his pants, which strained from his erection. It sprang free, and he sighed heavily as she wrapped one hand around him. She started moving it up and down, and his shivered under her touch. After a several minutes he spoke.

"Use your mouth."

It wasn't anything she hadn't done for him a hundred times, Calla told herself. This is no different. But it was. Those other times she'd wanted to pleasure him, and knew he would pleasure her in return. This wasn't her Seth, the Seth who had been so kind and loving. Had she hurt him even more that morning than she realized, or had she simply built him up in her mind? Maybe her Seth had never existed, she thought sadly.

Closing her eyes, Calla wrapped her lips around his hard length. She would do as she was told; she would earn her money.

* * * * *

Seth stared down at Devora's head, bobbing back and forth in his lap. The feeling of her lips on his cock was exquisite. Just the sight of her was enough to make him hard, ready to go any time, any place. Her touch was beyond description and he couldn't imagine getting tired of her. But that was an illusion, he reminded himself coldly. He had to push down any sympathy and tenderness her felt for her.

She was a paid companion; she had no loyalty to him. He was a Saurellian, genetically incapable of forming a long-term bond with a woman outside his own race. He'd started thinking of them as partners, imagining they were on a mission together. Hell, she didn't even know they were on a mission. He wanted to tell her that he was only using Calvin, that he'd protect Sarai and the children, but the stakes were too high for such revelations. Unless he could trust her absolutely, he couldn't risk the security of the Saurellian occupation by telling her everything. It would be criminally irresponsible, and despite their closeness he had only known her a few months. There were lives at stake, for love of the Goddess!

She continued to work on him, lips and hands moving smoothly together. The sensations were building through his body, but he could tell that when he came it would be no more than physical release. He'd come to expect more from their love-making, he thought sadly.

A snuffling sound caught his attention, and with shock he realized she was crying. Remorse hit him like a punch to the stomach.

"Devora, you can stop," he said quietly. Her head stopped moving, then she slowly pulled away from him. Her hair covered her face, hiding her expression, but the quivering of her shoulders and the sound of her sniffing back tears touched him more than anything she could have said. She looked defeated. Hating himself for what he had made her do, Seth pulled her gently onto his lap, cradling her against his chest. She turned to him like a lost child, wrapping her arms around his neck and sobbing quietly into his shoulder.

"Shhhhhhh," he said, trying to comfort her. "I'm so sorry, Devora. I don't know why I did that to you. I'm so sorry." His words, far from comforting her, seemed to open the floodgate. She started sobbing against him, crying as if her heart was breaking. Her pain stabbed through him. He couldn't stand it. "Please stop. I'm so sorry," he whispered again.

She cried for almost five minutes, then fell silent except for the occasional hiccup. Seth turned her to face him, gently tilting her face up toward his. He brushed her hair out of his eyes, gazing at her steadily.

"Devora, sweet, I can't explain to you what's going on here," he said. "There's more than meets the eye, but you're just going to have to trust me."

"Like you trust me?" she said darkly. Seth didn't respond, unable to meet her gaze. Finally she spoke again.

"Well, I guess that settles things," she said softly. "You don't trust me, but I'm supposed to trust you."

"Devora, it's not like that," Seth said. "I have responsibilities. This is about more than just you and me... Please try to understand."

"Oh, I understand," she whispered. She dropped her head back down against his chest, cuddling against his warmth. He held her, brushing her hair occasionally with his hand. Eventually she fell asleep. Seth continued to cuddle her body against his, staring out at the stars and realizing that while he had had sex with countless women, Devora was the first he'd ever made love to.

Things weren't going as he'd planned at all.

* * * * *

Calla awoke slowly. Something was tickling her face. Something soft flitted from her forehead and across her cheeks before settling against her mouth. Seth was kissing her, she realized. She was still tucked in his arms, up in the cockpit.

His lips moved against hers, nipping lightly at her mouth. She stirred a little, eyes closed, then tilted her head up to give him better access. His mouth touched her more firmly, enticing her to open her lips. When she did, his tongue tentatively touched hers.

"Mmmmmmm," she moaned, encouraging him. It felt so good to be held in his arms tenderly. So different from what had happened earlier. She reached her hands up behind his head and neck, pulling his head down against hers more firmly. His cock, pressed against her hip, twitched in response.

Seth responded to her encouragement eagerly, arms pulling her tightly to him. His mouth slanted open against her, and his tongue thrust harder into her mouth. Calla clung to his large frame, her legs moving against each other restlessly. She could feel her cunt growing hot and moist.

Sensing her need, Seth reached one hand down to the sensitive area between her legs, rubbing her clit through her clothing. Calla squirmed against him, rubbing his cock and thrusting her own tongue back at his. She gave another little moan, and Seth stopped kissing her, resting his forehead against hers.

"We'll need to be quiet if we don't want Calvin and Sarai to hear us," he whispered. Calla stilled instantly. She'd completely forgotten their Pilgrim guests.

"Maybe we shouldn't-" she tried to say, but Seth silenced her by taking her mouth again. This time he was rougher, his tongue claiming her mouth and thrusting purposefully. Sliding lower in his chair, he shifted her weight so that she was fully facing him, and thrust one knee up between her legs to steady her. Calla, unable to control her movements, ground her clit against his thigh. One of his hands rested on her butt, pulling her hard against his leg. The other was glued to the back of her head, holding her tightly to his mouth. It took both of her hands to steady herself, using his shoulders for support.

Seth's tongue ravaged her mouth, his fingers digging tightly into her ass. Calla rubbed herself against him wantonly, pressing harder against his leg. It was almost enough, but not quite. She wanted his cock thrust into her.

Seth had other ideas. Reaching both hands down around her butt, he suddenly rose out of the seat, carrying her with him. Calla gasped as the movement pressed his erection between her legs, rubbing deliciously. She squirmed against him, anxious to feel more. Still holding her, he swiveled toward the main control panel, balancing her against the edge. He reached around her to press a button, and a flat security panel slid over the controls, locking them out of reach and protecting them from their activity.

Seth pressed Calla down against the panel, bracing her with his body. The position kept their sexes in close contact. Standing tall above her, Seth started slowly to grind his body against her.

She gasped with pleasure as his hard cock slid slowly back and forth against her clit. The friction was exquisite, almost painful in its intensity.

Leaning down over her, Seth took first one and then both of her arms and pinned them gently over her head with one strong hand. He kissed her softly on the lips, and then started unzipping the front of the light jumpsuit she wore. His lips followed the motion of the zipper, kissing her bare flesh until he was just below her breasts. Then, nosing aside the fabric of the suit, his lips found her nipple. He licked around the small, pink nub in a circle, and Calla strained toward him. In answer, his mouth closed around her peak, sucking gently.

The pull of his mouth sent a quiver through Calla's body that ran from her breast down between her legs, and she pressed herself against him urgently. His rock-hard cock responded, pressing up against the fabric of her suit. She whimpered, begging him to give her relief, but Seth just continued to suck slowly.

After a minute, he moved to the other breast, sucking, kissing, and running his tongue around the sensitive center.

Calla wanted more, and she tried to free her hands to pull him to her. His grasp was like a band of iron around her wrists, though, and she couldn't move. In desperation, she thrust her hips against his violently and for one second the hard length of his manhood was poised at the entrance to her cunt. Only the thin fabric separated them.

It was too much for Seth, and his hips plunged against hers involuntarily, driving a small bit of the suit fabric that held them apart up into her moist opening before he regained control. Seth paused, gasping for air. She had taken him off guard with that thrust, and he'd almost been lost. He wanted to stay in control

"For that," he whispered seductively, "I'm going to have to punish you."

She quivered at his words. She had no idea what he meant, but she didn't doubt her punishment would be delicious.

Standing up straight, he abruptly released her hands. She grasped as his shoulders for support as he pulled her off the panel. Using quick, efficient movements, he stripped off her jumpsuit, gesturing for her to step out of the pant-legs. She did so, anticipation at his next move filled the air.

He had her hop back up on the flat surface, and then–using her own soft fabric belt–tied her by the wrists to a loop at the top, normally used to secured things in zero gravity. He paused to survey her, running his eyes over her exposed body.

Calla realized she was utterly helpless against whatever he might choose to do to her. It scared her, but it was also exciting to lie before him naked and open to his touch. What if the others heard them? A thrill raced through her–it seemed so wrong to be doing this within hearing of Sarai and Calvin. But it was thrilling, too...

Seth smiled at her darkly, then knelt between her legs. Gently lifting them over his shoulders, he blew softly on her exposed clit.

Calla shuddered, and bit her lip to keep from making any noise. A hysterical giggle almost burst out at the thought of Calvin and Sarai would think if they came to investigate any noises.

Seth gently pulled apart the lips on either side of her sensitive nub, then slowly and deliberately touched the very tip with his tongue. He felt Calla jump slightly in response. Flicking his tongue back and forth against her a few times, he then sucked her clit into his mouth. When Calla's hips heaved in response, he pulled back from her with a chuckle.

"You're not going to get it that easy," he whispered.

Taking one large finger, he gently thrust into her, massaging her from within. After a second, he thrust in a second finger and lowered his head to her clit again. Moving with excruciating slowness, he started building her into a frenzy of pleasure, only to back off each time before she came.

Calla twisted and turned against her restraints, desperate to pull him against her. She knew from experience that his own arousal must be fierce. If she could press herself against him, he'd finish things.

But Seth only laughed at her efforts, and the small vibration the noise made against her clit was almost unbearable. He continued to work her from within with one hand, while his mouth remained glued to her clit. His other hand, which he had used to hold down her stomach, now shifted. He dipped another finger inside her wet cunt, and slowly moved that hand from her wetness around her body. He massaged her ass gently, then slid his hand around to the crevice between her cheeks.

Calla paused in her squirming, unsure of what he planned to do next.

Seth intensified his efforts, sucking her entire clit into his mouth and working it viciously with his tongue. Her gasp was audible, and he felt her orgasm starting to build again. A still wet finger pressed against her nether opening, even as his hand and mouth continued to stimulate her front.

The unfamiliar feeling caused her to jerk her hips up slightly, right into Seth's mouth. Her breath whooshed out in a gasp as her hips fell back down on his finger, and the tip of it slipped effortlessly inside her previously untouched rear entrance.

It burned slightly, but the pain was exquisite. He wiggled his finger slightly and she moaned. Then he stopped working her clit.

"Tell me what you want," he whispered harshly, staring up across her heaving chest with dark eyes.

"I want you to fuck me," she managed to gasp out. He wiggled his finger again; she moaned in response.

"Who do you want?"

"You," she said. "I want you, Seth. Please."

He laughed triumphantly, then attacked her swollen clit with renewed vigor.

Calla gasped against the sensation, more stimulated than she'd ever been before. It was almost unbearable. Her body was tensing, preparing for her release, and she strained against the belt holding her down.

Seth sucked her fully into his mouth, and pushed almost viciously into her cunt with his fingers.

Gasping for air, Calla felt every bit of energy in her body building, and then Seth abruptly thrust the rest of his finger up her ass. The feeling pushed her over the edge and she exploded, every muscle in her body rock hard from the strain.

* * * * *

Seth stood up slowly, watching as Devora came back to herself. Her body was glorious in its arousal. Her small, freckled breasts heaved with every breath, and her nipples were tight and hard from his sucking. He noticed that her breasts had flushed red from the slight scratch of his beard, and one was slightly bruised. He liked the looks of his marks on her; she was his. He silently acknowledged that he could never let her go. For some reason, this small woman was his life mate, or as close as he would ever experience. He didn't understand how or why he needed her so much, and he didn't care. All he knew was that he would be keeping her by his side as long as he could hold her.

Seth watched as Devora opened her eyes and stared up at him, a small, satisfied smile playing around the corners of her lips. Deliberately meeting her gaze, he reached down and slowly pulled his own shirt off, exposing his bare chest to her view. Her eyes followed him appreciatively. He stretched in front of her, deliberately giving her a long, slow view of his rippling chest muscles. Then he dropped his hands down to his pants, where his cock still stood out from his body, surrounded by his open pants. He cupped its solid length and squeezed slightly, allowing his head to tilt back in pleasure at the sensation. A small bead of sweat started making its way across his forehead.

Opening his pants further, he allowed his full sacs to spring free. His swollen cock was flushed red with arousal, the head nearly purple. A small bead of moisture welled up at the tip. Reaching down with one hand, Seth grasped his own length and started to stroke it up and down while staring directly into her eyes.

"Do you know how much I want you, Devora?" he asked with dark intensity. "Do you have any idea how much I want to fuck you right now?"

The woman splayed in front of him shook her head, mesmerized.

"Did you know that the week I waited for you back at Discovery station I had to do this every day?" he continued, deliberately moving his hand over his cock head, then rubbing his fluid down his length. "Every night I thought about you, dreamed about you, and I did this a hundred times. I couldn't wait to fuck you."

Calla's eyes widened at his revelation.

"Do you want me now? Do you want this?" he asked, smoothly caressing his own flesh. "Now that you've had your pleasure, do you want to give me pleasure?"

"Yes," she whispered quietly.

"Not just because I'm paying for it?"

"No, I'd want you no matter what," she said. And a surge of triumph washed through him. She wasn't lying, no one could fake the look on her face. She was truly his. When this mission was over, he'd take her away somewhere and never let her out again. He'd spend the rest of his life making love to her... there would be no children, of course, but they'd make due. It was more than he'd ever dreamed he'd find.

Smiling at his thoughts, Seth stepped forward between her legs, leaned over, and untied her hands. Devora raised her arms and wrapped them tightly around his neck. Their mouths met fiercely, his tongue thrusting in and claiming her. He lifted her body, fitting the tip of his cock against her moist lips, and plunged into her in one smooth motion. Devora gasped against his mouth.

Seth rose, then carried her back to the pilot's chair and sat down heavily. Devora, still astride him, started moving quickly, and his body tensed at the hot, tight fit of her. She squeezed him, milking him with her inner muscles. She threw her head back, breasts bouncing in time to her motions, and Seth groaned.

Abruptly she stopped moving, and with a wicked smile placed one finger across his lips. Shhhhhh," she said in mocking imitation of his own words earlier. "We don't want to wake up Calvin and Sarai."

Seth glared at her as she laughed softly. Grasping her waist with both hands, Seth lifted her and plunged her back down on his length. Devora took the hint, and started riding him again. The pleasure built in him, then–when it seemed like he could take no more–his hips jerked spasmodically and he came, grinding himself against his small woman. She kissed him deeply as he sat back, massaging him with her inner muscles as his erection started to fade.

"Thank you," he said after a minute, grasping her head in both hands. He kissed her again, then she responded.

"Thank you," she whispered back, dropping a kiss on his nose. "I have to say, that wasn't half bad."

She burst out laughing at the look indignant look Seth gave her.

"All right," she said, still giggling. "It was pretty damn good. So, do you think they heard us?"

"Probably," he said. "Do you care?"

"No," she replied, sobering. "I don't really care at all. Being with you is too good to worry about things like that." After a brief pause, she looked over at the star maps he'd pushed aside earlier. "You said we're going to Bethesda base. Where is that?"

"It's further into the belt," he replied. "We're about a third of the way around the belt from the main station's orbit. Bethesda is actually just about as far from Discovery station as you can get and still be in the asteroid belt. It's actually on the opposite side of the sun. Calvin won't tell me exactly where, he says he'll help guide us in when the time comes."

"And you actually trust this man?"

"I know what I'm doing," he said with finality, not really answering her question. He wished he could explain what was going on, but it wasn't worth the potential risk. He would explain everything to her later. Too much was at stake to take to tell her right now, he thought morbidly. He didn't think she would deliberately betray him, but it would be so easy to say the wrong thing to Sarai or one of the children...

"I guess we keep coming back to the issue of me trusting you without you trusting me," she said, gazing into his eyes searchingly. "Of course, I'm just your employee. I need to remember that, right?"

"You're more than that to me," he replied. "I'd think you would have realized that by now. Haven't I treated you well? I know I was an ass earlier, but I haven't forced you to do anything."

"No, you haven't," she replied with a sigh. "I can't fault you for that. We should probably get some sleep. I have a feeling that as long as Calvin's on board, things aren't going to be very restful. You will protect Sarai and the children, won't you?"

"I said he wouldn't harm them on my ship, and I meant it," he said. "But don't provoke him. I need this man to finish my business deal. It's very important."

"I guess I never thought of you as a dealer in explosives."

"Well, there's a lot you don't know about me," Seth gritted out, wishing she'd just drop the subject. He wanted to go to bed and hold her warm body close to his through the night. He didn't want her analyzing his actions. He was well aware how bad he must look to her right now.

"I'm realizing that," she said quietly. "Let's go to bed."

Chapter 8

It would take them a little over a week to reached Bethesda base, but by the fourth day Calla was ready to strangle Calvin with her bare hands. He complained constantly, berating Sarai and glaring at Calla. He'd discovered she and Seth weren't married shortly after he'd arrived, and made it clear he didn't approve. He was just like Jenner, Calla thought. A hypocrite, through and through. He had no problem beating and starving his own wife, but he condemned her as a loose woman. It was sickening.

Equally sickening was Seth's refusal to do something about the man. Every night they would drink *bakrah* and talk for hours, laughing and making crude jokes. He had even asked Calvin to explain his religion further, and seemed fascinated by the teachings of the "Celestial Pilgrim" who had founded the sect. Yet he was tender with Calla, and somehow managed to deflect Calvin whenever it seemed like he might hit his wife or children. His behavior was truly puzzling, she thought.

They had developed a new routine. Each day, she and Sarai would rise and prepare the morning meal for the men. Seth and Calvin would eat, then retire to the cockpit to discuss their "business" and look at maps of the mining belt. She and Sarai would clean up, then play quietly with the children.

The first day or two, Sarai, Mali and Able seemed afraid of Calla. She tried to find some vids for them in the ship's digital library, but Calvin had burst into an angry diatribe the first time she turned one on. He didn't want his children and wife "corrupted" by the outside world.

Instead she started reading to them during the day. Calvin didn't seem to notice as long as they were quiet, and every time he came down from the cockpit she would stop, hiding the book behind her pantsuit. First she read them nursery rhymes and myths of past civilizations. Then they moved on to tales of the Emperor's harem and stories written by a woman who had grown up in an early space colony. The children sat in fascinated silence, eyes widening at her tales. Sarai would busy herself with small tasks, but Calla knew she listened, too.

One evening, as they prepared dinner for the men, Calla asked her how she had come to be with Calvin.

"My father arranged it," Sarai said shyly, not meeting Calla's eyes. Now that she was clean, with her light blond hair held back in a thick braid, she looked rather pretty and very young. She had tendency to blush, adding color to her pale face. "We were married when I was fourteen."

"Did you grow up in the asteroid belt?"

"Yes, I was born here," she said. "My parents lived at Bethesda base. They're dead now, though. Their transport decompressed and they were killed. It was after Able was born."

"I'm so sorry," Calla murmured. Perhaps there were some advantages to never having had parents. At least she only had Jess to lose ... and Seth, of course. But he hadn't ever really been hers in the first place, she thought morbidly.

"It's all right," Sarai said, flashing her a quick smile. "It's been a long time. I think it was kind of a blessing for mama, anyway. My little sister was with them. She was supposed to marry a man who was not... kind. Sometimes I almost think she was lucky to go the way she did, quickly and without pain before she got married."

"You aren't happy with Calvin, are you?" Calla said, her heart melting at Sarai's story. "Have you ever considered leaving him?"

Sarai stopped working, and Calla realized she was trying to control her emotions.

"I could never leave him," she said finally, her smile faded. "I used to think about it, but there is no way. This is the first time I've been off the rock since we got married, you know. The children have never left before now. There's no way I could get away from him. I don't have any money, I don't have anywhere to go and I've only ever been to Bethesda base and the rock. There's no place for someone like me out there, and I have my children to think about."

Calla cast a glance over toward the children. They sat at the table, drawing pictures with an unnatural quiet. Both had been eating heartily, but were still painfully thin. Mali's skin looked like white parchment stretched across her pale face. Able was delicate too, although he seemed tougher than his sister. Calla had noticed how protective he was of the little girl. Just like Jess was with me, she thought longing.

"What if you could leave?" she asked Sarai finally. "What would you do then?"

"Then I would leave," the woman replied in a faint voice. "I would leave and take my children somewhere else. He's already started talking to some of his friends about Mali. They're going to marry her off, and I'll never see her again... It will be another six or seven years before they do it, but I think about it all the time."

"Maybe you'll have a chance someday," Calla said after a long pause.

"I doubt it," Sarai answered. She looked at Calla with haunted eyes. "He'll kill me before he lets me go, and no one will stand in his way. I've come to accept that."

Turning away from Calla abruptly, Sarai walked across the room to the fresher. Calla moved over to the table and sat down next to Mali. The little girl had drawn a picture of four people standing together, holding hands. Two adults and two children. Mali looked up at her and smiled, the expression transforming her small, thin face.

"This is mama and me and Able and you," she said. "We're going to the palace to visit the emperor's harem. When we get there, we're going to have roast *baka* bird and eat candy all day long!"

"Don't be silly," Able said, looking at her scornfully. "We're not going there. We're going to Bethesda base, and then we'll head back to the Rock. That's what daddy says."

"I want to go to the palace," Mali said. "I hate the Rock, I don't want to go back there."

"It's not about what we want," Able said. "Isn't that right, Devora? We gotta do what the men say. That's the way things work."

"Yes," Calla said softly, her heart aching for them. "Unfortunately, that's the way things seem to work."

* * * * *

Seth kept a close eye on Calvin as they approached Bethesda base, just as carefully as he'd watched the man all week. He wouldn't put it past the man to attack him when they landed. He'd been eyeing the ship since they'd first arrived at his camp. Seth had done everything in his power to convince the crazed fool that he was sympathetic to the Pilgrim cause, but there was no way to know if he'd fallen for it or not. Seth wanted to get as much information as possible out of him before his cover was blown. Calvin was his key to finding the rest of the Pilgrims.

"It don't look right," Calvin said as they got closer, pointing toward the asteroid's surface. "I told you them Sarelins took 'em out. See that?"

Seth did see. On the surface was a small cluster of habitation domes. Two of the three had been blown open. The third appeared to be intact, but there were no signs of life. No activity, no moving vehicles, no lights. The landing field was completely empty of ships. Seth cautiously double-checked to make sure their shields were at their highest setting; he wanted to take as many precautions as possible before landing.

Calvin worked the radio, trying a variety of frequencies and codes. There was no response. By the time they'd landed, the man's expression had grown ugly. Making his way down out of the cockpit, Seth thought through his options carefully. He hadn't been able to detect any signs of life using his scanning equipment, but there were ways to fool a scanner. It would be best to leave the women on board. He would set the autopilot to take the ship back to the main base, so that if something happened to him, Devora, Sarai and the children would escape. He'd have to keep an even closer watch over Calvin. He seemed so unsettled by what had happened at Bethesda that Seth believed he might snap.

"We're going to try and figure out what happened here," Seth said as soon as he was off the ladder and in the main room. The women and children watched him anxiously, Devora's eyes full of questions.

"What did you see?" she asked quickly.

"Two of the domes have been blown open," Seth replied, moving quickly toward the airlock. "The third seems to be intact, but we don't know if there are any survivors. We'll be back soon. If anything happens, or anyone approaches the ship, you can call us on the com. I'll leave the feed open so you can hear us."

"But don't call us with your stupid women's crap," Calvin muttered as he entered the room. He paused to give them a harsh glare. "We've got more important things to do."

Quickly pulling on their pressure suits Seth and Calvin went through the airlock He had strapped his blaster onto the side of his hip. The slow cycle seemed to take forever as Seth peered out the small porthole toward the base. Something just seemed wrong. When the light flicked green, he and Calvin stepped through the door and descended to the surface. There were still no signs of life. Seth motioned his companion toward the still-intact dome, and they started lumbering their way across the uneven surface. It was as if someone had gone so far as to try and destroy any hope of repairing the base by attacking the rock itself. All around them, the landing field was pitted with craters.

As they came closer, there were more signs of violence. A pressure suit glove, spent energy blaster casings and scorch marks littered the surface. The main entrance to the dome was directly ahead of them, but Seth noticed a large, blackened pile off to the left. Telling Calvin to wait for him through the com patch in his suit, Seth moved closer to investigate. It looked as if some had used a proton gun to try and destroy whatever it was in the pile. Kicking aside some of the debris with his foot, Seth made a discovery that sent him stumbling back.

A sooty skull grinned up at him.

In horror, Seth realized he was probably staring at the remains of those who once lived on the base. Who had done this?

"Calvin, come here," he said. "I think we've found your friends. At least some of them."

"What the hell are you talking about?" Calvin muttered, walking toward him slowly and heavily. The man was not in good shape, and lumbering around the surface left him breathing unpleasantly loud into the com unit. "Holy shit. They slaughtered 'em."

They both stood staring at the mound. Most of it had been burned so fiercely that nothing but ash remained, but here and there a bit of bone was visible. Seth felt sick to his stomach.

"Drop your weapons and turn around slowly, hands where I can see you," said an unfamiliar voice through the com unit. "Otherwise I'll kill you. I don't have a damn thing to lose, so don't push me."

Seth dropped his gun, then raised his arms slowly. Calvin hesitated, then did the same. Seth hadn't actually trusted him with a charged weapon, but Calvin didn't know that and neither did their captor. Slowly, the two men swiveled to face the man who had come up behind them.

He was dressed in pressure suit that had definitely seen better days. It was scorched from blaster fire, and had been patched in several places.

"Who are you?" the man asked, seeming anxious. "What group are you with?"

Seth wondered if he was the only survivor.

"I'm a trader, just passing through," he said. "This is my colleague, Calvin."

"I'm a Pilgrim, and this is our base," Calvin said brashly. "Who are you? What happened here?" Seth could have strangled him for being so rude to their captor. The last thing they wanted to do was piss the man off, but Calvin was about as stupid as they came. If he wasn't lucky, he was going to get himself killed before too long. Hell, sometimes Seth was tempted to do the killing.

"Me?" the man asked. He chuckled to himself a bit wildly, and Seth wondered if the man was unbalanced. Being stuck alone in a burned out base for a month or two might do that to a man, he figured. "I'm the new owner of Bethesda base. It's my territory now, and you guys are trespassing."

"What the hell-" Calvin started to bellow, but Seth backhanded him across the chest in disgust. He fell to the ground gasping.

"My friend didn't mean to be rude," Seth said quietly, trying to engage their captor. "Perhaps we can come to some kind of arrangement? We aren't interested in causing any trouble."

"An arrangement?" the man laughed. "I don't think that's going to happen. I think we're past making arrangements." Without warning he fired his blaster. The shot took Seth off guard, then the ground next to him sported a new blast mark. He'd missed. With sudden insight, Seth realized the man didn't have much experience with a gun. There might still be some hope for the situation.

Calvin was still on the ground trying to catch his breath, oblivious to the drama taking place above him. Suddenly, he rolled over and vomited in his suit. The movement startled the man with the gun, and Seth leapt toward him. The man never saw it coming. One minute he was watching Calvin gasping and the next he was on his back, pinned down by Seth's bulk. Seth wrenched the gun out of his hands and held it against his neck.

"Now, let's get some answers," he said coldly. "What the hell happened here?"

"I told you, I've got nothing to lose," the man giggled. "Go ahead, shoot me. Then at least it would be over."

"It's not going to be that easy," Seth said. "I need information, and you're going to give it to me. We can do this the easy way or the hard way. The hard way will be extremely painful, and it could take a very long time. Now, who are you?"

"I'm Bragan," the man said after a minute. No longer giggling, he seemed to have grown suddenly morose. "I'm the doctor here."

"Now we're getting somewhere," Seth said. "What happened?"

"The slaves revolted," the man said. "They found a way to remove their implants and they revolted. The Pilgrims fought back and they died. Poor Pilgrims, they got a taste of their own medicine…"

Seth sat back on his haunches, keeping the gun trained on Bragan. All the fight seemed to have drained out of him, and he simply laid there in his pressure suit.

"Are there any other survivors left beside you?" Seth finally asked.

"Oh, no, I'm the only one," Bragan said. "It's really quite amusing when you think about it." He started giggling softly to himself again.

"What's amusing about it?" Seth asked, feeling nauseous. The poor man was out of his mind, but he was the only witness they had.

"That I had to stay behind, of course," Bragan said. His giggles grew louder, punctuated by snorts of escaping air. Then he started laughing out loud, uncontrollably. The sound was magnified as it passed through the com system, adding strength to the man's cackles.

"Why is that amusing?" Seth said. Bragan was laughing so hard now he could hardly speak.

"W-w-why, b-b-b-because," Bragan sputtered out between fits of dark mirth. "I'm the o-o-one who took out the implants, of course. I'm the surgeon. But when all the slaves were free, there was no one left to take out my implant and I had to s-s-s-stay..."

The man continued to lay on the ground, giggling at his little joke while Seth stared in horrified fascination. Bragan had helped his fellow slaves revolt, only to find himself trapped on the asteroid base. After a few seconds, the quality of his noise changed, and Seth realized he was sobbing. Bragan cried for a few minutes more, then lay still.

"They said they'd come back for me," he finally whispered. "But you got here first. It's all over, now."

Calvin, who Seth had all but forgotten about, chose that moment to launch himself at Bragan's prone figure.

"Who did it?" Calvin screamed. "Who did this? Which slaves? Where did they go? I'll kill the bastards!" He grasped Bragan's pressure suit and began banging his head against the ground.

"Jess..." the man gasped under his onslaught, pawing feebly at Calvin. "It was Jess and Logan. They were the leaders."

"Calvin, get control of yourself," Seth said with disgust, then wrenched the braggart off Bragan's prone body. "He can't give us any information if he's dead. Come on. Let's get him back to the ship."

"Oh, no you don't!" Bragan shouted hysterically. He started crawling frantically through the dust toward the dome. "I can't go on a ship. I can leave the base. My implant will go off! I can't go ... I can't ... please don't make me go, please!"

"Get on your feet," Seth said. "We're not going to leave the base yet. I'm just going to lock you up on my ship so we can explore." Bragan didn't seem to hear him. The man just kept scrabbling away from them, whimpering and crying.

"We should just kill him," Calvin muttered, casting a resentful look at Seth. Seth glared back, not bothering to answer. He continued to coax Bragan, who ignored him. Finally, seeing no other, Seth came up behind the gibbering man and hit him on the head with the blunt end of his blaster. Hoping he hadn't caused any permanent harm, he boosted his limp body up and threw it over his shoulder. Then he headed back to the ship, Calvin following him and muttering angrily.

* * * * *

Calla watched the man anxiously. Seth had bound and gagged him, tying him securely to one of the bulkheads in the main room. She and Sarai listened to the entire exchange between the men and Bragan on the com before they brought him in, and at the sound of Jess' name her heart had all but stopped beating. This man, still unconscious, might have information for her. She needed to find a way to get it out of him. Seth and Calvin had left to go exploring again. It would be at least an hour before they came back. It might be her only chance.

"Children, why don't you go into the bedroom," Calla said, smiling at them as if having a bound and bloodied man in the main living quarters was a normal thing. "Your mother and I are going to take care of this man and make him feel better."

Sarai looked at her anxiously, concerned that she was disobeying Seth. They were supposed to ignore the man, to not speak or come close to him. Seth had given them a gun, and told them to shoot to kill if Bragan did anything threatening.

"I know what I'm doing," Calla said, looking reassuringly toward Sarai. The two of them had developed a strange, secret bond over the past week. Hopefully she would be willing to play along, Calla thought. "Just trust me."

After a second, Sarai nodded her head. "Yes, I'll trust you Devora. What should we do?"

Calla was startled at Sarai's quick acquiescence, then realized she shouldn't be. Sarai always did as she was told... sometimes Calla wondered if the woman had a mind of her own at all.

"Bring me some warm water," Calla said, moving quickly toward the man. "I'll wash his face, and maybe that will wake him up. If he isn't seriously injured, that is," she muttered under her breath. You couldn't tell with a head wound. Sarai brought the water and a soft cloth. Calla handed her the gun, telling her to sit just out of the man's reach. "Shoot him if he tries anything, you understand?" Calla said. "And if he grabs me somehow, shoot anyway. It's very important to protect the children. Can you do that?"

"Protect the children," Sarai echoed back to her, lifting the weapon experimentally. She turned the blaster over in her hands several times, and a strange little smile came across her face. "Yes, I can do that."

"Good," Calla said, then knelt down beside the man. Dipping her cloth in the water, she brought it to his face, wiping gently at the blood. The worst of it was in his hair, but with one little washcloth she wasn't going to be able to get him truly clean. This would be to revive him, make him comfortable. Then maybe he'd tell her about Jess.

He didn't show any signs of life, and after several minutes she started to get worried. Then he made a small, moaning noise and his eyelids fluttered open. He looked up at her in confusion.

"Don't worry, we aren't going to hurt you," she said, trying to smile in a reassuring manner as she removed his gag. "I was just cleaning you up, trying to make you a feel a little better. How are you doing?"

"My head hurts," he whispered. "Where am I?"

"On our ship," Calla replied. "Seth and Calvin brought you here so they could explore."

"A ship?" he started struggling against his restraints. "I can't go anywhere on a ship. I still have my slave implant. I'll die if I leave the asteroid's electrical field."

Calla laid a calming hand on him.

"We're not going anywhere right now," she said quickly, keeping her voice low and soothing. "You're just here as a precaution. There's no plan to take off any time soon, so you don't have to worry about that right now." The man peered up at her, trying to judge whether she was speaking the truth. Something in her expression must have reassured him, because he stopped struggling.

"I'm very thirsty," he said softly. "Would you be willing to give me something to drink?"

"Of course," Calla said. "I'll be right back."

She brought him a glass of water, and tilted it against his lips so he could drink. After a few seconds, she pulled it away, but he reached for more.

"It's so good," he said finally, licking his lips. "I can't remember the last time I had fresh water like that. Years, maybe. You look like someone I've seen before."

"How long have you been here?" Calla asked quietly, even as she searched her mind, trying to remember if she'd seen him before. Had he ever come through the hostel?

"Five years," Bragan replied. "Five long years. It's been hell."

"I've never met a slave who was a doctor before," Calla said, attempting to draw him out. "Were you born into slavery?"

"No, I wasn't," he replied. His eyes darted nervously around the room. "Are you sure we aren't going anywhere?"

"Very sure," Calla replied. "I'm curious about how you came to be here, though."

"I was enslaved for breaking the law," he said. Calla caught her breath–she'd never heard of such a thing. Usually criminals were executed. Bragan must have sensed her confusion, because he gave a harsh laugh. "My crime was I sometimes removed slave implants illegally. Runaways, that kind of thing. When they caught me, I guess they figured the punishment would fit the crime."

Unable to stop herself, Calla, nervously reached around to feel the back of her neck, to the spot where her implant had been. There was no scar; her surgeon had been good. Bragan watched her closely, then gave a sympathetic smile.

"I guess you know what that feels like," he whispered. "Does anyone know?"

Calla glanced back at Sarai. The woman was watching them closely, although she doubted she'd been able to hear Bragan's comment. "No," Calla whispered back. "Only the one who did it, and he's far away from here. Are you going to tell?"

"No," Bragan said. "I've learned something from my time here. Slaves have to help each other. It's the only way any of us will ever survive. Why are you here?"

"I'm here because I'm looking for someone," Calla said. "I need some information from you."

"What kind of information?" Bragan asked, grinning wryly. "I'm don't really have much to offer at this point, I have to admit."

"I need to know about the revolt," Calla replied. It was her moment of truth. "You mentioned the leader was named Jess. Can you describe him to me?"

"Why do you want to know?" Bragan asked suspiciously. Calla took a deep breath. It was time to tell the truth; she had to know for sure.

"Because I think he may be my brother," Calla replied. Bragan's face froze.

"What's your name?" he demanded in a harsh whisper.

"I go by Devora," she replied, twisting the cloth in her hands. It was so hard to talk about her old life. "But I used to be called Calla."

Bragan looked stunned. He just stared at her for a moment, then broke into a smile. "That's why you look familiar. Jess had a hologram of the two of you together that he showed me. He kept it on a string around his neck."

Calla's breath caught in her throat. Jess had been here, so close.

"Where is he now? What happened?" she asked desperately.

"He's gone," Bragan said. Strong emotion flickered across his face. "He was going back for you. How did you get here?"

"I escaped," she said, tears building in her eyes. "I escaped and came to rescue Jess. I guess he had the same idea. Can you tell me how it happened?"

"I will, but you can't give the information to those men," Bragan said. A cough took him by surprise, and his body doubled over, spasming, for a minute. When it finally stopped, Calla gave him another drink of water. "Sorry about that, asthma," he muttered. "I got it from living here in all this dust... You'll have to be patient with me. I've been here a long time, and after the others left I started hallucinating a lot. It's hard for me to tell what's real anymore."

"I give you my word, I'm real and I won't tell anyone," Calla said, closing her eyes briefly. It would be one more lie to Seth, but she'd gone too far to stop now. Remember, she told herself firmly, Seth is a pleasant interlude, but Jess is your family. Don't forget your priorities.

"Jess hadn't been here that long," Bragan told her. "But he was angry. Angrier than a lot of men who've been here for a year or more. He and another man, Logan, started talking. It wasn't too long after that they came to see me. They knew I'd been a doctor, and they wanted to know if I could remove their implants."

Bragan stopped speaking, apparently lost in thought.

"Bragan, do you need some more water?" Calla asked him after a moment. He looked at her, startled.

"Sorry, I forgot where I was," he said softly. "You know, I warned them it was dangerous, even with the right equipment and anesthetic. There was a good chance they'd die. They were willing to take the risk, though, and I was willing to do it for them. I had gotten to the point where I didn't really care if I lived or died, but I really liked the thought of Jess and Logan taking out some of those damn Pilgrims. Cruelest human beings I've ever met."

"I know," Calla said. "Jess and I belonged to one."

"Well, these ones were worse," he said. "They liked to use the energy whips on the slaves, and sometimes they'd get drunk and decide to go hunting. Then they'd pick someone, give him a pressure suit and sent him out without any food and water. They'd stalk him and kill him like he was nothing."

"Slaves aren't human to Pilgrims," Calla murmured darkly.

"No, we aren't," Bragan agreed. He paused to collect his thoughts, a far-away look coming into his eyes. "I did Jess and Logan, and they both lived. But that wasn't good enough for them. They wanted to escape, but they wanted the others to escape with them. And they wanted to destroy the base before they left. They didn't want any of the miners to be able to ever hurt another slave again.

"So they started organizing. Ultimately all the men agreed, they were willing to risk death to escape. It's not like they had any hope here, after all," he said. His tone had become strangely smooth, almost sing-song as his story progressed. "So one by one, I took out their implants. Some of them died–quite a few actually–but they disposed of the bodies in the mine. Made 'em look like accidents. It wasn't hard to fool the Pilgrim bastards. They never did give us enough credit for our intelligence.

"The ironic thing is that in the end, there was nobody to take out my implant. They're wrapped around the spinal nerves, you know, so you can't just cut them out. They offered to try, but I didn't see any point to it. So they decided they would escape, then come back with a doctor to free me if they could find one. I told them it was foolish, but they wouldn't listen. Of course, they haven't come back yet, either. I figured I'd wait until I couldn't take it any more, then kill myself. I don't know what I expected to happen." He paused, licking his lips. "Can I have another sip of water?"

"Of course," Calla said quickly, raising the cup to his lips.

"So they planned and waited," he continued. "One day, a bunch of the miners left to go to another base, some kind of meeting. When they'd gone, Jess and the others overpowered the men watching us. There were only two of them, and about fifty of us. They were so smug–they thought they could kill us with a touch of a button. You should have seen the looks on their faces when they realized the implants weren't working! It was beautiful to see, although I wasn't very close. I had to stay away, you know, because my implant was still active.

"When they realized their emergency activation wands weren't going to work, that's when they got scared. Then they started screaming, and one of them actually got down on his knees and begged for his life. This was the same guy who, just a week before, had killed a slave for walking too slow. Bastard.

"They killed him, of course, and they killed the other guard too," Bragan got a hard look in his eyes. "I still think they let them die too quick, but Jess and Logan were pretty clear from the start. They'd kill the Pilgrims, but they weren't going to torture them. Said they wanted to be better than them or something, I don't know. Anyway, once the guards were dead it was easy to take over the base. There were hardly any men left; they took all of them out and shot them."

"What about the women?" Calla whispered, a sinking feeling in her stomach. Seth had described the charnel pile he'd found to her. "What about the children?"

"They herded them all together in one of the transport ships. Sent them off toward the main base on a slow route, I guess. Told them to tell everyone what happened, and that Pilgrims better not sleep soundly anymore," he added with a vicious smile. The gleam in his eyes was almost feral. Calla was glad he was still tied up, because at that moment he scared her. She could see the madness in his eyes. "We didn't want to hurt them. Most of them were as much victims as we were, although some were real bitches. And there was one...well, anyway," he said, looking away from her. Calla sensed he was hiding something from her.

"What happened?" she pressed. "I want to know."

"You're not going to like it," Bragan said, still not meeting her eyes.

"Tell me," Calla said with quiet confidence. "I've survived a lot myself. I can handle it."

"Well, Jess was always watching her," he finally said. "He talked about her all the time, and when we finally took over the base, he took her."

"What do you mean, *her*?' Calla whispered. "Who was she? What did he do to her."

"She was the station leader's daughter, and what the hell do you think he did to her? Use your imagination," Bragan snapped. "He said she was his, that she wasn't going with the others. He was keeping her. For himself."

Calla felt sick to her stomach. The Jess she knew would never hurt a helpless young woman, but she could see the truth in Bragan's eyes. She pushed it out of her mind, it was too much to think about. Jess was gone-*free!* A part of her felt like singing with joy for him, the other like crying for him and the woman he'd taken prisoner. The Jess of her youth was gone beyond her reach, she realized with sorrow. She would never find him now. "Tell me the rest."

"Well, once they got rid of the women and children, they set a trap for the men. When those buggers returned, they ambushed them and killed them. All of them," he said with dark satisfaction. "I helped them do it, too. I've lasted a long time here because I'm a doctor and they needed me. The others weren't so fortunate. I've seen a lot of young men die on this rock. Killing those Pilgrim bastards was justice. I'd like to do it again," he muttered, dark pleasure lighting his face.

"When they got done, they had a council and decided to go their separate ways. Logan was taking a bunch of them with him, and I guess Jess was going to meet up with them later. He took that girl and went off to find you. There was another group who wanted to go hunt down more of the Pilgrims and rescue their slaves. They were the ones who were coming back for me with a doctor... I was going to go with them, to remove implants," he said. "I guess that's not going to happen now."

"I guess not," Calla whispered. "I don't know what to tell you. Even if I had a way to get you out of here, I can't do anything about the implant."

The two sat in silence for a while. Sarai watched over them, still holding the gun. Finally, the woman spoke, startling both of them.

"You aren't very good at keeping your voices down," she said. "I heard what you said. I had no idea you were a slave, Devora. Or should I call you Calla?"

"Devora," Calla said tightly. She squeezed her eyes closed, willing her situation to change. She didn't think Sarai would intentionally harm her, but the woman was weak. Eventually Calvin would find out, and then she'd be caught.

"Devora," Sarai spoke softly, reassuringly. "I know what it's like to be afraid. I've been afraid my whole life, but I've come to realize something." She set the gun down carefully on the table, then came across the room to sit with them on the floor.

"I've realized that I don't like living in fear, and I don't want my children to live in fear any more, either," she continued. "Until now, I never saw how I could change that. I see now, though."

"What do you see?" Calla asked dully. Jess was gone. They'd each found a chance at freedom in their own way, but they had no way to find each other. It was a big quadrant.

"I see that we don't have to stay here," Sarai replied. She looked more animated than Calla had ever seen her. "Those slaves revolted, and they left. We could have our own little revolt."

"You want to kill Seth and Calvin?" Calla asked, horrified.

"No, of course not," Sarai said. "But we could leave them here. I listen to all of you talk; I know this ship is capable of flying without a pilot. All we have to do is leave. Once we're gone we could send help for Seth and Calvin. But by the time they're rescued we'll be long gone. Don't you see? This could be our only chance. We'll sell the ship and make new lives for ourselves!"

"I can't do that to Seth," Calla said. "He doesn't deserve to be treated that way."

"I don't deserve to be treated this way, either," Sarai replied fervently. "Neither do my children. Seth hasn't done anything to help us."

"Think about what she's saying, Missy," Bragan added, watching her closely. "I don't know this Seth very well, but I do know that life isn't easy for a slave on the run. If he ever finds out, he could return you to your master for a reward, or even take you himself. You don't have any rights, you know."

Calla could see their logic, but leaving Seth seemed so wrong. She loved him. Of course, he didn't love her, she reminded herself. When their contract was up, she might never see him again. She'd have enough money to get herself set up somewhere, but that wouldn't help Sarai and her children. Just the thought of leaving them with Calvin made her blood run cold.

"I'll have to think about it," she said finally. "What about you, Bragan? What would happen to you if we did it?"

"You can just leave me here," he said earnestly. "It won't change anything. I'm stuck on this rock no matter what. While you're thinking, though, I would really appreciate something to eat."

"Of course," Sarai said, startled into giving a out a little laugh. She sounded happy, Calla realized. She'd never heard Sarai sound happy before. "I'll get you something."

Calla sat thinking as Sarai fed the man. Maybe she should take the ship. If she did, they could go somewhere and sell it. They'd get enough to start over, and if they went far enough away, Seth would never find them. Calla had no doubt his anger would be terrible. If she did do it, she didn't want to take any chances he'd find her... A whirring noise from the airlock caught her attention. The men were back. Sarai leapt away from Bragan, busying herself in the kitchen area.

"Think about it," Bragan softly, his eyes locking with hers. Then the airlock door opened, and Seth and Calvin walked were there. Seth's gaze flew to his prisoner, noting the gag had been removed.

"I told you not to talk to him," Seth said angrily to Calla. "He's dangerous."

Chapter 9

Devora stared up at him with guilt written all over her lovely face. Why was she talking to Bragan? Sarai was scuttling around like a mad woman, refusing to look at any of them. The children were nowhere to be seen. Something was definitely going on, Seth thought.

"Why were you talking to him?" He repeated his question.

"Um," Devora said, casting her eyes about. Then she gestured toward a small bowl of water and a rag. "I was worried about him. He wasn't moving, so I decided to clean off his face and make sure he was all right. When he woke up he wanted some water. We–I mean, I–gave him a drink and some food. That's all."

No one said anything, and silence fell over the room. Calvin glared at her, then muttered, "Stupid women," before turning to pull off his suit. A new stench–that of vomit–followed him. Seth tensed at Calvin's tone; he had long since realized the man was a fool as well as a menace, but he learned a great deal about the Pilgrims from him. In fact, he was pretty sure Calvin thought Seth was considering joining the cult. It was probably the only reason the man hadn't turned on him yet, Seth reasoned.

As for Devora, he would keep a close eye on her. She seemed to be up to something, but he had no idea what interest she would have in Bragan. Maybe she *was* just trying to help the man; he did look pathetic slumped there on the floor.

"Well, don't talk to him any more," Seth finally said. "I'll make sure he's fed from now on."

"What are you planning to do with him?" Devora asked bluntly.

"We'll kill the bastard," Calvin blustered. "He's a murderer, he deserves to die."

"Not so fast," Seth broke in quickly. "Bragan, if you give us the information we're looking for we may spare you."

Bragan's eyes grew wild at Seth's words. He tensed his entire body, then spat at Seth like a snake.

"I'll take that as a sign you don't want to talk right now," Seth said, sighing. His mission had grown far more complex than he'd ever anticipated. He'd come to the belt to collect information on a dangerous cult. Now he had a family to rescue, not to mention a band of revolutionary slaves running around. Not that he blamed them for fighting back; the working conditions in the belt were unbearable. Quietly he admitted some admiration for the men who'd risked their lives to fight back. He would have done the same in their situation. It created complications for the occupation and peace process, however. The Saurellians couldn't afford to look weak right now.

"Calvin, let's eat and we'll talk about tomorrow," he said finally.

"Woman, bring me my food," Calvin bellowed and Sarai jumped. "And *bakrah*!"

He missed eating with Devora, Seth thought as he sat with Calvin that night. The man was telling him the Celestial Pilgrim's theories on racial purity. Seth listened with one ear, keying a small pocket recorder to preserve everything the man said for the Saurellian intelligence analysts. Calvin's theories were so delusional and violent that they made him feel ill at times; it was hard to stay focused. Devora and Sarai eventually took small plates of food in to the children. Seth wished deeply that he could go with them. The evening, like every evening with Calvin, crept by with agonizing slowness. After an eternity, the disgusting man belched heavily and lumbered off to the bedroom. Devora and Sarai cleaned up his mess, then Sarai retired.

"Can I feed Bragan some dinner?" Devora asked quietly once the three of them were alone in the room..

"I'll do it," Seth said gruffly, wishing he hadn't come down on her so hard earlier. She still refused to look at him. There'd been something different about her for days now, and he suspected it had something to do with the way he was making friends with Calvin. She didn't trust him and she hated Calvin. For the thousandth time, he wished he could explain everything to her. But each time he almost broke down, he reminded himself that she was a former imperial citizen who hadn't expressed any allegiance to the confederation. It was an unnecessary risk, one he had no right to take.

Once this was all over, he knew their life together would be hard. She might not want to live in Saurellian space. She would expect regular compensation, and he would have to keep a close eye on her. He'd have to be particularly careful around other men. She was a pleasure worker, she wasn't used to long-term fidelity. She would learn with time, though. He could make her happy; his family was both wealthy and of high social standing. He just needed to finish his mission and they'd be able to start over...

Dropping to one knee, Seth offered Bragan a bite of the hearty stew they'd had for dinner. Bragan took it and chewed it furiously. After several mouthfuls without incident, Seth let his attention wander. His gaze came to rest on Devora, who was sitting at the table studying some star charts. It seemed like such a long time since they'd looked at the charts together; she loved to learn about the geography of the quadrant and navigation, but since Calvin had been on board they hadn't done anything together. She was so beautiful just sitting there that it made his heart ache to watch her.

His reverie was broken by a warm splat against his face. Stifling a roar of surprise and anger, he slapped one hand to his cheek, pulling it away to see what hit him. Bragan was giggling at him. With disgust, Seth realized the man had spit chewed-up stew at him. He glared at the man, raising a hand to cuff him for his insolence. Then the absurdity of the situation hit him, and he dropped his arm slowly. He replaced the gag in Bragan's mouth...

"That's it for tonight, Bragan," he said, forcing himself to ignore the incident. The man was clearly crazy. He rose to his feet, washed the mess off of his face and went to join Devora at the table. She didn't look at him directly, but he could see her shoulders shuddering with suppressed laughter. "I'm glad I could do something to entertain you."

"I'm sorry," she said. "The look on your face was priceless." She sobered after a minute, then asked him, "So what did you find today?"

"Well, it looks like things got pretty bloody," Seth said, relaxing back in his chair. It felt good to sit and talk with her. It had been too long. "I did a scan of the bodies we found, and none of them were women or children. I don't know what happened to them, though, so we have to assume they're hostages."

"Bragan said they sent them to the Discovery station," Devora broke in quietly. Seth looked at her penetratingly, and Bragan gave a grunt of protest from his corner. "Bragan, he needs to know this," she told the prisoner. "You don't want them to think the slaves are more dangerous than they are, do you?"

"So you don't think they're dangerous?" Seth asked casually. Devora's words surprised him; he'd thought she would have been more frightened by the idea of a slave revolt.

"Well, they were being held under terrible conditions," she replied, looking away from him. "If you were a slave, wouldn't you try to get away?"

"Maybe," Seth said. "But I can't approve of they way they slaughtered these men."

Devora's eyes flashed in anger. He didn't understand why she cared so much.

"If they were just slaughtering people, why did they spare the women and children? It sounds to me like the men got what they deserved. You've heard Calvin talk–he doesn't even think of the slaves as human. I know why they did what they did."

"You know why they did what they did? What does that mean, exactly? It's not like you've ever been a slave," Seth said, one eyebrow raised. Devora looked away.

"I guess I meant I can imagine what it would be like," she said finally. Bragan gave a harsh bark of laughter from behind his gag as he sat tied in the corner, and Devora glared at him. "I'm tired of this. I want to go to sleep."

"Fine," Seth said mildly, promising himself he'd start this conversation with Devora again someday. He'd never seen her so flustered; she was definitely hiding something. She stood up abruptly and went into the fresher. With a sigh, Seth turned off the lights and made his way over to the pallet they'd been sleeping on ever since Calvin and his family had joined them. The ship was too small for so many people, Seth thought darkly. With Bragan in the room with them, he and Devora couldn't even have sex. He missed their times together.

After a few minutes she came out of the fresher and joined him in the darkness. He reached over and pulled her small body close to his, nestling his front against her back. She stiffened, then relaxed into his larger frame. Dropping his face down into her hair, he inhaled deeply. She smelled clean and fresh, and he hardened instantly. Her tight little butt wiggled involuntarily against his erection, and he felt his cock twitch in response. Bragan snorted loudly from across the room, and Seth stiffened.

It was going to be a long night.

When Seth awoke the next morning, Devora was already up and ready. Bragan had been grunting during the night and making himself generally annoying; neither of them had gotten much sleep. Calvin strutted out into the room a few minutes later. Sarai came out even more quietly than usual, her long hair hanging in her face. Both children were equally subdued, staying as far away from their father as possible.

He must have hurt her last night, Seth realized. He was going to have to do something about Calvin today, he decided. The man's value wasn't worth tolerating his behavior any longer. He needed Calvin to help him move some of the barricades left over from revolt, but tonight the Pilgrim would join Bragan in captivity. Perhaps he could convert one of the two cargo holds to serve as a make-shift prison cell, he mused. Devora dropped his breakfast in front of him on the table with a thunk. She was angry with him, probably about Sarai's condition. He sighed heavily, wishing it was just the two of them again.

After they'd eaten, he allowed Devora to feed Bragan, and escorted him to the fresher. Then he and Calvin donned their suits and made their way to the airlock.

"The hand blaster is still fully charged," he reminded Devora as they left. "Don't hesitate to shoot him if he gets out of hand. We'll be back in a couple of hours."

"You shouldn't leave them stupid bitches with a weapon," Calvin muttered as soon as they started walking toward the ruined domes. "They'll probably end up hurting themselves. And I don't figure why you want to keep that murderin' bastard alive. He ain't got no more information for us. He don't deserve to live."

"It's not up for discussion," Seth coldly, and abruptly turned his radio down so he wouldn't have to listen any more. The man really was a monster, he thought. It would be a pleasure locking him up. He had more than enough evidence to convict him for plotting against the occupation.

They reached the main bubble where Bragan had been living first, but that wasn't Seth's target today. He wanted to explore the second bubble, where the families had been. Calvin stumbled along beside him, muttering to himself. They didn't have far to go, although the craters and debris made walking hard. The second dome's entrance was still relatively intact, its airlock doors shut tightly. There was no power to open them, but it wasn't a problem. They simply walked around, stepping through one of the many holes that had been blasted in the wall.

What they found inside was an eerily quiet war zone, a ghost colony. The interior rooms and corridors that remained were scarred with blaster fire and pocked with holes. It was hard to tell what had happened, but as they moved through the various rooms it appeared the men had fought their way out room by room. Darkened blood spatters could be seen in several places. It had been an ugly fight.

Nearly two hours later, Seth made their first useful discovery. Just outside one of the apartments was a holo-camera, the kind used often used as a security device. It looked like it had once been trained on the apartment's caved-in door, although it was now dangling from a single cord.

"It's probably where Bose, the station leader, lived," Calvin said as Seth examined the device. "He would've wanted a record of who came to see him, even when he wasn't around."

Gesturing for Calvin to boost him up, Seth managed to grab the recorder and pull it down from its precarious perch. He turned it over in his hands several times, searching for signs of what happened. As far as he could tell, it was fine except for a power source.

"It's amazing it wasn't more damaged during the attack," he finally said. "I wonder if there's anything on the recording. Let's hook it into a power source and see. Turn around."

Calvin turned, giving Seth access to the small power pack on the back of his suit. It took Seth a couple of tries before he managed to splice a connection between Calvin's suit and the camera. Then it flickered into life. Seth started the playback mode, and a small holographic representation of the apartment entrance appeared in the air before them.

Apparently the camera had been set to slowly pan back and forth between the apartment door and the corridor, and for several minutes they watched shots of nothing happening. No one walked by; it had been a quiet day on the station. Calvin grew impatient, and made to pull the camera away from his suit, but Seth held up a hand to stall him. The picture before them was changing. There was a flash of movement, then the camera's view slowly panned from the apartment entrance to the corridor, revealing a horrifying struggle for survival.

First there was simply a shot of empty corridor as it once appeared, unmarked by blaster fire. Then a group of filthy men–presumably the slaves–came creeping up into the camera's vision. Several carried homemade weapons, while a few held blasters. Their leader gestured them to stay back, and cautiously stuck his head around the corner at the far end of the corridor. A flash of blaster fire came back, and the men froze. Then the leader stood and yelled something. Seth and Calvin had no idea what he was saying–the camera wasn't sophisticated enough to record sound–but whatever it was put life into his men. As a group they charged around the corner. There was more blaster fire, then the camera's angle started to change as it swept back toward the apartment entrance.

At first there was nothing, then an obviously terrified child came running up to the door, pounding on it for entrance. The door opened, and a young woman wearing a dark dress opened it quickly and pulled the child in. She glanced down the hall, then slammed the door shut. After a few seconds another woman, this one older and carrying an infant, came running up. She too was allowed into the apartment, then nothing.

The camera swept back to the corridor, where several men–different than those who had been there before–were setting up benches to form a makeshift barricade. They seemed to be Pilgrims. They shot down around the corner several times, with blaster fire answering them. After a few seconds of intense firing, one was hit and he went down. Then a second was hit. The final man continued to shoot desperately until his blaster stopped responding. It must have run out of charge, Seth thought grimly. The slaves sensed his weakness and swarmed him in an instant, one of them slitting his throat savagely. The fight appeared to be over.

The camera slowly panned back to the door, which remained shut. Seth and Calvin watched, mesmerized, as one of the bloodied men came up to the door and hammered on it. The man was tall, his bare arms roped with muscles. It was the leader who had lead the charge around the corner earlier. He turned his head, said something to the men behind him, then hit the door with one fist. A weapon came into view, passed to the escaped slave from one of his companions, and he yelled again. Then he stood back, took careful aim and shot at the locking mechanism.

It held out for a minute or two, then exploded in a shower of sparks. The man shoved the door open and stalked into the apartment purposefully. Several men followed him, their mouths open in silent whoops and screeches of victory. After a second the child who had taken shelter in the apartment came running out, chased by two of them. The woman with the baby walked out next, surrounded by several more. They quickly disappeared from the camera's view. Then, to Seth's frustration, the camera's view swept out into the hallway again, maintaining its steady surveillance schedule, oblivious to the traumatic events it recorded.

Seth and Calvin stared at the empty hallway for a minute or two. Every once in a while someone would come running through–a child, a jubilant slave. One looked like Bragan, although he moved to quickly to tell for sure. There was still no sign of the man who had broken through the door however, or the other woman who had been hiding in the apartment. Finally the camera turned back to the apartment door. Seth sucked his breath in at what he saw next.

The young woman in the dark dress was struggling to escape the man who had blasted his way through the door. She was pressed up against the doorway, pinned by the weight of his large body. One of his hands was twisted into her hair, and he crushed her mouth against his in a brutal kiss. The woman was fighting him with all her might but he was too strong. With a sickening feel in the pit of his stomach, Seth wondered if they were about to witness a rape. It wouldn't be the first time such a thing had happened in the heat of battle.

The woman flailed against her captor desperately, one hand catching against something tied around his neck. She pulled at it, trying to choke him. Seth held his breath, wondering what she could hope to accomplish; even if she subdued the man, there were fifty more just like him. He already knew how the story ended–the slaves had won. The poor girl didn't have a chance.

The man lifted his head from hers to wrench whatever she had grasped out of her hand. They fought for possession of it, then it broke and something small and bright came off of it and flew out of the camera's range. The man looked around for it, but apparently he couldn't tell where it had gone. The woman, sensing his distraction, chose that moment to try and break free. She kicked him savagely in the groin, and he doubled over in agony. She jerked away from him but was pulled up short by her long hair. A chunk of it was tangled in what was left of the shattered door lock. She pulled at it frantically, but before she freed herself the man had recovered enough to realize his prey was escaping.

He grabbed her arms, savagely twisting them so she couldn't move. Then he pulled out a homemade knife from his belt, a sharpened piece of metal with fabric wound tightly around one end. He brought it toward the woman's head, and Seth caught his breath. The man raised the knife and slashed through the chunk of hair holding the woman to the door. She fell forward against him. Dropping the knife, he grasped the back of her head and crushed her mouth to his again.

Once again, the camera moved back to view the corridor. This time it was empty. Then the man came into view, dragging the woman with him. He searched several minutes for whatever it was that had flown out of his grasp, but the woman struggled against him fiercely. He finally swung her up over his shoulder, her upper body flopping down against his back. She kicked out helplessly and he swatted her butt hard in response. The camera swung away from them as he strode around the corner, his cargo having given up her fight.

As the camera focused once again on the apartment door, a large hand came around in front of it. It grasped the camera, darkening the picture, then the recording ended. Someone had ripped it away from its power source.

"It makes me sick to think of honest Pilgrim women being touched by scum like that," Calvin growled into the silence that followed. "Even if we could get them back, they're no good now. Once a woman's tainted, she's ruined for life. It's a damn shame."

Seth grunted in response. There was nothing to be said to Calvin's statement, and the woman's plight–frozen in time–haunted him. He turned around, surveying the corridor. Something had flown off the man's necklace, and he wondered what it was. Probably just some little keepsake, but it would be interesting to know. He appeared to be one of the leaders; any clues Seth could find to his identity would be helpful when he returned to Discovery station.

Simply looking around, Seth found nothing, so he keyed the suit's scanner to help him. Moving slowly and deliberately, he covered every inch of the corridor, pausing to investigate every anomaly. Unfortunately there were quite a few, as each blaster burn and piece of debris registered separately on the scanner.

"What the hell are you doing that for?" Calvin asked, clearly disgusted. "We should get back to the ship and kill that bastard. Then we need to hunt the rest of 'em down. They're killers, and there's only one way to deal with killers."

"Shut up, Calvin," Seth muttered. The sensor chirped in his headset as it picked up something. It was crystalline in structure. Following the readings, Seth made his way across the corridor. The remains of the small barricade were still there, although they had been torn apart–perhaps the man had come back to find his pendant? Using the sensor as his guide, Seth narrowed in on a broken bench made of hollow plast-crete. Cheap and easy to form, plast-crete was used in construction throughout the empire. In most cases it was brightly colored or shaped to resemble some other material. This was simply plain without ornamentation.

Using the sensor as his guide, Seth turned the plast-crete bench over. There was a rattle inside. After several tries, he realized he wasn't going to be able to get it out by simply maneuvering the bench. Calvin, who had come up behind him to watch, spoke.

"Why don't you just cut the damn thing open?" he asked. "That's the best bet for getting' it out."

For once, Calvin was right. Removing a small laser-cutter from his tool belt, Seth carefully lined the tool up on the bench leg. Making his cut well above the place indicated by the sensor, Seth slowly made the cut. The leg came off easily.

He grasped the newly-freed leg and tilted it. A small, shiny object fell out into the open palm of his glove.

"What is it?" Calvin demanded.

"It's a holographic pendant," Seth said, turning the bauble over in his hands. "You know, the kind you can get taken in booths for a half a credit."

"I ain't never seen one of them booths," Calvin admitted slowly. "We don't hold with that kind of thing."

"Have you ever been out of the asteroid belt?" Seth asked curiously.

"Nope, and I don't wanna ever leave, either," Calvin said harshly. "There ain't nuthin' for an honest Pilgrim out there. Me and my family plan to stay put on our rock."

Seth sighed, wondering briefly what kind of man Calvin might have been if he'd grown up somewhere else, or had access to education. How did a person become so filled with hate?

"How does that thing work, anyway?" Calvin asked, trying not to look too curious.

"Watch," Seth replied. Gripping the little disk between his thumb and forefinger, he held it up in the air. Then he took a small light from his pouch and aimed it at the disk. "You shine the light through it, and the hologram will appear right in front of us."

With a flick of his finger, he turned on the light. The beam hit the disk, and an image of two people took shape in front of them. One was the man who had lost the pendant, although he looked different in the hologram–younger, not as hard. Seth turned his attention to the woman with him, and his heart stopped.

It was Devora, smiling brightly. Her head was tucked snugly against the man's neck, his arm holding her gently around the shoulders. Both seemed to filled with happiness. Below, written clearly in the wavy, gimmicky font often used by public holo machines, was "Jess and Calla, Celebration of the Accession of his Imperial Majesty, Belpharian IV."

The holo was less than two years old. It was as if he'd been kicked in the gut. She'd duped him, been lying to him all along. She *was* the slave, Calla, and she'd used him to escape and look for her husband, the one Jenner had sold.

Calvin cackled into the silence.

"Looks like there's more going on here than I realized," he said with evil glee. Ignoring the man, Seth snapped off the light with tight, controlled movements. He placed the holo-disk into his pouch, then started toward the ship. It was time to ask "Devora" a few questions.

Chapter 10

"Something's wrong," Sarai said quietly. She and Calla were sitting in the cockpit, watching the men approach across the barren landing field. "Look at how Calvin is walking, he's almost bouncing. He's happy about something."

Calla followed Sarai's pointing finger. Calvin was strutting like he'd discovered gold. Seth walked with strong, deliberate steps beside him. Whatever had Calvin going hadn't excited him.

"I'll call Seth on a private channel," Calla said as the two women watched them approach. "Maybe he can tell us what's going on."

She toggled the com switch, then carefully entered the correct transmitter coordinates and hailed Seth as he had shown her. She and Sarai had listened in on Seth and Calvin when they'd first landed, but it had grown tedious after Bragan's arrival. Calvin talked enough while he was on the ship; both women treasured their breaks from his noise.

"Seth, do you read me?" she asked. "It's Devora."

Seth didn't reply at first. Then, just as she decided to give it another try, his voice crackled over the speaker.

"Really?" he said tightly. "Because it sounds like Calla."

The bottom dropped out of her stomach, and her hand wavered over the com switch. Sarai gasped, then reached across to cut off the transmission.

"He found out," Calla whispered. She looked up at Sarai with a lost look. "How did he find out?"

"I have no idea," Sarai said in a quavering voice. "But you're in trouble. He's angry, and when men get angry they get violent. We've got to do something, it may be our last chance."

"Seth isn't violent," Calla said, but her heart sank as she said it. A vision of him slamming his fist through the wall at the hostel raced through her mind. He'd been in battle hundreds of times. He had enforced the occupation with cold calculation, sentencing more than one man to death. He was more than capable of violence…

"What am I going to do, Sarai?" Calla whispered, looking to the woman hopelessly. "I'll never be free now."

Sarai's face hardened.

"We should leave, like Bragan suggested," she said after a brief pause. "We should just leave, and never come back. I don't know how we'll survive, but we will. I can work hard, and you know all about what it's like outside the belt."

Calla bit back a harsh laugh. "Sarai, all I know anything about is being a slave at a Discovery station hostel. Besides, we don't have any money."

"If we steal the ship we can sell it," Sarai replied, somewhat shocked by her own audacity. "This is a valuable ship, and I'm sure we could get enough credits for it to start over somewhere. We could work together, and maybe the kids could go to school. It would be like a dream come true for both of us, and you know it."

"What about Calvin and Seth?" Calla asked. "We can't just leave them here. They'll die."

A dark look came over Sarai's face.

"I don't care if Calvin dies," she said bitterly. "I hope he does die. He's an evil bastard, and I want better for me and the kids. And I don't care about Seth, either. He hasn't done a damn thing for us. You're the only one who seems to care what Calvin does to me."

It was true, Calla realized. Sarai tried to hide her bruises with her hair and clothing, but she had seen them. Calvin really was evil. But Seth ...

"No, I don't wish harm on Seth," she said. "I don't know why he hasn't done anything about Calvin, but he doesn't deserve to be left on this asteroid. He's been good to me. And despite everything, I love him."

"What's love?" Sarai asked, gazing at her with haunted eyes. "I don't see any promises from Seth. At least he was paying you to fuck him, but now he won't have to. If you're lucky he'll keep you for a while. If not, he'll sell you or turn you back in. That's all Calvin is doing, too. We're in the same situation, Calla, whether you like it or not. We're both slaves, and we both want to be free."

"I still don't like it," Calla said stubbornly.

"Well, you better make up your mind quick, because they're coming," Sarai said. "You may never get another chance like this one. I know I won't, and neither will my children."

Sarai was right, Calla thought. She had known from the start that her relationship with Seth could only be temporary. If she wanted to survive as an escaped slave, she had to be ruthless.

"We could send help for them, couldn't we?" she said thoughtfully.

"Yes, we could," Sarai said. "Although I don't know who we'd send."

"We could send a message to the Saurellian command on Discovery station," Calla replied. "Seth is Saurellian."

Sarai looked startled.

"I didn't realize they'd look so much like regular people," she said finally. "I've heard they're monsters."

"Well, I'm a former slave, and I'm perfectly human," Calla said. "You Pilgrims have some messed up notions of humanity."

"It's hard to know what to believe when you've only ever known one way to live," Sarai said softly. "Do you understand why I want something different for my children? I don't want Mali to grow up to be like me, and I certainly don't want Able to become like Calvin."

"I can see that," Calla replied. She didn't want to leave Seth behind, but it really was the best choice. Jess was beyond her reach now, but at least he was free. It was time to take care of herself, not to mention the children. Sarai was right–they deserved better than a lonely life on an asteroid. "All right, I'll do it. But we have to leave them some supplies, and we have to send them help."

"All right," Sarai said. "What about Bragan?"

"We'll let him out with the supplies," Calla said. "I think we're going to have to use the blaster to control the men. We can try locking them out, but Seth can manually override the doors from the outside. We'll have to let them on board the ship, then hold them prisoner while we get supplies ready for them. Can you do that?"

"Oh, I can do it," Sarai said. A fierce light had come into her eyes. For the first time in her life, she was in control and she liked it. "There's no going back now. I'd rather be dead than back on that asteroid."

"I'd rather be dead than become a slave again," Calla replied. "Let's do it."

* * * * *

Seth was seething the entire trip back to the ship. Calvin bumped along beside him, chuckling at his situation.

"Women'll do it every time," he said with satisfaction. "You can't trust them bitches."

"Shut up," Seth told the man tersely. Once they got back to the ship, Calvin was getting locked up in the cargo hold. Seth had had enough of the him.

153

When they reached the ship, Seth strode into the airlock and immediately started the cycle that would allow them to enter the ship. Calvin, scuttling along behind him, barely made it through the door before it slammed shut behind them.

"Watch it," Calvin blustered, "Or I'll give you something to watch."

"Are you threatening me?" Seth asked coldly, turning to face the man. His face was black with anger, and Calvin flinched.

"Sorry, no harm meant," the man muttered, flinching. Seth turned from him in disgust. The airlock finished its cycle and the green light flashed over the door. Seth punched the button to open it, and strode into the room. It was time to confront Calla.

She and Sarai were standing there waiting for them, their faces pale. The children were nowhere to be seen, and for the thousandth time in the past couple of days Seth wished the two of them were alone. Soon he would be rid of Calvin, and Sarai would be resettled. He had hoped he could build a future with Devora–Calla, he corrected himself–but that had been nothing more than a foolish dream. She wasn't his life mate, and she wasn't Saurellian. Even if she was, even if he could forgive her for lying to him, she had a husband. The mere thought of her and Jess looking so happy together in the hologram was almost more than he could bear.

"Calla, we need to talk privately," he gritted out. Just saying her true name was almost too much–he wanted his Devora back. But there never had been a "Devora," he told himself. All of it was a cold, calculated ploy. He couldn't forget that.

"I'm so sorry, Seth," Calla said quietly. She raised her hand slowly, and for the first time he realized she was holding a small blaster. He had never seen the gun before. She gazed steadily at him, her brown eyes unreadable. "But that won't be possible. I need you to sit down quietly on the floor and place your hands behind your head. You, too, Calvin."

Seth just stared blankly at her for a minute, confused by her words. Then Sarai spoke.

"Sit down," she said tightly. She was holding a blaster, too, the one he had left with them to guard the escaped slave. Bragan laughed from his place in the corner, then spoke.

"They're going to escape," the man said in a high-pitched voice. "They're going to escape and you're going to die!"

Seth looked at Calla in confusion, unable to believe the man's words. Would she really kill him? She blinked rapidly, eyes filling with tears. Her hand remained steady, however. The cold barrel was aimed directly at his heart.

"You're not going to get hurt as long as you do what you're told," Calla said quietly. "I don't want to do this, but I don't have a choice. Sarai and I need to get away, and we need your ship to do it. If you do what we say, we'll leave you here with enough supplies to last until help arrives. We'll send word to the Saurellian command that you're here. You'll be fine."

Seth peered into her eyes, looking for some sign of softness. All he saw was determination, though. His soft little Devora had become hard, unrecognizable.

"We'd better do what they say," he told Calvin, then started sinking toward the floor. Calvin had a different idea.

"Put down that blaster right now you stupid bitch," he growled, and started moving toward Sarai. Seth could see the woman was terrified of him, but she held her ground. Calla's eyes darted between the two men, and her hand wavered.

"Calvin, I'm not going to live like this any more," Sarai said softly. Her face was pale and her lips trembled. Her grip on the blaster, however, remained firm. "You have to sit down over there or I'm going to shoot you."

"You aren't strong enough to shoot me," Calvin said. "Now shut up and put the damn gun down."

"I can't do that," Sarai said. Calvin gave a snort of disgust and launched himself at her. Calla shrieked as the large man came flying toward them, but Sarai didn't even flinch. She simply took aim and pulled the trigger on the blaster, sending a bolt of energy right into Calvin's chest. A look of surprised shock came over his face, and he stumbled to the ground before slumping over. Then he was still.

"I think you killed him," Calla whispered in horror. "I think he's dead."

"I had to do it," Sarai replied. Tears were running down her face, but she still held the blaster steady. "I had to do it for me and for the children. I couldn't let him take us back."

"I can see that," Calla replied. She paused to catch her breath, unsure of what to do next.

"Watch out!" Bragan shouted, and both women looked up. Seth had taken advantage of their distraction to start raising himself from the floor. Calla fumbled for her weapon, panicked.

"Get back down there," Sarai snarled, catching all of them off guard with her ferocity. "You stay on the floor or I'll shoot you, too."

Calla felt sick to her stomach–she hated this violence, and Sarai seemed to have become another person entirely. The woman's expression was feral, and Calla had no doubt she'd be ready and willing to kill Seth if he tried anything. The thought of Seth dying made her breath catch; she had to do something to protect him.

"All right," she said, trying to bring everyone's tension level down a notch. Her own gun was lowered–she knew she'd never be able to harm Seth. Sarai might, though. It was up to her to get them all out of this alive. "Sarai, we just need to get some supplies together. Seth, we'll be leaving you and Bragan with enough food and water to last until someone gets here to rescue you. Who do you want us to call?"

Seth glared at her coldly for several minutes, refusing to answer. She'd never seen him so angry.

"Well, just think about it," Calla finally said. "Sarai, you keep your blaster on him. I'll get his things together."

Walking quickly through to the sleeping room, she grabbed a carryall from the storage closet. Mali and Able were watching her with wide eyes. Suddenly realizing their father had just died, Calla paused in her motions.

"You need to stay in here no matter what you hear, all right?" she said. "You're being very good children, and your mother and I will explain everything to you as soon as we're done. Are you going to be okay in here?"

"Yes," Able said, putting a protective arm around Mali. "Did something bad happen to papa?"

Calla hesitated, then decided to tell them the truth.

"Yes, something did happen to your papa," she said slowly. "There was an accident, and he's dead."

Mali snuffled softly against Able's shoulder, and the little boy's face paled.

"I'll take care of Mali," he said, steeling his shoulders. "You take care of mama."

"You're being very brave," Calla said, tears welling up in her eyes. "I know your mama will be proud of you."

Able rubbed Mali's head with one small hand, comforting the little girl. His eyes followed Calla's movements as she started stuffing the bag with clothing and blankets.

"Are you making Seth leave?" he finally asked.

"Yes, I am," Calla said.

"Maybe he wants his pictures," Able said after a minute. "Those kids look really happy. If I was him, I'd want them pictures."

The boy was right, Calla thought. She should pack Seth's pictures for him. She walked quickly around the room, pulling Seth's pictures off the wall as she went. When she had them all, she wrapped them carefully in a small plastic sheet and tucked them in the side of the carryall. Then, wondering if she was crazy, she tucked the small blaster into the pocket with the pictures. He wouldn't find it right away, she told herself, but he might need it to survive. Able's eyes widened as he watched, but the boy said nothing.

"I'm leaving now, so you keep taking care of your sister," she told Able, then she swung the sack over her shoulder and carried it out into the main room.

Seth was still sitting there, staring sullenly at Sarai. The slight woman continued to hold the blaster on him steadily. Her face was still pale, but the look on her face was determined. Bragan remained in his corner, standing. He was still tied, but they had loosened the bindings to make him more comfortable.

"How are you doing, Sarai?" Calla asked cautiously. The woman was so tense she looked as if she might break into a thousand pieces at any minute. Her husband's lifeless body still lay on the floor between her and Seth.

"I'm fine," she said. "Just keep moving, because I want to get this over with."

"All right," Calla said. "I'm going to get the food and water packs now."

It took her about twenty minutes to build a little pyramid of supplies sufficient to feed and water Seth and Bragan for several weeks. Help should arrive long before then, she kept telling herself. Seth would be just fine.

Once all the supplies were ready, she walked over and let Bragan out of his bonds. The man grabbed her suddenly, causing her to gasp in shock. Sarai's voice came anxiously from across the room, "What's wrong?"

Bragan gave Calla a smacking kiss on her cheek, then let her go.

"Nothing to worry about," he said. "I just wanted to wish her luck. Now what do you need me to do?"

"I want you to drag Calvin's body and the supplies into the airlock," Sarai said.

"My pleasure," he said, grinning broadly. Then he spoke to the angry man across the room in his sing-song way, "Oh, Seth, we'll become great friends in our time together. You'll see, you'll see."

The tone of his voice alarmed Calla–would Seth be safe with Bragan? The man was definitely unhinged. She made a snap decision to cuff Bragan before allowing him off the ship. Seth deserved that much at the very least. She glanced over at him quickly, afraid to meet his eyes. He sat there, hands above his head, staring at her steadily. There was a promise of retribution in his eyes.

It only took Bragan a short while to load all the supplies, but Calvin's body was too much for him to handle by himself.

"Seth, help him," Calla said. Seth stood slowly and deliberately, flexing his arms as he rose. His hands were clenched into fists tight with anger. Calla shivered, backing up a couple of steps.

"I won't hesitate to shoot," Sarai said. "I've already done it once, I'll do it again. I have nothing to lose, so don't tempt me."

Seth believed her, because he turned to grasp Calvin's body under the armpits. Bragan took the feet, then together they lifted the man and carried him out into the airlock. The Seth spoke for the first time.

"Leave the Jansenite here," he said. "It's too dangerous to take with you."

Calla was startled, and she looked to Sarai, unsure what to do.

"He's right," Sarai said. "Calvin always handled it very carefully. He could use it to blow up this ship, though. Do you think he'd rather die than let us escape? It would be a suicidal move."

Seth merely glared at them, but Calla spoke.

"I don't think he'll do that," she said, hoping desperately that she was right. "Remember, Seth, the children are completely innocent. They don't deserve to die, no matter what you think of us."

"I give you my word I won't use the Jansenite against you," Seth finally said. "But it's very important that you leave it behind. I don't want it out there on the open market."

"I thought you were going to sell it," Calla said, startled.

"I thought you were going to trust that I knew what I was doing," Seth replied pointedly.

"Just get the damn Jansenite," Sarai said, confused by their exchange. "No, have Bragan do it. I don't want to let you out of my sight."

"I'll get it," Calla said, breaking in quickly before things got out of hand. "I'll bring it out here, then Seth and Bragan can take it off the ship."

"Be careful," Seth said, trying not to look at her. "If you drop it, we're all dead."

Calla carefully dragged the boxes out into the main room, then Seth and Bragan placed them in the airlock. Sarai's gun never wavered.

When they had finished, Sarai gestured toward the pressure suits hanging in the airlock bay. Seth was still wearing his, but Bragan needed one. Seth pulled on his helmet, then he and Bragan quickly checked each other's suits.

"Bragan, come over here," Calla said. Sarai looked at her in surprise, but gestured with the gun that the man was to follow her instructions. "Hold your hands out in front of you."

Calla quickly clasped a pair of restraints around the man's wrists. She had been concerned he'd make a fuss, but he simply cocked one eyebrow at her.

"Afraid I'm going to hurt your lover?" he asked with a smirk. "Don't worry about it. I don't hold it against you."

"Just go out into the airlock," she said, unable to meet his eyes. Then she tossed the restraint key to Seth, who caught it in one gloved hand. "You, too. Into the airlock."

Seth turned and stalked into the airlock, then turned back to face her.

"I won't forget this," he said coldly. "You'd better start running, because Goddess help you if I catch you."

"We'll send someone for you," Sarai said tightly. "You have all you need to make it until they arrive. Once the airlock cycles, we'll give you twenty minutes to get everything out and get away from the ship. Then we're leaving."

"I'm sorry, Seth," Calla said. "I don't have a choice. I won't go back to slavery."

"Your husband has a new girlfriend," Seth said with disgust. "You might want to think twice about trying to join him."

His words sent pain shooting through her.

"He's not my husband," she said. "I just said that to get rid of you at the hostel. You've got to go now."

Seth's eyes widened, but before he could say anything Calla punched the button that shut the airlock. The door swung closed, and the light went red as the ship started pumping out air.

Twenty minutes later, Seth had unloaded the supplies and was standing with Bragan at a safe distance. Sarai checked to make sure the children were strapped into their chairs, then joined Calla in the cockpit. Seth had left the autopilot set to take them back to Discovery station. Together, they pressed the key to initiate their takeoff sequence, then braced themselves as the ship lifted away from the asteroid. Calla forced herself to watch Seth's still figure for as long as he was visible from the ship's window, then turned to Sarai.

"I guess it's time to start working on re-programming the auto-pilot," she said. "The last place I want to go it Discovery station. I have the codes and manuals in my hand-held computer."

"When will we send the rescue message?" Sarai asked quietly.

"I think we should clear the asteroid field first," Calla replied after a brief pause. "We'll send the message before we make the leap to light speed."

Chapter 11

"Fifty thousand credits. That's my final offer," Karinvass said, eyeing the two women standing before him. Their ship was worth at least 150,000 credits, but they obviously didn't have any idea what they were doing. Clearly, they'd never been out of their home systems. Every time they saw an alien, their eyes widened. As he watched, the little one–the one with the brown hair and freckles–bit her lip, and looked at her friend for guidance. If he wasn't careful, he might lose the sale...

"Here now, I don't have all day," he said roughly. It was always better to keep the upper hand in a negotiation like this. He didn't want them to feel bullied, but he also didn't want to give them too much time to think. They were ripe for the taking, and he wanted that ship.

"Either you like the deal or you don't. I have other customers to help," he added, despite the fact that they were his only prospects at the moment. It wasn't often that he had the chance to acquire a ship like theirs, especially for such a price. It was stolen, of course, but that wouldn't matter if he moved it quickly enough. There were plenty of customers who'd be interested in buying a prize like that one.

"All right," the freckled one said, looking panicked at the thought of him losing interest. Karinvass gave her a broad smile, then held out his hand to shake on the deal. She looked at him, confused at the gesture, and for a moment he almost felt sorry for her. She really was green. These two were going to be eaten alive if they weren't careful.

"I'll be right back with your credits," he said, and they smiled at him nervously. Shaking his head in bemusement, he turned and went into his back room. Once the door was locked, he activated a small control panel on the floor. A tile moved noiselessly across the floor, revealing his safe. As he counted out the thousand-credit chits, he briefly considered short-changing them. He'd bet they'd never seen a credit chit worth so much–it would be easy to pawn off some counterfeits.

Then an uncharacteristic wave of compassion came over him. He was already making a fortune off of them, he reminded himself. They were on the run, any fool could see that. Besides, if he let them go now, he could always make more money later if someone came looking for them. He smiled again at the thought, then closed up the safe and walked back out into his shop.

"Here are your credits," he said, counting the money out carefully before them. "Fifty thousand, just like I promised."

Their eyes widened, and the quiet one–she was taller–gave him a smile so lovely it took his breath away. She really was quite pretty, he realized. Maybe he could... Then he laughed to himself. He was getting *too* greedy, now. He'd already taken enough from these two little birds. Better to let them go.

"Here are the access codes," the little one said, pressing a piece of paper into his hands.

"I'll find you if they don't work," Karinvass said, although he wasn't concerned. He was sure it had never occurred to them to double-cross him. They were too innocent.

They left the store quickly, turning out into the main corridor and out of Karinvass' sight. Calindra station wasn't really that large of an outpost, he reflected, if you knew the right people. If he changed his mind and wanted to find them again, he would be able to.

Deciding he had worked enough for one day, Karinvass left the store–locking it carefully, as always–and headed across the wide corridor. The station's open gallery rose four stories above him, stretching as far as the eye could see. Either side of the gallery was lined with shops. Up two levels was his favorite drinking house, where the *bakrah* was cheap and the women were friendly. It was time to celebrate his newfound wealth, he thought with satisfaction. It had been a most profitable morning.

* * * * *

"Calla, I don't trust that man," Sarai said, looking at her friend anxiously. They were walking quickly along the wide boulevard that was the station's center of commerce. Earlier that day, Sarai had watched all the activity around them with wide eyes, but now all she could think about was escape. "I think he knew we weren't the real owners of the ship."

"I think you may be right," Calla replied. She clutched their bag of precious credits closer. People seemed to be watching them; they weren't safe, she could feel it. "But we'll be gone as soon as we find a transit. We just need to figure out where we want to go."

"And what we're going to do when we get there," Sarai said faintly, her expression troubled. "Calla, I don't know how to do anything. How am I going to support my children?"

"Sarai, we've been over this before," Calla said, trying to stay patient. "If we can just find the right place, we'll open a hostel. I know all about hostels, I've worked in one all my life. We're going to be fine."

"I'm sorry, Calla," Sarai said. "I know, I've got to trust you."

"That's all right," Calla said, flashing her a quick smile. She and Sarai had grown close in the two weeks since their escape from Bethesda base. A wave of sadness came over her, the same feeling she got every time she thought of the day she had left Seth behind on the asteroid. She missed him so much. Suppressing a sigh, she said, "Here we are–I think the hostel is down that corridor."

Together they turned into the quiet corridor. In contrast to the busy boulevard, this area of the station was more residential. There were blocks of apartments, small food shops and even a book and vid store. Their hostel was nestled in the middle, a little gem of hospitality. A kind-looking pleasure worker at the space port had directed them there the night before. Not only was it quiet, it was inexpensive, which was important. They couldn't afford to waste the few credits Calla had from Jess' stash, or those from the sale of the ship, either.

When they walked through the door, a chime rang but no one was at the front desk. Calla could hear voices, though. Able and Mali were in the back, talking with someone animatedly and laughing. She looked over at Sarai, whose face had grown cold. They had told the children not to open the door for anyone, and now Able and Mali were out of the room completely.

Moving quickly through the small lobby and living area, Calla and Sarai walked into the kitchen. Mistress Bannings, the hostel's owner, and her daughter, Erika, were sitting at a table with the children. Erika's children were there, too, and the entire group seemed to be playing some kind of board game. Erika looked up and smiled.

"I hope you don't mind that we invited the children into the kitchen to play," she said brightly. "We don't usually get guests with children, and my girls were so excited to meet them."

Calla's heart melted at the sight, but Sarai's lips were tight. Erika shot a concerned look to her mother for support.

"Now, Sarai," Mistress Bannings said kindly. Her gentle face was covered in wrinkles, most of them from laughing. She looked every inch a beloved grandmother; Mali and Able had been utterly charmed by her from the start. "Don't worry. The children were perfectly safe, and I knew they must be hungry. Speaking of which, neither of you have had anything to eat yet today. Would you like something?"

Mistress Bannings so obviously meant well that Sarai couldn't stay mad. She sighed, then said, "Yes, that would be very nice. Thank you."

Erika immediately jumped up and started fixing them some food, while Mistress Bannings gestured for Calla and Sarai to join her at the table.

"Why don't you girls take Able and Mali into your room to play," she told her grandchildren. They jumped up, and all four ran off together laughing. "The girls will keep them occupied while we talk. You have lovely children, Sarai."

"Thank you," Sarai replied, unable to keep herself from smiling at the compliment. Erika brought them plates of food, then joined them at the table.

"Mother and I wanted to talk to you," she said, glancing at Mistress Bannings. "We're worried about you."

Calla's head snapped up, and she looked at the women suspiciously.

"Now, don't get all defensive with me, young one," Mistress Bannings said, her face kind and understanding. "We're on your side. Both of us know what it's like to be a woman alone in the world. I'm concerned about you."

"Why would you be concerned?" Calla asked, trying to evaluate their motives. Both Mistress Bannings and Erika met her eyes with calm, friendly expressions. They seemed to be genuine...

"I can tell you're running from something," the elderly woman said after a moment. "Or *someone*. And I can tell that you don't know where you're running to."

Sarai opened her mouth to protest, but Mistress Bannings just smiled and raised a hand to silence her.

"I don't want or need to know the reasons," she said. "If I don't know, I can't tell anyone. But I would like to offer to help you, if there's any way that I can. I know you sold your ship this morning-"

Calla looked up at her, startled. "How could you possibly know that?" she asked.

"This station is smaller than it looks," Erika said with a smile. "One of my friends works in a tavern not far from

Karinvass' shop. He was in there, buying rounds for the entire house not ten minutes after you left. She called to tell me all about it before you got home. If you had let us know you were trying to sell it, we probably could have sent you to a more reputable trader."

Calla and Sarai exchanged startled looks. This wasn't what they had expected.

"What we're trying to tell you," Mistress Bannings said quietly, "Is that if you're hiding from someone, you're not doing a very good job. We can help you. Now tell us what you plan to do with yourselves."

Calla looked to Sarai for guidance, but the young mother simply shrugged her shoulders. Then Calla decided to take a chance and trust her instincts. Mistress Bannings and her daughter seemed like good people, and they really did need the help.

"Let's just say we're trying to rebuild our lives," Calla said slowly. "We're looking to move somewhere far away, and start a business."

"What kind of business?" asked the elderly woman.

"I'd like to open a hostel," Calla replied. "I have some experience in running one."

Mistress Bannings nodded her approval of the idea.

"Running a hostel is a good trade for a woman on her own," she said. "Do you have enough money to buy a hostel?"

"I think I might," Calla said slowly.

"Good," Mistress Bannings replied. "Now, how about location? Do you know where you want to go?"

"No," Calla said slowly. "We haven't decided yet."

Erika and her mother exchanged knowing looks.

"My aunt, Lilith, has a hostel on Hector Prime," Erika said after a brief pause. "It's a lovely planet, an ecological preserve and wildlife sanctuary. There's a great need for hostels, because so many students go there to study each year. The population is constantly changing, and it's quite far from here. It might be a nice place for two women to build a new life for themselves."

"Is it in Saurellian space?" Calla asked quickly.

"It's actually in a neutral zone," Mistress Bannings replied, one eyebrow raised questioningly at Calla. "It's not really of any value to the either the Saurellians or the empire. Neither side has taken the time or interest to garrison it. It's under the political control of one of the trans-system universities, which has branches on both sides of the conflict. I doubt you'd run into any Saurellians there, if that's a concern."

"We need to talk about this privately," Calla said. "I don't know if that's the right place for us or not."

"Think about it," Erika said. "You can learn more about the planet from the terminal in your room. It's called Hector Prime. If you're interested, let me know. We can help you arrange to travel in an inconspicuous way, and I know that Aunt Lilith would be willing to help you get settled when you arrive."

"Thank you," Calla said. "We'll let you know."

She and Sarai exchanged small talk with the women until they finished their food, then went up to the room.

"What do you think?" Sarai asked as soon as they were alone.

"I don't think they mean us any harm," Calla said slowly. "And I don't feel like we have that many options. I can't believe they heard about the ship so quickly. If they know all about it, who else will? I don't think we're safe here."

"I agree," Sarai said. "I don't see how we can afford to stay here much longer, and I have no idea where to go if we don't take their advice."

"Let's do it, then" Calla replied, closing her eyes. An image of Seth's face came into her mind, and she ruthlessly pushed it away. "There's no reason to stay here any longer than we have to. Let's go tell Mistress Bannings that we'll take her up on her offer."

Chapter 12

"Do you want a food pack?" Bragan asked Seth, holding up one of the small plastic pouches. "This is the last sweetened one."

Seth looked over at Bragan with amusement. The man seemed like such a child at times, although Seth knew he had survived terrible things. Despite his suffering, Bragan still took joy from something as silly as a sweetened food pack.

He had gotten to know Bragan pretty well over the past three weeks, and no longer worried that the former slave would turn against him. They were actually doing pretty well for themselves, although it was tedious to sit and wait for rescue in the small, portable pressure bubble Calla had left for them. Of course, they were grateful for the bubble, part of the ship's emergency survival kit–otherwise they would have been forced to live in their pressure suits, not a pleasant prospect.

"Are you sure you're a doctor?" Seth asked Bragan. "I thought those sweet packs were supposed to be unhealthy."

Bragan swallowed his food, then grinned at him. "No, getting trapped on asteroids with no hope of rescue is unhealthy. Sweetened food packs are the least of our worries." He cackled quietly at his own joke, then took another bite.

"You're right about that," Seth said, his mood darkening. Calla had promised she'd send for help, but in reality Seth knew she might not have. There certainly hadn't been any sign of rescue so far. If he and Bragan died alone in the ruins of Bethesda base, no one could ever learn how the women had betrayed them. Of course, if Calla and Sarai had wanted the men dead, they could have killed them weeks ago. It was hard to know what Calla's motivations were, Seth realized. For all he knew, she in love with Jess, and the two of them had coordinated the whole thing. The thought filled him with anger, and he scowled into the silence.

"Snap out of it," Bragan said. He took another bite of his food, them wiped his mouth on his sleeve. "I'm tired of your moping. Either we'll get out of this or we won't, but pouting won't make it any better."

"I am not pouting," Seth said coldly, glaring at the doctor.

"Really?" Bragan replied. "I wouldn't bet on that. She did what she had to do, you know. I told her to do it. An escaped slave can't afford to have feelings for a man like you. If she'd been smart, she would have killed us. She loved you too much for that, though."

Seth turned away, unwilling to let Bragan see how much his words hurt. If Calla had loved him, she wouldn't have left him to die.

"It was her only choice," Bragan continued. The man was perceptive as hell, something that didn't always endear him to Seth. "She had to save the children. She had no idea that you were planning to lock Calvin up. It takes a strong woman to give up the man she loves to save a child."

"I don't want to talk about it," Seth said, gritting his teeth in frustration. Thinking about Calla made him crazy. He wanted to strangle her. He wanted to roll on top of her and thrust into her again and again. He dreamt of them having a child together, something that was biologically impossible. At times he thought he might lose his mind.

Abruptly standing, Seth stalked across the small open area to their sleeping mats, inflatable cots from the same survival kit that had contained the pressure-bubble. For the thousandth time, Seth thanked the Goddess for leading him to outfit his ship with the highest quality survival equipment available. At least he and Bragan were relatively comfortable in their exile.

"I'm going to take a nap," he said shortly, lying down on the mat. Turning away from Bragan, he closed his eyes and tried to sleep. He knew he would dream of Calla, something he both anticipated and dreaded. Her silken thighs, her sparkling laugh, even her freckles… She was always with him in some way. Trying to reign in his anticipation, Seth closed his eyes. The dreams were all he had left.

* * * * *

"Seth, wake up," Bragan whispered in the darkness. Seth was alert instantly, his warrior instincts honed from a thousand battles. "There's something going on at the landing field. That little motion alarm thing you set up is blinking."

A burst of adrenaline shot through Seth's body–were they about to be rescued? A list of all those it could be raced through his mind: Pilgrims, Saurellians, the escaped slaves … Perhaps even an innocent trader, as he had pretended to be. Each possibility carried its own risks.

"We need to get into our suits, then head for our hiding place," Bragan whispered, furiously shoving supplies in a little bag. "Do you have your blaster?"

Seth did. He'd found it in his carryall, right next to the photos of his niece and nephews. Its presence was just another piece of the complex puzzle that was Calla. In the dark times, when he wondered whether she had ever cared for him at all, he looked at it. At least she hadn't wanted him to die, had given him something to defend himself with. That was something.

When they were both dressed and ready, the two men checked each other's suits, then quickly made their way through the bubble's tiny air lock. It was manually operated, and Seth chafed at the delay. It took ten full minutes for each of them to pass through, time that their new guests might use to discover them.

"Here's the plan," Seth said tersely once they were both free. "I'll go down and scout. You go into the mine and guard and hide the food. I'll call you when things are clear, otherwise stay out of site. No matter what happens, we can't let them get the Jansenite. If I'm captured, I'll key my headpiece twice, so they won't know you're out here."

"If I'm going to stay with the Jansenite, you should leave me the blaster," Bragan said. "You know that, don't you?"

"I'll need the blaster," Seth gritted out. He didn't say what they were both thinking–that he didn't trust Bragan with a weapon.

"I can use the blaster to detonate the Jansenite if things go wrong," Bragan reminded him. "We both agreed that as a last resort, that's what needed to be done. We can't let the Pilgrims get their hands on it. Neither of our lives is worth saving if they use that stuff against our people."

Seth knew the man was right, but he couldn't quite bring himself to give up his weapon. Bragan sighed in frustration

"Well, if you won't give me the blaster, that's fine," Bragan finally said. "But then you'll have to stay with the Jansenite."

"You have no idea how to scout without getting caught," Seth gritted out.

"Well, one way or another, you've got to trust me if we're going to get through this," Bragan said heatedly. "Believe me, if I wanted the damn blaster I could have taken it a thousand times over the past few weeks. Hell, we both know those restraints Calla put on me weren't worth anything. She didn't even know how to fasten them all the way, but I didn't jump you when I had the chance. Face it, Seth, we're in this together. Let me do my part."

Wordlessly, Seth handed the blaster to Bragan, biting back a sharp reply. They both knew he was right. Without each other, they didn't stand a chance. It hurt to give up his only weapon, though. He felt naked without it.

Bragan, muttering something about "fool's pride," started moving quickly toward the abandoned mine shaft where the explosives were hidden. Seth turned toward the ridge that lay between them and the landing field.

When they'd first found themselves trapped on the abandoned asteroid, they had considered setting their camp up in the ruins of the station. But locating the bubble on the other side of the ridge had given them several advantages. They were hidden from view, and there was a place to hide the Jansenite. Additionally, the rock formations were such that it seemed unlikely any intruders would be able to detect them with a standard sensor sweep. That alone had made hauling all their equipment across the ridge worthwhile.

Within minutes, Seth had reached the top of the ridge. Crawling on his belly, he raised his view-scope to his eyes and looked out over the landing field. There were four ships there, all of which looked ancient. Either the escaped slaves or the Pilgrims, he decided. The Saurellians would have better equipment. He keyed his comset four times, the signal he and Bragan had worked out ahead of time. Seth hoped the doctor would remember what it meant; a steady diet of nutritious food and companionship had done wonders for the man's mental health, but he still had a tendency to forget things. Turning his attention back to the landing field, Seth saw a large group of the men had gone over to the remains of the funeral pyre. They were gesturing angrily. Others made their way through the ruins.

Were they Pilgrims or escaped slaves? Seth wondered. Hard to tell, although he hoped they were escaped slaves. They, at least, would be friendly to Bragan. The two of them had agreed that if the slaves came back, Bragan would go with them without telling them about Seth or the Jansenite. If the Saurellians came, they could both be rescued. They had yet to come up with a successful plan of action to deal with the Pilgrims.

Seth watched for another forty minutes, still unable to tell who the men were. But then about ten of them started digging a large hole near the pyre. Another man started sorting through the burned remains, making a series of complicated, ritualistic gestures over them. They were burying their dead, Seth realized; the men had to be Pilgrims. He had seen enough.

Scooting back until he was well below the crest of the ridge, Seth walked quickly down the hill toward Bragan's hiding place. They needed to get their camp packed up, and they needed to figure out a plan of action.

Bragan jumped out of the shadows as Seth approached, blaster ready to fire. For a moment, Seth froze. Was the man going to double-cross him after all? But Bragan lowered the weapon as soon as he recognized Seth.

"It's the Pilgrims," Seth said, and Bragan's face fell.

"Let's get the camp packed up, and then we'll try to figure out what to do next," Bragan said quietly.

The survival bubble was designed to be portable, but it still took them nearly an hour to deflate and move it. They wasted precious air in doing so, but it needed to be done. From now on they would live in their suits. The bubble, even hidden among the rock formations, was too visible. When all was ready, the two men went into the mineshaft. Sitting next to each other, they eyed the boxes of Jansenite.

"It's amazing that something so small could do so much damage," Bragan said into the silence, gesturing toward the explosives.

"There's enough here to destroy this entire asteroid, and quite a few around it," Seth replied. "Hell, this is more than enough to destroy Discovery station. I wonder what they were planning to do with it."

"Overthrow the Saurellian occupation," Bragan said. "We both know how they feel about you guys. One of their core teachings is that 'humans shall not be governed by non-humans.' Words of the Celestial Pilgrim himself, if I remember correctly."

Seth grunted in response, then they both sat in silence.

"I don't see too many options here," Seth said. "Not good options, anyway. If we really want to stop them, perhaps the best thing would be to detonate the Jansenite. At least that way they couldn't use it against anyone."

"There's another option," Bragan said quietly. "You could steal one of their ships. That way you could contact your people and warn them about how dangerous these Pilgrims really are."

"You can't leave the asteroid, your implant won't let you," Seth said harshly. "And I'm not going to leave without you."

"You sure as hell can leave without me," Bragan said, his voice firm with conviction. "You can steal a ship and go for help. I'll stay hidden. You can come rescue me once you've found help. It's our best hope."

"That could take weeks," Seth replied. "Do you really think you can last that long? They'll find you sooner or later, we both know it."

"If they find me, I'll blow the Jansenite," Bragan said. "I've been living on borrowed time for years now. At least this way I'll get to choose when and how I die. Very few people are that fortunate. I kind of like the idea of taking some of those bastards with me..."

"I don't like it," Seth replied. "Saurellians don't leave each other behind. We're brothers, we live together and we die together."

"Well I'm not a Saurellian," Bragan said harshly. "I'm an escaped slave, and I'm going to die on this rock. I've known that for five years. Do you know I'm not even a man any more? They castrated me for looking at one of their women. Give me this, Seth. Give me the chance to fight back, like a man. I don't want you to stay with me.

"I want you to warn your people," he continued. Seth could see the man's face was twisted with emotion, despite the helmets they both wore. "Don't fool yourself, Seth, it's not out of any love for you. I don't want these bastards to ever buy another slave. I don't want them to ever hurt another woman. You saw what Calvin did to Sarai. There are thousands of women out there just like her. Take this chance to escape, to save them. It isn't about leaving a comrade behind, it's about saving people's lives. If you refuse to do that out of some misguided sense of honor, you're as much a criminal as they are. And an idiot, to boot," Bragan added, disgust in his voice.

Bragan was right, Seth realized. Leaving him behind went against everything he believed in, but saving his people was more important. In fact, saving his people was really all he had to live for. It wasn't as if there was anything waiting for him if he survived. Calla was gone. From the time he'd realized he would never have a life partner, Seth had lived only to fight. It was time to continue that battle.

"All right, I'll do it," Seth said. "But I want you to wait until the last possible moment to detonate the Jansenite. I'll do everything in my power to rescue you."

"I know you will," Bragan said quietly. "Seth, I want you to make me a promise."

"What?"

"I want you to try and understand why Calla did what she did," the man said, staring fixedly at the Jansenite. "I think the two of you should give each other another chance."

"It's impossible," Seth said tightly. "Even if I found her, she isn't my life mate. Our relationship could never grow into anything real or permanent."

"At least answer this," Bragan replied. "Do you hate her for what she did to you?"

"No," Seth said softly after several minutes of silence. "No, I don't hate her at all."

"Remember that," Bragan whispered. "We don't all get a chance to be happy in this life. Don't be afraid to take whatever joy you can find, regardless of whether or not you understand it."

"We need to get ready," Seth said tightly, refusing to look at the man he'd once thought crazy. "If I'm going to steal a ship, I should do it as soon as possible. The longer we wait, the more likely it is they'll find us."

Bragan just laughed, which confused Seth.

"I'll pack you some supplies," the doctor finally said. "You'll need them to get back to your people."

* * * * *

Darkness came over the asteroid suddenly. Seth, his carryall strapped to his back, crept silently toward the waiting ships. They were all in poor condition, but the smallest one looked slightly better than the others, and had the added advantage of being parked on the edge of the field. Seth was willing to bet it was faster, too. Realizing that his life might depend on his ability to outrun any pursuers, he decided it would be his target.

He had been watching the Pilgrims for hours, ever since he and Bragan had parted ways. Bragan had packed enough food and water to last Seth a week, more than enough time to make his way to a friendly station, assuming he made it off the asteroid at all.

Making his way carefully, Seth moved quickly. The darkness would only last a few hours, as the asteroid's cycle of day and night was extremely short. Fortunately, the Pilgrims had been working long enough to warrant taking a break. Most of them were probably asleep.

Seth skirted the landing field until his target ship was directly before him. No one seemed to be around. The Pilgrims had set guards in front of the two larger ships, but apparently this one wasn't considered important enough. Using a small tool from his suit's all-purpose set, Seth quickly removed the service access panel by the ship's door. Positioning himself so his body was between the panel and the other ships, Seth shined a tiny light on the controls. The ship was locked, of course, but he could override a simple palm-activated locking device like this one easily enough. As long as no one caught him in the act, that was; anyone seeing his light would know something was up.

Fortunately, none of the Pilgrims seemed to be paying attention to the smallest of their ships. Connecting two of the circuits manually, Seth shorted out the locking system and the hatch slid open. He was relatively certain the ship was empty—no one had entered it the entire time he'd been watching. Moving quickly, he climbed though the opening and closed it behind him. The ship was so small there was only the cockpit and one small hold for cargo. Seth checked the hold, confirming he was alone, then settled himself in the pilot's seat.

He breathed a sigh of relief as he realized the controls were standard; he'd piloted a thousand other shuttles just like this one. He saw that whoever had piloted the ship had left it on standby. At least he would not have to wait for the engines to come online from a cold start. He wouldn't have time for a pre-flight check, either, so hopefully everything was still operational. Whoever owned the ship should be shot, he thought wryly, because it clearly hadn't been properly serviced in years. Whispering a prayer to the Goddess, he strapped himself in and toggled the starter.

The ship came to life with a whine and he slammed the control rudder forward. He was airborne before he could even check to see how much fuel she had. The roar of the engine would alert the Pilgrims; they would be after him within minutes. Not pausing to pull up a navigation chart, Seth pushed the tiny ship to its maximum speed. Dodging debris, he zigzagged sharply through the cloud of asteroids surrounding Bethesda.

It took every bit of his skill as a pilot to control the tiny ship as it careened through the field of debris. Seth dodged rocks ranging in size from pebbles to small moons as he sped away from the Pilgrim base, barely breathing for the first ten minutes of his flight. He was positive they must be after him by now, but the little ship's sensors weren't sophisticated enough to check for pursuit at full speed. Instead, Seth focused on putting as much distance between himself and the Pilgrims as he could. Once he was safely away, he'd send for help.

Five hours later he was still racing, although his hands trembled from the strain of piloting the ship. He needed to find a place to land, a place where he could hide and rest up. There was no way they would be able to find him now, he reasoned. Not unless he did something truly stupid to attract their attention. Slowing his speed, Seth guided his small ship toward a large asteroid. It seemed to have some good-sized overhanging rock formations; perfect for hiding a ship of like this from both sight and sensors. After several minutes of careful navigation, Seth managed to land the ship just under the lip of a massive crater. Forcing himself to release his grip on the controls, he sat back in his chair and massaged his hands. He was exhausted; it was time to get some sleep. He also needed to eat.

Grabbing the carryall, he dug out a food pack. Ripping off the end, he sucked the ration tube's contents down without bothering to identify the contents. Then he reached for a fluid bulb. As he pulled the bulb out of the bag, a small piece of paper came with it. He read it quickly, his blood running cold as he realized what Bragan had intended to do from the moment the Pilgrims had landed...

Seth–I am including this note because I want you to understand why I've chosen to do what I'm going to do. I am not going to wait for you to return. There is too much danger that the Pilgrims will find me. It's better to kill them now and destroy the Jansenite while I still can. I will wait until you've had enough time to get away, but then I plan to detonate it and destroy this place. If I have not waited long enough, then I am sorry. You have become a friend to me and I wish you no harm. I consider myself fortunate to die on my own terms, for something I believe in. It is enough.

When would it happen? Seth wondered desperately. Why was Bragan doing this? Realizing there was nothing he could do for the man, Seth checked his instruments and ran a few quick mental calculations. He should be all right in his hiding place, he realized, but he wasn't as far as he'd like to be. When that Jansenite blew, it would destroy everything within a thousand square miles.

Seth started powering up the ship again; he needed to get further away. But before he could do more than initiate the procedure, and alarm trilled a sharp warning. Something big had happened, there had been a sharp wave of radiation. Slapping his hand against the control panel, he activated an emergency beacon. He didn't have time to do anything else before a shock wave blasted the asteroid. His last thought before he lost consciousness was to wonder whether the ship's landing tethers would hold. Then blackness swept over him as his was slammed by the explosion's impact. Seth sank into the darkness.

* * * * *

"I think he's waking up," a voice said. Where was he? Seth wondered. What the hell had happened?

"Seth, can you hear me?" It was Jax's voice. Memory rushed back to Seth–he had been in a ship, trying to escape from the Pilgrims... and then Bragan had blown up the Jansenite. It was a miracle he was still alive, Seth realized. Barely alive, though. His entire body ached, a thousand small pains making themselves known.

"Jax?" he whispered, trying to open his eyes. He couldn't see anything. "Jax, is that you? How did you get here? Why can't I see anything?"

"Don't worry, you've got bandages over your eyes," Jax said, excited relief in his voice. "Don't worry, your eyes are fine. You got radiation burns, though, and they had to do surgery.

You'll need to keep your eyes covered for a few weeks, give them time to heal. Someone blew up half the quadrant using Jansenite. Who the hell would do such a thing?"

"Bragan," Seth whispered. "He did it. He blew it up to keep the Pilgrims from getting it."

"Can you give me any more information than that?" Jax asked. "I got a message a few weeks ago from some woman saying you were trapped. She included some coordinates, and told me to bring a surgeon. Weirdest thing I've ever seen, but that's how we found you so quickly. Otherwise you would have died."

"That was Calla," Seth said. "Can I have some water?"

"Um, let me ask" Jax said. "Can he have some water?"

"Of course," said another voice. "Let me help him with it."

Seth felt a straw touch his lips, and he sucked the water down greedily. His throat felt like sand paper. "Don't drink too much at once," the voice said.

"I've got to tell you what happened," Seth said finally. He tried to raise a hand, to grasp Jax, but he couldn't move. "We've got a problem. There's this group called the Pilgrims. They're planning an attack against us."

"I know," Jax said. Seth felt his friend's hand touch his own lightly through the bandages. Jax suddenly sounded very tired. "They've already moved against us. You've been out for nearly two weeks, Seth. They attacked several days ago."

"What?" Seth whispered. "I don't understand."

"When we found you, you were hardly alive," Jax said, his voice filled with strain. "We put you into stasis immediately. You never would have survived, otherwise. We took you directly to the station hospital, and you've been in and out of surgery and regeneration chambers ever since."

"What about the attack? What brought it on?"

"As far as we can tell, they decided that the explosion was some kind of sign from their leader," Jax said.

"The Celestial Pilgrim?" Seth asked.

"I don't know what they call him," Jax said harshly. "He's been dead for a thousand years, but the bastards still think he's talking to them. They attacked from small bases throughout the asteroid field. There were even some of them living on Discovery station. In fact, that old bitch, Jennings, was one of them. They killed nearly a hundred people before we managed to stop them. She escaped, by the way."

"I was trying to let you know how dangerous they are," Seth whispered, sorrow washing over him. How many of his friends were dead? "I'm sorry I didn't get here in time to warn you."

"We can still use whatever information you have," Jax said with feeling. "There are thousands of them still out there. Hunting them all down will take months."

"It's time for Commander Seth to go back to the regeneration chamber," the other voice said. "Commander, I'm going to give you some medication to make you sleep now."

"Take care, Seth," Jax said quietly. "They say you'll be ready for regular duty in about a month, but I'll get some of the intelligence specialists in to speak with you the next time you wake up. We need to know everything that happened, everything you've learned about them..."

Jax kept talking, but Seth could no longer understand what he was saying. He tried to ask him to speak louder, but the darkness was too much. It was time to sleep again. Seth let unconsciousness wash over him. To do anything else would have been too exhausting.

Part III: The Sanctuary

Six Months Later

Chapter 13

Bitch.

Seth lifted his glass of bakrah and took a long swig. The lovely blond sitting in the booth beside him reached over and tried to fondle his leg, but he pushed her hand away. He didn't want her, he wanted Calla—six bloody months since Jax had rescued him from the asteroid, and he hadn't been able to think of anything else. It was killing him. With a frustrated sigh, he gestured for the woman to leave him alone.

Calla's presence was with him always. the smell of her hair, her smile. The feel of her tight opening around his cock and the little noises she made when she came. Was she making those little noises for Jess now? Seth clenched his fist around the glass, his vision clouding over with black rage.

Bitch.

She'd left him to die, and now she haunted his every step. He could hunt her down; he'd thought about it a thousand times. But what would be the point? She didn't want to be with him, and he didn't want to be with her. At least, that's what he kept telling himself. At night, though, he ached for her touch...

It had been a hard six months. He had spent the first seven weeks recovering from his injuries, a process made more difficult by the constant stream of Saurellian intelligence analysts sent to pick his brains for information on the Pilgrims. Then he had joined his brother warriors in the fight. They were successful and the rebellion was over, at least for now. But casualties had been heavy on both sides, and the Pilgrims were still out there. They were hiding, licking their wounds and preparing to fight again.

Once upon a time, Seth had found the thought of new battles and new enemies exhilarating. Now he was simply tired.

A whooping cry came from across the seedy tavern, startling him out of his thoughts. Seth looked up at the source of the noise with little interest. Jax and the others were excited, slapping each other on the back and laughing. Whatever it was, Seth didn't care. He drained the rest of his glass, threw a credit down on the table and got up to leave.

As he made his way across the room, Jax caught sight of him and bounded over, literally leaping over a table to get to him.

"Seth, I have great news!" Jax yelled, grabbing his arm. Seth shook him off, disinterested. "No, you need to hear this! Sit down."

Realizing he wasn't going to get rid of Jax that easily, Seth resigned himself and dropped into a chair.

"What is it?"

"Something wonderful has happened," Jax said. His face was flushed with excitement, and something else. Hope? "You've heard of General Nikolas Tresky, haven't you?"

Seth nodded tightly. Tresky had been among the leaders who negotiated the truce with the emperor. He had a solid reputation.

"Well, several years ago, before the war started, Tresky met a woman during a diplomatic mission to the Imperial court on Tyre, the capital planet," Jax said excitedly. Seth glanced at his time piece, willing Jax to go away. He had no interest in the younger man's stories. "He had a brief affair with her. I guess he was never really able to shake the thought of her, and after the war he hunted her down. Guess what he found? She had a child by him, a girl no less, and the baby is Saurellian! He found a life mate who wasn't Saurellian!"

Jax's words caught Seth off guard. No Saurellian man had ever found a life mate outside their homeworld.

"Are you sure?" he whispered. If what Jax said was true, the implications were incredible. Suddenly there was new hope for all of them.

"Yes, the news came in an official dispatch from the Temple of the Goddess on Saurellia. Apparently he took her there to confirm their bond in front of the priestesses," Jax said breathlessly. "Do you know what this means? We have a chance! We could all find life mates. It's almost too much to imagine."

The younger man fell back against his chair, all but glowing with happiness. Jax's words kept running through Seth's mind again and again. There was hope. Maybe he could have Calla, if she was his life mate. Some of his anger fled at the thought of holding her, thrusting into her warm flesh. He wanted her so badly...

"Tell me about this woman," Seth said suddenly, leaning forward. "Where did she come from? What do the priestesses say about this?"

"Well, she didn't look Saurellian, but they did a genetic analysis, and she's definitely of Saurellian stock," Jax said, grimacing. "I know, it sounds incredible, but she was actually the daughter of two freed slaves. Genetically she's a real mish-mash, because both her parents came from an imperial slave farm. But somewhere in there was a Saurellian. Thank the Goddess for dominant genes!"

"Calla came from a slave farm," Seth said softly. Jax stared hard at him.

"She left you to die," he said harshly after a minute. "You can't think that she might be-"

"Maybe," Seth said. He looked down and realized his hand was trembling. He held it up before him, fascinated at his reaction. "I haven't been with another woman since I was with her. I can't stop thinking about her. And when we were together, I wanted to stay with her, even after months of only one woman. Doesn't that sound like a life mate?"

"Yes," Jax said slowly. "But Seth, she lied to you. For all you know she's already married to that slave rebel. I know she told you she wasn't, but she lied to you all along. If she was your life-mate, she wouldn't even contemplate being with another man after meeting you."

"But how else do you explain it?" Seth said after a moment's thought. "Being with her felt so right, so different from any other women I've ever been around. She came from a slave farm. Maybe the Goddess chose her for me."

Jax sat quietly for a minute, then looked up at him.

"If what you say is true, you have to go get her," he said finally. "You have to know the truth. But why would the Goddess pair you with a woman you could never trust?"

"The Goddess has ordained stranger things," Seth replied thoughtfully. "If she's truly my life mate, I'll simply have to learn to deal with it. And if I find Jess, I'll take care of him, too. But if she's really my life mate, then maybe she was telling the truth about him. I can't imagine the Goddess would give me a woman who already belongs to another man."

"She's yours by law," Jax said, warming to the idea. "You have the right to take her, regardless of whether she's already with another man. If it's the Goddess' will, you don't have a choice."

No, he didn't, Seth thought. He was filled with the most amazing sensation. Sudden joy ran through him as he realized that he, too, might have children. He could build a life for himself, rejoin his brother on Saurellia. He could have Calla. The thought of her, with her soft skin covered in freckles and her long, brown hair wrapped around his fingers made him instantly hard. He had known from the start she was his, he realized, there was simply no doubt about it. He just hadn't believed such a thing was possible. Now all he had to do was go and get her.

Jax read his thoughts. "I take it you're going after her?" he asked with a grin.

"Oh, yes," Seth said with dark determination.

"Want some company?" Jax asked. "I'm ready for another trip. Beside, the more I travel, the more likely it is I'll run into my life mate. I want her, Seth. I'm ready for her, wherever she is."

"Then let's go."

"Any ideas where to start?" Jax asked.

"I'll start by tracing the ship," Seth said with a smile. "It shouldn't be too hard to find out where they sold it. We'll take it from there. Neither of them had ever been out of the system before. They'll stick out no matter where they go. We'll find them."

Chapter 14

Damn, it was hot. Jax wiped one arm across his brow. It came away wet with sweat. Why the hell had Seth's life mate chosen a planet like Hector Prime to live on? Granted, it was a nature preserve and kind of pretty in its own way. But she could have chosen to live in the north, where it wasn't so hot and humid.

Looking around him with disgust, Jax studied the small slip of paper one last time. She was living with a woman named Sarai, a Pilgrim. Sarai probably wasn't a threat, but Jax wasn't so sure. Pilgrims couldn't be trusted. They had all learned that the hard way. He'd keep a close eye on this Sarai while they were there, because the last thing Seth needed was a knife in his back. From Seth's descriptions, she was one tough bitch. She had even killed her own husband.

Jax pushed through the door of the hostel. Seth had asked him to check things out before he contacted Calla, which had seemed a solid plan back on the ship. That was before Jax had realized how damn hot it would be. Now he was doing the grunt work while Seth waited for a full report in comfort.

The hostel's lobby was even hotter than the street outside, if such a thing was possible. He could feel a bead of sweat running down his back–what had ever possessed him to come here with Seth? This planet was a hell-hole … The hostel's entryway was small, with a counter across from the door where presumably the women served their customers. No one was behind it, though. In fact, there were no signs of life at all in the hostel.

"Hello?" Jax called. "Is there anybody here? I'm looking for a room."

Thank the Goddess he wouldn't actually have to sleep here, Jax thought as he looked around them. They had rooms booked in a comfortable inn at the center of town. Rooms with climate control.

Jax called out again, but there still wasn't any response. After a few minutes waiting, he decided to go and find someone. There were two choices–a stairway that went upstairs and a hallway behind the counter. The stairs seemed more public, so they probably provided access to the guest rooms. The hall seemed a better bet.

Making his way down the hall, Jax stuck his head in several rooms along the way. He saw an office and a small living area before the hall opened into a large kitchen. It, too, was empty. Against the back wall was a door, however, and the faint sound of a woman singing. Jax went to the door, pushing it open quietly. A small, walled garden was revealed, filled with lush tropical plants and rows of vegetables. A woman was kneeling among the vegetables, facing away from him. Her song was light and happy, and while her voice wasn't strong, it was pretty.

What caught his attention, however, was her heart-shaped ass. She wore a long, sturdy gray skirt. In kneeling, the fabric was pulled tight, clearly outlining the shape of that enticing butt. She leaned forward on her knees, pulling the fabric even tighter, and his cock leapt to attention. Jax's breath stopped momentarily. He felt dizzy. He grasped the door frame to steady himself and his eyes narrowed. The sound of her soft singing wound its way through him, and his gut clenched in excitement.

He was struck by the urge to stalk across the garden, push her down in the dirt and fuck her hard right on the spot. He could just imagine what her tight little cunt would feel like, how that tinkling singing voice would sound when she screamed in pleasure. He would do her quick and dirty first, then slow and hard. The thought brought a smile to his face. She would be startled, when he grabbed her, but then she'd sigh in satisfaction at his touch. He'd take her home, and they would …

Jax caught himself up short. What the hell was he thinking? For all he knew, this woman could be Calla. Sure, he had stayed at the same hostel where she was a slave back at Discovery Station, but he hadn't noticed her. She had been one slave among many. If this woman was Calla, he was a pervert, and a bad friend. Shaking his head, he tried to will his erection away and then cleared his throat.

"Excuse me," he said. The woman's song broke off and she turned to face him, startled by his presence. Then she gave him a friendly smile, and his teeth clenched as another wave of arousal coursed through him. This was going to be difficult.

"Can I help you?" she called. "I'm sorry; most of our guests come at the beginning of the academic term, so we don't man the front desk all the time. Are you looking for a room?"

"Um, yes," Jax said. "I need a room. Do you have anything available?"

"Of course," she replied. "We're pretty full, but we almost always have one or two empties. Let me get cleaned up, and I'll be right in to help you."

Jax nodded, then moved back into the kitchen. What was wrong with him? It was taking every bit of his control not to run out there and jump the poor woman. Forcing himself to breath evenly, he made his way back down the hall and into the lobby. He waited impatiently, wanting to see her again. Was she Calla or Sarai? The thought of her being Calla, of her lying under Seth's hard body, send a wave of rage through him. His vision grew red around the edges, and he imagined what it would feel like to drive his fist into Seth's face. Shaking his head, he caught himself. What was going on?

"I'm sorry you had to wait," she said, walking into the room briskly. She was relatively tall, with light blond hair tied back loosely in a bun. Her eyes were green and sparkling, and for several long seconds Jax just stared into them. She blushed prettily, then cleared her throat. There was a smudge of dirt on her cheek. Without pausing to think, Jax leaned across the counter and lifted one finger to the smudge, touching her lightly. A jolt went through him as he made contact, and she looked startled.

"You have some dirt," he said quietly. The woman lifted one hand to her cheek, then blushed again.

"It's from the garden," she whispered, then she shook her head a little. Jax felt the spell that was over them lift a little, and they both stepped back. "I'm sorry, I didn't catch your name?"

"I'm Jax Falconer," he said. "And I need a room for the night. What's your name?"

"I'm Sarai," she said, smiling at him. Relief flooded through Jax–this woman wouldn't be claimed by Seth. "My friend Calla and I own the hostel. Where are you from?"

"Saurellia, at least originally," he said. She looked up at him sharply. He smiled, trying to look innocent. "I haven't been there in years, though."

He looked at her face again, and she caught one light pink lip nervously in her teeth. She seemed unable to meet his gaze, and Jax knew instinctively that she was every bit as attracted to him as he was to her. But she was scared, too. He was going to have her, he decided. Whatever it took, he wasn't going to leave until he had her and was tired of her. Seth wouldn't need him once he had Calla, anyway.

"I'll take a room for at least a week," Jax said tightly, trying to control himself. His cocked throbbed with anticipation. "Perhaps longer, depending how things go."

"It is just you, or do you have a wife or family with you?" Sarai asked, entering his name into her terminal. She wasn't looking at him, but he could see her hand tremble on the keyboard. Definitely interested, he thought with satisfaction.

"I'm alone," Jax said, and she let out a breath of relief. Then she blushed yet again, and Jax had to stifle a chuckle. Seducing her wouldn't take long, which was good. He didn't know how long he would be able to stand the damned heat of this blasted planet. He was willing to bet, however, that it wouldn't seem so oppressive from the comfort of her bed...

"We ask you to pay at least one night in advance, although there's a discount if you choose to pay for the entire week up front," she said, looking up at him nervously.

"I'll pay for the entire week," Jax said, holding out a credit chit. She reached for it and their fingers brushed against each other. That spark of electricity arched between them again, and she gasped. Both of them were breathing heavily now, and the tension stretched out for several long, silent seconds before she took the chit and slid it into the computer terminal. Once the credits were deducted, she printed out a receipt and handed him an access card.

"Just take this and use it to program your palm print into the room," she said. "Climate control is optional, although I think you'll find that you get used to the heat pretty quickly. We don't usually even bother with the cooling system any more."

Jax gave a sigh of relief at that welcome information. He had no intention of sticking around long enough to acclimate to the heat, but he definitely planned to use his role as a guest to get closer to Sarai. A climate control system would go a long way toward making that wait more comfortable. Of course, the passion would burn itself out quickly once he bedded her, he knew that from experience. Until then, things would be very pleasant for both of them. He knew how to please a woman.

"Can you show me the room?" he asked, glancing toward the stairs. Sarai looked startled, then nodded.

"Yes, please follow me," she said, moving quickly from behind the counter and across the room. She moved lightly up the stairs in front of him, giving him an excellent view of that shapely bottom. The hard length of his arousal stirred in response, and he all but groaned aloud. He needed to get in this lady's pants fast, he thought. This was ridiculous.

"Here's your room," she said, pushing open the third door on the right. Jax followed her in, pleasantly surprised by the accommodations. There was a large bed with a wicker frame, as well as a desk and several chairs. There was a large window as well, and a ceiling fan stirred the air. Sarai walked across to the window, then turned to look at him.

"It's a rather nice view from here," she said. "You can see across the garden to the forest. At night, if you open it, you'll be able to hear all kinds of animals. A lot of the students who stay with us like it here because we're so close to nature."

Jax nodded, disinterested. How far was her room, he wondered? Sarai walked across to one of two doors on the wall. She pushed one open and stepped in. Jax followed behind her, then stopped short when he realized the small room wouldn't accommodate both of them.

"This is the fresher," she said, turning back around. He was still standing behind her, and she almost ran into him before she realized he was there. She was so startled that she threw up her hands to catch herself, and both palms came to rest firmly against his chest. That exquisite sensation ran through Jax again, and he smiled.

"I can see that," Jax said, reaching his own hands up to cradle her head with them. Her eyes, wide with surprise, gazed up at him. Her pink lips were open in a small "o" of surprise. She was so beautiful that he couldn't think. He had to kiss her.

His lips closed over hers and her hands clenched against his chest reflexively. She was soft and warm, and Jax slanted his head against hers, hoping to probe her more deeply. He thrust his tongue into her mouth and she moaned. His loins surged in response, and his grasp on her tightened.

Grinding his mouth over hers, Jax pressed her back against the wall. She slid her hands up around his neck and pulled at him, whimpering against his mouth. The sound almost undid him, and he thrust against her lower body with his rock-hard erection. What would her hot flesh feel like closing around his length? He couldn't wait to find out.

Continuing to hold her head with one hand, he reached the other down to the rounded globes of her ass, which he'd admired in the garden. Her muscles were sleek and firm, and he dug his fingers into them, pressing her against his body. Wrenching his mouth away from hers, he swept her up in his arms and carried her purposefully across the room to the bed. He set her down, coming down on top of her and kneeing her legs roughly apart. Then he fell on her like a starving man, plunging his tongue into her mouth. She moaned and bucked against him. He felt like he was going to explode in his pants. He had to get into her tight cunt or he was going to die.

"Mommy?" a child's voice called. "Mommy, where are you?"

Jax stilled at the sound, and Sarai frantically tried to push him off her. "Get up," she hissed. "That's my son. I can't have him find me like this."

Jax rolled to one side, and she stood up quickly. Running her hands over her clothing, Sarai turned to the door. A small boy was standing there, watching them.

"Mommy, I want to get a snack," the boy said, looking at Jax suspiciously. "Is that all right with you?"

"Yes, sweetheart," Sarai said, her voice trembling.

"Will you come with me?" the boy asked. From the child's glare, Jax knew he suspected something was wrong about the situation. He was trying to protect his mother from a strange man, Jax realized.

"Thank you for showing me my room, Sarai," he said, trying to sound innocent. The boy gazed at him coldly, then turned to his mother and held out his hand to her.

"Of course," Sarai said. "Please let me know if you need anything." Then she walked out of the room with her son. Jax lay on his back for several minutes, watching the fan on the ceiling. Her smell was still in the air, like flowers, and his aroused cock throbbed with frustrated desire. He had never wanted a woman so badly. She wanted him, too, he knew it. It was just a matter of time before he would be able to take her, he told himself. Otherwise she might be the death of him.

Chapter 15

"Calla, I need to take a rest," Mali whimpered. The little girl had already taken several "rests" along the way, but she was weak. In another six months, Calla hoped she would be strong enough to skip along beside her. Until then, she was content to take as many rests as the child needed.

The gravity on Hector Prime was slightly higher than any of them were used to, but the nature preserve had been the perfect place to start over in every other way. Erika's aunt had welcomed them with open arms, insisting that they stay with her until they were on their feet. The money from the ship had been more than enough for them to buy a little hostel in one of the many tourist towns hugging the vast rainforests.

All that Erika and her mother had told them was true. Hector Prime was an ecologist's dream, and it attracted hundreds of thousands of students each year. All of them needed inexpensive places to stay for a few months while they took classes. These young men and women were the ideal guests for their hostel. Many were homesick, and they were happy to be "adopted" into Calla and Sarai's small family unit.

Calla had even offered a reduced rate to one of them in exchange for tutoring the children. For the first time in their young lives, Mali and Able had started school. She and Sarai studied with them. Things would have been perfect if she could just stop thinking about Seth.

"Come on, Mali," Calla said, rousing the girl. Mali smiled up at her sweetly.

"Can I get a candy?" Mali asked, pointing to a little shop across the street. They almost always stopped off there on their way home, so the child's request wasn't a surprise.

"Will you get one for Able, too?" Calla asked.

"Yes, m'am," Mali said, trying to hide her excitement. It was amazing to Calla just how much joy the simplest things gave the children. They had never tasted candy before.

"Then yes, you may," Calla said. She handed Mali a credit chip, trying to push down the twinge of guilt she felt every time she spent money.

They'd made a tidy sum from selling the ship, but she'd paid a high emotional price. She would never forget the sight of Seth standing there on the asteroid's surface. *I did what I had to do*, she reminded herself firmly. *We sent someone to rescue him, and someday we'll pay him back.* Both she and Sarai agreed on that. From the first, they'd set aside a percentage of every credit they earned in a fund to repay Seth. It might take them years, but they would get him his money. Credits would never be enough to repair the damage she'd done, though. Calla knew that instinctively.

The thought of Seth made her ache, both in her heart and in other places. Every other man paled in comparison to him. Not long after they'd arrived, one of her male neighbors had invited her out for dinner. Just the thought of spending time with him made her long for Seth. Deep in her heart, she knew she'd never get over him. At times, the knowledge was almost too much to bear. She wanted children, she wanted a husband. But at least she had her freedom, and Sarai and her children had gotten a chance at life. It was more than any of them could have dreamed of a year ago.

She and Mali arrived home to find Sarai working in the small garden behind the hostel. One of the students showed them how to plant some vegetables and flowers, and all four of them were still amazed at how the little plants pushed themselves through the dirt and into the bright, natural light of the sun. None of them had ever lived anywhere that plants would grow before; that small miracle of life was just one of many they encountered every day in their new home.

Sarai saw her and rose to her feet, wiping the dirt off her hands on to her apron as she stood.

"We have a new guest," she said as Calla came up next to her. She blushed as she spoke, piquing Calla's interest. "Did you get a candy, Mali? Why don't you take it over to Able."

Mali nodded her head happily, then scampered off to find her brother. Sarai waited until she was out of hearing, then said, "He's Saurellian."

Calla felt a coldness rush through her. Then reason took over, and she fought her panic back.

"There are millions of them all over the quadrant," she said. "I'm sure it's nothing to worry about. We've checked the criminal alerts–they aren't looking for us."

"Well, I just wanted to let you know," Sarai said, blushing more deeply. "His name is Jax Falconer, and he said he'll be with us for at least a week."

Jax. She recognized that name–Dani had had a client named Jax, back on Discovery station. Of course, there were probably thousands of Saurellians named Jax. Don't let it bother you, she told herself firmly. She couldn't live the rest of her life in fear.

They were all the way across the quadrant from where she'd left Seth. They'd traveled through ten ports after selling the ship to cover their tracks. She and Sarai would be safe here, in the back of beyond. Hector Prime was so insignificant that neither the Empire nor the Saurellians had bothered to send an occupation force. Then she noticed Sarai was blushing so much she was bright red.

"What's up with you?" Calla asked suspiciously.

"He, well," Sarai gave a girlish giggle, and Calla stared in astonishment. "He *kissed* me, up in his room!"

"Who did?" Calla asked in confusion.

"The Saurellian. Jax."

"Watch your step, girl," Calla replied. "Those men are hard to handle. Trust me on this one."

Sarai gave another giggle, then looked away. Calla sighed. What was it about those Saurellian men, anyway?

Chapter 16

"Well, at least we've found her," Seth said tightly. The two men sat in a bar, sipping *bakrah* and discussing their next move.

"They're set up pretty nice," Jax said. "They seem to have a lot of students staying with them. I took one of them out to a bar this afternoon, bought him a few drinks. He can't say enough good things about them. They take good care of their guests, are quiet, the children seem happy. And no men, either."

Jax seemed uncharacteristically pensive as he made his report, and Seth stared at him suspiciously. What the hell was he up to this time? It didn't matter, of course. Nothing mattered but finding Calla.

It was a good thing there weren't any men, Seth thought darkly. He didn't want to have to kill anyone, but he'd long since come to the realization that anyone who touched Calla would face his wrath. The very fact that she was running a hostel was more than he'd hoped for–a small part of him had been terrified that she'd decide to continue her career as a pleasure worker. Normally a life mate wouldn't be capable of being with another man, but the whole concept of mating with non-Saurellian women was too new to know if the old rules would hold true.

"So what do you want to do now?" Jax asked.

"We'll go and get her tonight," Seth replied thickly. The realization that within hours she would be his again was almost too much for him. He leaned his head back and took a deep breath. "I need her."

Jax looked at him sympathetically.

"It's going to be hard," he said quietly. "Somehow you're going to have to work through all that's happened if you ever want to have a decent life for yourselves. It's not a good thing to be at war with your life mate. You have to let your anger go."

"I know," Seth said. "But it's not that easy. Even if she comes with me voluntarily, I don't know that I'll ever be able to trust her again."

"At least you have a life mate," Jax said after a long pause. His customary good humor seemed to be fading. "The Goddess is merciful, but there are still so many of us who can only hope."

"Well, we have hope, now," Seth said. "So many of our brothers have gone to their deaths without even that much."

Jax took another long drink of his *bakrah* without responding. Seth gave him another penetrating look, but the younger man refused to look at him. With a shrug, Seth turned back to his own drink, content to think about his reunion with Calla.

* * * * *

Jax hadn't come home that night, although Calla had monitored their guests' arrival from the office all afternoon and evening. It was paranoia, she told herself wearily, but she just couldn't shake the feeling that something was wrong. Until she saw for herself that he wasn't one of the Saurellians who had been at Jenner's hostel, she wouldn't be happy.

Finally, though, she needed to sleep. Sarai and the children had retired hours earlier. The alarms were set; the door was locked. It was time to go to bed.

After making sure all was secure, she made her way to the private part of the hostel. She and Sarai had rooms that were separate from the guests rooms. Her room–a luxury that always sent a thrill through her–was cool and dark as she stepped inside and locked her door. She kept a window open in the evenings because she loved the sounds of the animals in the darkness. Small insects chirped, and occasionally a night-loving bird would call in the distance. She would never get over the simple pleasure that came from living on a planet.

Pulling her dress off, Calla stepped over to the window wearing only her shift. The darkness was alive, she could feel it outside. Their small hostel was on the outskirts of town, and she could see the rainforest behind their small, walled garden. At first, the sight of all that teeming wildness had frightened her. Now she loved it. She raised her arms and stretched, enjoying the stretching sensation that raced through her muscles. This was freedom.

"Hello, Calla," a smooth, familiar voice said in the darkness. Her heart stopped, and she froze, excitement coursing through her. It was Seth, somehow he was there, in the room with her. Her eyes moved frantically over the window, trying to decide if she could jump to the ground. Was it was too far?

"Jax is out there, just in case you try something stupid," Seth said softly. "Why don't you turn around so we can talk."

Slowly, Calla turned. She couldn't find him at first, then she realized he was actually lying on her bed, leaning back comfortably against her pillows. How long had he been waiting for her?

"What do you want?" she asked, feeling foolish. The sight of him sent a tingle of sensation through her traitorous senses. She knew his presence wasn't good, but her body was overjoyed to see him again. She wanted him.

His face was like stone in the darkness. He simply stared at her for a long moment, and the tension rose between them. He wanted her, too.

"We never finished things, Calla," he said.

"Seth, I'm sorry," she whispered. "I did what I had to do. We'll pay you back for the ship, I promise."

"I don't care about the damn ship," he said tightly. "I have enough money to buy a hundred ships. What I care about is the fact that you lied to me, that you left me behind. Why didn't you trust me? I would have helped you."

Calla snorted in disbelief.

"Right, like I should believe that," she muttered. "You were plenty interested in fucking a slave, but I didn't see you offering to set me free."

"You never gave me that option," he said quietly.

"Why would I take that chance?" Calla replied. "Do you have any idea what happened to slaves who didn't meet Jenner's standards of morality? They got sold to pimps. Would you risk dying on your back in a mining camp to have a fling with guest in a hostel?"

Seth caught his breath; the thought of her being subject to men like Calvin made his skin crawl.

"No, I can understand that," he said finally. "But all that time together–why didn't you confide in me then? You can't believe I would have sent you back to her."

"I had to think with my head, not my heart," Calla said bitterly. "And I had to rescue Jess. Would you have understood that?"

A flash of jealous anger went through him at the name.

"Jess," he said slowly, dragging the name out on his tongue. "What about Jess? Did you ever find him? Did he send you away? How is your *husband*?"

"I didn't try to find him," Calla said quietly. "I had no idea where to begin looking, and Sarai and I needed to get away. It was enough to know he had escaped."

"You would leave behind a man you love so easily?"

"Jess is not my husband. I already told you that. He was my crèche-brother, we were raised together on the slave farm. He always wanted to escape, but he wouldn't go without me. If I hadn't been so scared he never would have ended up in that mining camp. That's why I had to find him."

"He was never more than a brother to you?" Seth asked, jaw tight. His tension was a palpable presence in the room.

"No, never," Calla said, willing him to believe her. "Even when we were younger, we never experimented together. We were too close for that, even if we weren't related biologically. Of course we might have been, for all I know. Both of us were synthesized out of the same genetic material."

"I don't know whether to believe you or not," Seth said finally. He sat up and swung his legs down off the bed.

Calla sank to the floor, trying not to look too closely at him. It was too hard to be in the same room as him, feeling his hatred. He remained silent for several minutes, contemplating her as she sat. Then she grew angry. Who was he to judge her?

"Why should you care whether or not I'm telling the truth, now or then?" she finally asked. "All we had was a contract. I provided you with sex, you provided me with money. I know it didn't work out quite right and that I still owe you, but in the long run why should you care, as long as I repay you? It's not like we could ever have had anything more together. You must have told me a hundred times that a Saurellian could never stay with a non-Saurellian woman."

"Maybe I was trying to convince myself of that," Seth said finally. "But it didn't feel that way. I wanted to stay with you."

Calla stared at him, unsure of what to say. Part of her thrilled to his statement, but another part wondered if it was just some vengeful game he was playing.

"Well, you never told me that," she said finally. "How was I supposed to know? If I'd told you the truth, I would have been totally in your power. I've seen what men can do to women. And I noticed you didn't do a damn thing to help Sarai or her children. Why should I believe anything you say?"

"I needed to get information from Calvin," Seth said after a long pause. "I wasn't going to let him seriously harm Sarai, and I was going to help her escape from him."

"After you'd gotten what you needed from Calvin, right?" Calla said skeptically. "And just when, exactly, was that magic moment going to arrive? Did you see the bruises on her face? I don't know how you could have missed them."

"I saw them," he replied. "I'm sorry to have to say this, but the information was more important. I needed to know if the Pilgrims were a threat to the occupation."

"Well, it looked to me like the Pilgrims were all dead," Calla muttered. "Sarai and her children were still alive, but at the rate Calvin was going they wouldn't have been for long. I don't regret what I did."

"The Pilgrims weren't all dead," Seth said, eyes glittering with anger. "They arrived not too long after you left, actually. Bragan and I had to hide out in the mines to survive. Oh, he's dead by the way. He died saving my life, no thanks to you.

"And this may interest you, too," he said, growing harsher. "They also attacked Discovery station. More than a hundred people died in that attack alone. It might have been prevented if I had been able to get more information back to the Saurellian council in time. It took us six months to regain control of the system. In fact, they're still out there, just waiting for us to show a weakness. Then they'll attack again."

Calla's face turned pale in shock.

"W-was anyone from the pleasure house injured, or the hostel?" she whispered, thinking of her friends.

"Not that I know of," Seth said, sighing heavily. His anger seemed to evaporate in the face of her distress. "Most of those killed were Pilgrims."

"What about Mistress Jenner," Calla said. "Was she part of it? She's a Pilgrim."

"I don't know what happened to her," he replied. "I heard she disappeared shortly after the attack. They were coming to arrest her."

"I'm so sorry," she whispered. "I didn't know."

"Well, I did," Seth said. "All you had to do was trust me."

"And all you had to do was trust me," she whispered back. "So, now what? Do you want your money back? We can sell the hostel. Or are you going to turn me in as a runaway slave?"

"Come here," Seth said, patting the bed next to him. "What I really want to do is touch you again."

Calla gave a brittle laugh. "Well, sex is certainly one thing we've always been good at. But forgive me if I say I'm not in the mood. I'm a little preoccupied with what you plan to do. How did you find me, anyway?"

Seth decided to ignore her little bit of rebellion. "It wasn't hard," Seth said. "The only time we had any trouble at all was with your friends at the hostel on Calindra Station. They managed to throw us off the trail, at least for a while. But you and Sarai were pretty noticeable no matter where you traveled. I guess people took note when neither of you understood how to do simple things, like catch a flight or use a credit transfer chit."

He was right, Calla thought with disgust. They'd had to ask for directions and help no matter where they went. Neither had traveled before, never mind selling a space craft. It had been naive to think they hadn't left a trail a quadrant wide.

"So, you didn't answer my question," she said. "What are you going to do? Whatever it is, I hope you'll let Sarai and the children go. She was only trying to protect herself and the kids. The whole thing was my idea."

"No, as far as I can tell, the whole thing was Bragan's idea," Seth said with a harsh laugh. "He and I had plenty of opportunities to discuss your actions while we were hiding out together. And as for Sarai, I don't blame her for what she did. I can understand it."

Then why can't you understand why I did what I did? Calla felt like asking, but she didn't want to push him.

"Come here," Seth said again. His voice was smooth and persuasive. She wanted to sink into his arms, have him hold her. Realizing she had nothing to lose, she stood and made her way over to the bed. If she *was* headed back to slavery, at least she would feel his arms around her one more time.

Seth pulled her down on top of him as he stretched back on the bed, reaching both hands up to cup her face. She could barely see him in the moonlight, but she could feel the tense urgency in his body. He was rock-hard against her, and she felt an answering rush of sensation course through her own body.

"I was so angry with you," Seth said quietly. "I told myself that if I ever saw you again I'd strangle you. But now that I'm here, now that I can feel you, all I want to do is be with you. Do you know what that means for a man of my culture? To only want to be with one woman?"

Calla shook her head. She had no idea, but she understood how he felt. Just touching him was enough to bring her to life again. This time there were no lies between them, and whatever the morning held was no longer important. She dropped her lips against his, pressing little kisses against his mouth. He kissed her back hungrily, then broke off the kiss.

"Usually, when a man and woman in Saurellia feel this way about each other, it's because they're life mates," he said.

"What are you saying?" she whispered. Horror filled her; he had come to get his revenge. Nothing else could explain such cruel teasing.

"Not long ago, our priestesses confirmed that at least one Saurellian has found his life-mate outside of Saurellia," Seth said. "She was the daughter of slaves. Imperial slaves."

Tears welled up in Calla's eyes. "Please tell me this isn't some kind of joke. Are you saying what I think you're saying?"

"It's not a joke," Seth said. He lifted his head to kiss her lightly. "You're my life mate. I knew it before, but I just couldn't bring myself to believe it. But now I know. The Goddess created us for each other."

"So what does that mean? What do we do now?"

"I would like it if you'd come back with me to Saurellia," Seth said. "Once we have a child, we can be officially bonded at the temple. That's what any other Saurellian couple would do."

"But we're not just any other couple," Calla said after a brief pause. Seth's body tensed under hers. "We've both lied to each other, and we've both hurt each other."

"I guess we'd have to learn to trust each other," he replied slowly. "I'm willing to try if you are."

"Do I have a choice?" Calla asked, gazing deeply into his eyes. "It seems like I've never had a choice before. Do I have one now, or are you simply going to take me with you whether I want to go or not?"

Seth's jaw clenched. He hadn't considered that she might not want to go with him.

"I can offer you a great deal," he finally said slowly. "My family is one of the foremost in Saurellian society, and we would have our own estate. You would always be well cared for; our children would have every opportunity to succeed in life. It's more than you'll ever get here."

"But do I have a choice?" Calla asked again.

"Yes," Seth said tightly. He stared up at her, begging her with his eyes to come with him. If she said no, he was lost.

"Seth, I love you," she said quietly. "But I don't want to go with you unless you feel you could love me, too. I'd rather stay here than live with someone who hates me, despite whatever quirk of the Goddess has made us biologically compatible. Can you understand that?"

Seth blinked up at her in confusion. What kind of question was that? She'd felt his response to her a thousand times. What more did she need?

"Of course I love you," he said after a second's hesitation. "Why else would I have let you go as long as I did? I would have hunted down anyone else who did what you did and punished them. I would never have let you get away. I only came for you when I realized I had something to offer you."

"Are you serious?" Calla whispered, still unable to fully believe him. It was too much like a dream, and a part of her expected to wake at any minute.

"Goddess, what do I have to do to convince you?" he muttered. "I've traveled across the quadrant for you. I've spent three times what the ship was worth to find you. I haven't been able to think of anyone but you since we parted. What will it take?"

Calla opened her mouth to reply, but before she could say anything he crushed her mouth against his. His kiss was hard and harsh, completely different from those light kisses he'd given her just moments earlier. Then he released her mouth, rolling her under him in one smooth motion. His knees thrust between her legs, and he ground his aroused flesh against her desperately. He had to show her, he had to prove himself. If she refused to come with him, he wouldn't want to live.

Calla tried to speak again, but once more he crushed her mouth against his even as he reached down with one arm to pull up her shift above her breasts, revealing all that he had been denied for so many months. Unable to speak, she threw her arms around his neck, then brought her legs up to clasp his body. His rock-hard cock pushed against her moist opening, and she gasped under his movements. Then he released her mouth and dropped his head against her shoulder.

"I'm sorry," he said in a rasping voice. "It's just been so long since I've felt you against me. I need you."

"I need you, too," she whispered. He looked at her, hope in his eyes.

"Then you'll come with me to Saurellia?"

"Yes," Calla whispered. "I would be honored to come with you."

"I promise, I'll never mislead you again," he said, dropping hot kisses across her face. He brushed against her eyelids, then down to her lips again. They kissed for several more minutes, then paused for breath.

"And I promise I'll never lie to you again, either," she said.

"I'll always take care of you, you never need to be afraid again," he replied touching her face in wonder. "You're so beautiful, Calla."

"I'll always take care of you, too," she replied. A smirk came over her face. "It seems like you have a pressing problem that needs urgent care right now." She moved against him suggestively.

Seth groaned at the sensation, his hips moving involuntarily in response. "What do you suggest?" he asked.

"I suggest you take off your clothes, then come show me what it means to have a Saurellian life-mate."

"I'm happy to oblige," he said, kissing her again deeply. He pushed himself up off the bed, standing quickly and stripping off his clothing. Then he reached down and pulled her shift over her head, letting it drop to the floor. She lay before him, open and trusting in the darkness. In what little moonlight there was, he could see her breasts rising and falling in time with her breath. She was just as aroused as he was, he noted with satisfaction.

He lowered himself to the bed between her splayed knees. He dropped his mouth to her breasts, but she thrust one hand into his hair and pulled his face to hers.

"I'm way past needing that," she said thickly. "I want you in me, now."

"Oh, giving orders now, are we?" he asked archly. "I think that you need to learn a little patience. After all, I've been waiting for this very patiently for months."

"And I haven't been?" Calla whimpered. "Seth, I need you."

But he merely smiled, then dropped his head to her breasts. He laved her nipple slowly, circling the pink nub with the tip of his tongue. Her stomach clenched in tension, and she gasped. Seth lifted his head and gave her a slow smile.

"I take it you like that?" he said. "How about this? Do you like this?"

He slid lower on the bed, dropping small kisses across her stomach as he moved toward her waiting clit. After what seemed an eternity, he reached the small nub that was the center of her pleasure. Using both his thumbs, he held her exposed to his view, then blew softly on the sensitive flesh. Calla rolled her head back and forth, then lifted her hips toward him, begging for more.

Seth chuckled, then allowed his tongue to graze her flesh. Calla stiffened, pleading with him wordlessly for more. Lowering his head, Seth allowed his tongue to play with her clit, flicking it sensuously. She pressed up against him once more, and with a sigh he sucked her into his mouth.

She gasped. "Oh Goddess, don't stop," Calla said, twisting against him. Waves of desire built in her, and she strained to achieve that pinnacle of pleasure she knew was waiting for her.

Seth laughed again, and the vibrations from his laughter stimulated her almost beyond endurance. Then he leaned back abruptly.

"I don't want to make this too easy for you," he said. "I think you need to earn your pleasure. Make it worth my while to finish things."

Leaning up on her elbows, Calla stared at him blankly.

"What do you want?" she finally said, her voice husky with desire. "I'll do anything for you. Anything."

Her words sent a twist of agonized longing through his groin. She was so beautiful, lying there with her legs splayed wide open and her eyes glazed with lust. She was fully his, he realized. This was his life mate, right in front of him, and she wanted to bring him pleasure. It was more wonderful that anything he could have imagined.

"I'll let you decide," he said finally. "You do whatever you feel you need to do. I'll trust you to be fair," he added with a smile.

"I'm honored that you would trust me," she whispered. "I won't betray that trust, now or ever. Now come up here."

She gestured imperiously to the bed, and he bounded up beside her. Pushing him back against the covers with one hand on his chest, Calla knelt between his legs.

"I think you need a taste of your own medicine," she said, looking up at him slyly. Then she allowed her head to drop slowly toward his jutting cock. It pulsed in anticipation, and Seth let out of a low groan. When she was just an inch from the head, she stopped moving. Then she slowly flicked out her tongue, allowing the tip to swirl lightly around the swollen helmet.

Seth gasped, then reached his hand toward her head. She looked up at him, abandoning his hard length to glare at him warningly. He dropped the hand to his side and let his head fall back with a sigh.

"That's better," she whispered. Reaching out with her tongue, she found the small groove on the underside of his penis, exploring it for several seconds. Seth gasped, then thrust his hips up at her.

"Take all of me," he gasped. Calla laughed huskily, then allowed her mouth to encase his length. Massaging the base of his cock with one hand, she bobbed her head quickly up and down on him, sucking steadily to give him as much pleasure as she could. She could feel him tensing beneath her, and realized he was close to coming. Then he gave a stifled moan, grasped her arms and dragged her up his body.

"Cover me," he said, looking in her eyes fiercely, then he slanted his mouth across hers in a powerful kiss. She pressed down against him, teasing his cock with her hot, wet lips. He felt so good, and as she slid down his length she felt tears build in her eyes. Then, fully impaled, she rocked vigorously against him, still locked in his embrace as he kissed her. His cock thrust high and hard, right to her womb. It was too much to bear. With a cry, orgasm washed over her.

"I love you," she moaned as she spasmed against him.

"I love you, too," he grunted, thrusting as hard as he could. She was going wild on top of him, and it was all he could do not to come on the spot.

"Seth, there's something I should tell you," she gasped.

"What?"

"My birth control implant is expired," she said.

An image of her stomach swelling with their child washed over him, and it was too much. He came in a burst, collapsing under her. "I'm sorry," he whispered. "I guess it's been a little too long."

"I don't think that will be a problem," she said, flexing her muscles around his length. He hardened instantly, then moved against her experimentally.

"No, I guess it won't be," he replied with an answering smile, then he rolled both of them over, so she was lying under him. He gave an experimental thrust, his sex still fully erect within her.

"Oh, that feels good," she whispered. She raised her legs around his waist, cradling him with her body.

Taking the hint, he started moving rhythmically within her. With each thrust, his length scraped along her engorged clit. She was so stimulated by the exquisite sensation that she felt as if she might explode. Then another orgasm hit her, and her body arched beneath his.

Seth laughed triumphantly as she came, then thrust against her even harder. He knew he wouldn't be able to last too much longer. The feeling of her muscles locking up around him as she took her pleasure was beyond anything he'd ever felt. If he could just get her to come one more time before he exploded...

He reached down with one hand, grasping her hip and adjusting the angle slightly. She gasped in response, and he pressed his advantage. Within seconds she was coming again, screaming out her pleasure and milking him with her internal muscles.

Finally, when it seemed he could hardly breath, he gave in to the pleasure. As his sperm shot deep into her body, he thought about their child; a child who might be created that very moment. Tears of joy ran down his face as he collapsed on her. She was crying too, whispering his name over and over. He rolled one side, cradling her against his body, and sighed. Then they were both asleep.

* * * * *

Sarai couldn't sleep. She was restless, almost as if she was waiting for something.

Jax? She still couldn't believe what she'd done with him, what it made her feel like when he'd touched her. It was so different than anything she'd ever experienced before...

For the first time, she had some small understanding of the power that Seth had held over Calla. Calla still missed him; Sarai could see it in her eyes every day. A woman who got involved with a man like Jax would be left mourning, too. He was dangerous. Too dangerous to allow herself to have any further contact with, she thought sadly.

After several hours of tossing and turning in bed, Sarai sat up and pulled on a light robe. She would go out to the garden. The night air never failed to calm her, and the soft sounds of night insects enchanted her. She had missed so much, growing up in the mining belt. Not a day passed when she wasn't grateful that Able and Mali would have more in their childhood than she had dreamt possible.

Her room was on the ground floor of the hostel, the only one with a private entrance to the side garden. It was a small, overgrown area they had yet to tame, but Sarai liked it that way. The air was heavy with the scent of tropical blossoms. Small creatures rustled in the bushes, little furry things that she secretly fed scraps from the kitchen. With their brown eyes and fluffy tails, the animals had quickly grown used to her presence, at times following her and begging for treats.

She wandered over to a small bench, seated herself and looked up at the stars. Somewhere, among that glittering trail, was the asteroid belt. Somewhere there were more Pilgrims, more children raised without joy and married off at early ages. It all seemed so far away, now... Her life with Calvin was more of a vague nightmare than reality.

"Hello, Sarai," a deep voice said softly in the darkness. Sarai's head whipped around, and fear ran through her. Who was out there?

"Don't worry," the voice said. "It's just me, Jax." His tall, solid form materialized from the overgrown foliage. His face was shadowed, and the pale, glistening moonlight made him look almost unreal. What was he doing here, in her garden?

"I couldn't sleep," he said, as if reading her thoughts. "I thought the night air might refresh me. Are you having trouble sleeping, too?"

"No," she said quickly, trying not to look at him. The last thing she wanted was for him to realize how much he had disconcerted her. Of course, as soon as she said it she realized how silly it sounded.

"So you often wander the garden in the night?" Jax asked, his voice filled with gentle humor.

"Yes," she said tightly. He sat down beside her on the bench. She kept her eyes fixed straight ahead, but she could sense his imposing presence next to her. His smell, masculine and slightly sweaty, filled her nose. Her body clenched, and a wave of lust swept through her. She remembered the feel of his lips against hers that afternoon. He had all but taken her in his room, would have taken her if it wasn't for Able.

"About this afternoon..." she started, but he cut her off.

"Sarai, look at me," he said.

Reluctantly, she turned to him, looking up at his face. The moonlight was reflected in his eyes - eyes hard and filled with desire. Without realizing what she was doing, Sarai gave a small whimper.

Jax's arms came around her and his lips came down on hers, hard.

He thrust his tongue into her mouth, sweeping the inside of her mouth with rough determination. His arms were like bands of steel around her body. She whimpered a half-hearted protest, but he pulled her roughly across his lap, head slanting against hers.

He kissed her with a desperate energy, refusing to let her free long enough to catch her breath or consider the consequences of her actions. One hand pulled apart her robe, then reached down into the neckline of her gown. He found her breast, rolling the nipple between his fingers until it tightened with need.

It was as if there was a direct line between her breast and the sensitive area between her legs, because the need his touch created in her was almost agonizing in its intensity. She moaned against his mouth.

He responded by standing quickly, pushing her robe off her shoulders. His mouth left hers long enough for him to pull her gown over her head, then he pulled her to the ground. Within seconds, he was on top of her. He kissed her again, one hand moving between her legs to massage her clit.

It felt like nothing she had ever experienced before. Sarai was out of control, there was a need building in her for something, but what was a mystery to her. Sex with Calvin had been nothing like this. She wanted more of Jax, and pressed herself against him. She twisted wantonly, searching for some kind of release that she knew instinctively only he could provide.

"Please," she gasped. "Jax, please, help me."

Jax muttered something, then his hand left her clit for a moment. She cried out in protest, but he kissed her, promising it would be better soon. She could feel him fumbling with the fastening of his pants. Then the hard, hot length of his shaft pressed against her and she gasped.

He pressed down, skewering her with his cock.

Sarai realized that Jax was much larger than Calvin, and the stretching sensation of his entrance both hurt and gave her unbearable pleasure. She twisted against him, and he stilled, resting his chin against her forehead and breathing heavily.

"Do you need me to stop," he asked, pain etched in his words. "Because if you do, you'd better say so right now."

"Oh, Goddess," she whispered. "No, I need more, Jax. Fill me more."

He growled in triumph, then thrust his entire length into her in one fierce motion. She tried to scream, but he swallowed the sound with his mouth, slamming into her again and again. Her body felt as if it might split from the force of him, but her clit was hard with arousal and every movement sent waves of agonizing stimulation coursing through her body.

Then it hit her–the most incredible sensation she had ever experienced. It felt as if she was shattering into a thousand pieces, the world seemed to dissolve around her. Her entire body stiffened in ecstasy, every muscle spasming simultaneously. A part of her realized that Jax, too, was in the throes of orgasm. She could hear his cry, and somewhere deep in her body she could feel his seed entering her. It was too much to take in, though, so she simply let the waves of her own pleasure wash over her.

Sarai came back to herself after a few minutes, realizing she was lying naked on her back in the garden. Jax, still fully clothed, pinned her to the ground with both the weight of his body and his still-hard cock. He was gasping for breath, cradling her face against his chest with one strong arm. The other was supporting his upper body so she wouldn't be crushed.

"Did I hurt you?" he asked. She stretched experimentally, trying to tell. She would be sore in the morning. His still felt massive within her–how had she taken it all inside? Yet she was all right, she realized. He hadn't injured her.

"I'm fine," she said quietly, trying to process what had just happened between them. "Could you get off me, please?"

He rolled to one side, and she sat up, nervously crossing her arms across her breasts. Horror filled her. She was naked, had rolled in the dirt with a strange man like a complete wanton. What had come over her?

Wordlessly, Jax handed her the discarded robe. She pulled it around her, and started to get up.

"Why don't you lie in the grass with me for a while," Jax said. "We've already had sex. I can see you're upset how quickly it happened. Let's take a little while to just be together and enjoy things, rather than you rushing back to your room to be angry with me."

He pulled her back gently against him, and together they lay in tense silence, watching the stars. After a while, she felt some of that tension ease.

"Where is Saurellia?" she asked eventually.

Jax pointed to the northeast, where a patch of stars shone brightly.

"Right there," he said. Then he pointed to another bright patch. "That's the asteroid field where you and Calla came from."

Sarai stiffened beside him, cold fear punching through her. "How do you know where we came from," she whispered in horror. "I didn't tell you that earlier. How do you know that?"

"Because Seth told me," Jax said quietly. "He's a good friend of mine."

Sarai moaned wordlessly, realization rushing through her.

"Where is he?" she asked in a panicky whisper. "Is he with you? Are you here to punish us for what we did to him?" She sat up, scooting away from him as quickly as she could. She had to get the children, wake Calla. They had to escape right away, or they were finished. Where would they go this time?

Moving more quickly than she had ever seen a man move, Jax caught her and held her against him.

She struggled against him like a wild woman, lashing out with her fingernails and teeth. She had to get away! Jax was too strong for her, though. Within seconds he had her pinned to the ground. One leg was thrown across hers, and both wrists were bound firmly by his hands. He loomed over her in the moonlight, his face shadowed. Against her belly she could feel the hard length of his arousal, and she shivered with fear.

"I'm not going to hurt you," he whispered harshly. "But I'm not going to let you run up there and ruin things for Seth."

"He's here, at the hostel?" she asked in a tremulous voice. "Jax, I have to protect my children! They aren't safe."

"Of course your children are safe," Jax said. "Seth has no interest in your children. He's come for Calla."

"What is he going to do to her?" Sarai asked. "You have to make him understand, it wasn't all her fault. I made her do it."

Jax laughed harshly. "He isn't going to do anything to her," he said. "Seth loves her. She's his life mate. He's going to take her to Saurellia and marry her."

"And what are you doing here?" Sarai asked suspiciously. "Why did you check in to the hostel this morning?"

"I was scouting things out for him," Jax replied. "He didn't want to scare the two of you off before he had a chance to talk to Calla, so he sent me to make sure we'd found the right women."

Sarai was filled with understanding. Jax had tried to seduce her that afternoon, and successfully completed his task at the most crucial moment, while Seth had come for Calla. She was a fool. He'd used her to get to Calla, then distracted her while her friend needed her most. To her horror, tears started welling in her eyes. This was too much, too cold-blooded. She had to get away from this man.

"Let me go," she said. "I'm not going to do anything, I promise."

"Why would I believe that," Jax said. "I'm staying with you for the rest of the night, whether you like it or not. How we spend that time is up to you, but I won't let you interrupt Seth and Calla."

Sarai tried to think what her options were. They seemed limited. Even if she could somehow overpower him and escape, he would be able to easily catch her. She was beaten, at least for now. She hated being manipulated by a man. It was like being with Calvin all over again...

"If you let me up, we can go back to my room," she said finally. Her voice was cold with anger. "We can't stay out here. The children almost always play in the garden before the rest of us wake up in the morning. I can't have them finding us like this. I won't have sex with you again, though, so you can just keep that out of your mind. Unless you feel like rape?"

"If I want a woman, I don't need to rape her," Jax said, his voice equally cold. "Next time we do this, I'll make you beg for it. And you will."

He rolled off her, and they stood up. Sarai led the way to her room with dignity, refusing to give him the pleasure of seeing how upset she was. As far as she was concerned, Jax could go straight to hell. She was determined that there would *not be* a next time.

Chapter 17

Calla came awake slowly. She felt wonderful, but something was different. She could smell Seth, male and slightly spicy. He was with her, his arms holding her. What had happened? Memory flooded back to her, and she realized he still in her bed. She sat up, leaning on one elbow, and examined his face.

He was smiling in his sleep, but around his eyes were new wrinkles. The night before they had been in shadow, but now she could see that on one side of his face was a fine web of newly-healed scars. A similar grouping of scars covered his shoulder, and spread across his chest. A wave of sadness and guilt swept over her as she realized that she might have been the cause of that pain. Would he have been injured if she hadn't left him on that asteroid?

She looked back up at his face to find his eyes following her.

"Good morning," he whispered.

"Good morning," she replied. "I thought last night was a dream at first, but it was real, wasn't it?"

"Yes, it was," he said. "Now that you realize it wasn't a dream, do you still want to go with me to Saurellia?"

"More than anything in the world," she replied, kissing him softly. He returned the kiss, pulling her over his body and rubbing against her sensuously.

"You may already be pregnant with my child," he said with satisfaction, once they surfaced for air. "How do you feel about that?"

"There is nothing I would love more," she said. Her hair had fallen forward in her face, and she pushed it back impatiently with one hand. "Although right now I would definitely enjoy a shower. Care to join me?"

Seth didn't need to be asked twice. Together, they jumped out of bed and moved into the small fresher room attached to Calla's room. Calla flicked on the warm water and stepped in. Before she could even turn around, Seth was with her, kissing the back of her neck. He reached both hands around her body to grasp her breasts, then pulled her back against him. His erection, already fierce, pressed against her backside as she wiggled against him and giggled. She pretended to try and escape, and he growled fiercely at her.

Turning in the circle of his arms, she reached up on her toes and kissed him. He responded by gripping her butt with both hands and lifting her. Then he slid her down over his rampant sex, bracing her against the wall of the shower. She wrapped him with both arms and both legs, then their mouths met again.

Starting slowly, he thrust in and out of her warm flesh. After a minute she stopped kissing him, too enthralled in the sensations between her legs to focus. He thrust faster and faster, until both of them were panting with exertion. She grunted rhythmically, then bit at his shoulder. The slight pain seemed to set him off, because he went wild, slamming into her again and again, until she thought she would explode.

Finally she did explode, a thousand stars breaking apart inside of her aching sex. She clawed at his back in ecstasy, and he groaned in response. Then he came too, pinning her against the wall with all of his weight as he shot load after load of hot, potent seed into her waiting flesh.

He allowed her legs to slide down his body, and she stood shakily on her own. He continued to stand above her, bracing his arms against the wall on either side of her. Gasping, he dropped his chin against the top of her head. They both stood for several minutes, then he shoved himself back and stood, facing her.

"When can we leave?" he asked, searching her face with his eyes. "I can't wait to start our life together. I can't wait for you to meet my family. And I can't wait to have our union confirmed at the temple, although we'll have to wait until you're pregnant for that."

Calla looked startled, then thought.

"I don't know that there's any reason I can't leave right away," she said slowly. "Sarai needed help getting on her feet here, but she can run the hostel alone."

"Then let's leave today," Seth said, pinning her with his dark gaze.

"Can I at least have some time to pack?" Calla said, laughing. "I'd like to say goodbye to our guests, too. How about tomorrow?"

"I'll give you until then," Seth said. He leaned down caught her mouth in a deep, soul-searching kiss. "But no longer."

"All right," Calla said happily.

She smiled up at him, and his heart caught. She was finally his. What would their child look like, he wondered. All Saurellian children looked similar, but Calla was different than any other Saurellian mother had ever been. Would they have a little girl? Would she have freckles like her mother? Only time would tell...

"If we're going to leave tomorrow, I have a lot to get done today," Calla said. "First, I'll need to tell Sarai and the kids. I think it might be better if you got out of here for a couple of hours. I'd like to tell her in private.

"All right," Seth said. "But I'm coming back this afternoon, and I'm definitely staying here tonight. You're never going to sleep alone again."

"That's something I can handle," Calla replied with a laugh. "Now finish your shower and get out of here."

* * * * *

"Are you sure you want to do this?" Sarai asked tightly. Jax had left her room early that morning. Unsure of what to do, she had started her day as usual, waiting for Calla to appear. Her friend had come in to the kitchen looking like Sarai felt–sore and worn out from being fucked long and hard. Calla, however, had a glow about her that made Sarai realize she was a lost cause. She was in love with Seth, and Sarai was going to lose her. It was too late to do anything to change the situation. Sorrow filled her heart.

She and Calla sat at the kitchen table. The children had already eaten their breakfast and had gone outside to play. Calla had decided to take them out for treats later that morning and tell them.

"I'm sure," she said. "I love him, Sarai. He had good reasons for behaving like he did before. If I had trusted him, none of this would have happened."

"If he had trusted you, none of it would have happened, either," Sarai muttered darkly.

"Well, we have a choice," Calla said briskly. "Seth and I can spend the rest of our lives hating each other for what happened, or we can learn from our mistakes. We choose to forgive ourselves and start over. I want happiness, Sarai, and Seth and I will only find it together. It's time to put the past behind us."

"I'll miss you," Sarai said, dropping her composed facade. Losing Calla was almost too much to bear. "Oh, Calla, you've been like a sister to me. I don't know what the children and I will do without you!"

"Oh, I think you'll do just fine," Calla said. "Sarai, you're a new woman now. You own your own business, and your children have a future, just take life one step at a time. And remember, we can always visit."

"I guess I just don't want anything to change," Sarai said with a sigh. She would save her tears for later, when Calla couldn't see them. "Are you sure you can trust him? A bad marriage is a terrible thing, Calla. I don't wish this upon you. It would be better if you stayed here with us, where it's safe."

"I'll be safe with him," Calla said, tears building in her eyes. She and Sarai stood and held each other for several long minutes. Then Able burst through the door. They both jumped in surprise.

"Think about it, Calla," Sarai whispered. "It isn't too late to change your mind."

"My mind's been made up from the minute I saw him," Calla replied, smiling happily. Sarai didn't return the smile. Instead, she held out her arms to her son.

"Sweetheart, go get your sister," Sarai said, giving him a quick hug. "Calla is taking you out for a treat. There's something she needs to tell you."

Able turned and ran out the door, and Calla followed. Sarai waited until they were gone, then sat down at the table. She lay her head down on her hands and let the tears flow. The thought of Calla leaving was too horrible. Worse yet, she was leaving so soon. She would be alone with the children again, all by herself against the whole world.

* * * * *

"Sarai?" a male voice asked. She whipped her head up–Jax had come into the kitchen so quietly she hadn't heard him at all. Sarai quickly wiped her face, then looked away from him. She didn't like looking weak in front of any man, let alone this one. He was too quick to take advantage of a woman's weakness.

"You're upset because Calla's leaving, aren't you?" Jax asked softly, coming to over to her bench. He swung one leg over, settling himself in a straddling position facing her. "It's going to be all right. She's his life mate–in Saurellia there is no greater bond that can exist between two people. They'll be happy together, they'll make each other complete."

"I don't care," Sarai said, still refusing to look at him. *Bastard.* He'd used her, and now he had the nerve to try and comfort her. "I'm going to miss her, and I don't like him. He's not good enough for her."

"Seth is a good man," Jax said softly. "I've known him for more than ten years, and I know that he'll always love her."

"You know, I'm sick and tired of men who think they need to take care of women," Sarai said harshly, finally looking at him. Her eyes blazed with the force of her emotions. "I had a husband who 'took care' of me regularly, and I wouldn't wish marriage on any woman. It's a trap, and Calla's falling into it. It's a trap." She repeated quietly, more to herself than to Jax.

"That's not true," Jess replied. "For a Saurellian-"

"Don't give me your crap," Sarai said, standing abruptly. She paced across the kitchen, then turned to lean against the counter with her arms folded in front of her. "Get out of my kitchen, get out of my hostel. You brought him here, you're responsible for this. Go back to Saurellia, because I don't ever want to see you again."

"I can't do that, Sarai," Jax said with determination. The intensity of his gaze frightened her. She turned away from him, willing him to disappear. He came up behind her, she could feel his presence, just as any creature can feel the presence of a predator. Taking a deep breath, she turned back to confront him.

"Get out," she repeated coldly, staring at a spot in the middle of his chest. "If you don't leave right now, I'm calling the authorities to remove you."

It was an idle threat, they both knew it. She couldn't move more than a few inches without running into him, and Jax was more than powerful enough to stop her. But he stepped back, raising his arms in mock surrender.

"I'll give you some space, Sarai," Jax said. "But I'm not ready to leave Hector Prime just yet. I'll see you again."

"Don't threaten me," Sarai gritted out between clenched teeth.

"I would never threaten you," Jax replied with a strange smile. "And I'll never lie, either. I'm not your ex-husband, Sarai. I'm a good man, and I won't hurt you."

With that, he turned on his heels and strode out of the kitchen.

* * * * *

The next day, after all the hugs were given and all the tears were shed, Calla and Seth sat alone in the cockpit of his new ship. It was bigger than the old one, with a more sophisticated design. The cockpit in particular was larger, with a small, cushioned couch behind the pilots' seats. Calla raised one eyebrow in question when she saw it, and Seth laughed.

"I decided that we could improve on the old design a little," he said with a shrug. "If I remember correctly, we could have used something like that several times in the old ship."

"It sounds like a great idea to me," Calla replied archly. "Of course, we'll need to do some testing, to make sure it works properly."

"By the Goddess, woman, can't you give me a break long enough for us to take off?" Seth asked, groaning in mock exhaustion.

"Oh, we can wait as long as you like," Calla replied with laughter. "Besides, if we don't take off pretty soon we'll miss our launch window. That could delay us for up to a day."

As she spoke, she deliberately propped both legs up on the control panel. Then she leaned back in her chair and stretched her arms above her head, causing the fabric of her shirt to tighten across her breasts. Seth growled warningly, and she laughed, reveling in her ability to arouse him.

"You know," she said languidly. "A good friend once told me that all men think with their cocks. Particularly Saurellian men. Is that true?"

Seth stared straight ahead, starting his checklist for take-off without replying. Calla took one toe and delicately pushed a small clip off the control panel, causing it to fall to the floor with a pinging noise.

"Oops, I dropped something," she whispered. Then she stood up, and turned away from him before slowly and calculatedly bending from the waist to pick it up. Seth breathed heavily as he watched her, and Calla had to bite her lip to keep from laughing. Then she sat down again, turning to meet his gaze.

"It's true," Seth said.

Calla looked at him with surprise.

"Right now, my cock must be doing the thinking," Seth said, giving her a slow smile. "Because I don't give a damn if we miss our launch window. Let's see how efficient the new cockpit design is. Come over here."

"Why don't you come and get me?" Calla asked. Then she scrambled off her chair and over to the low couch. Seth came after her, laughing like a child, and they rolled together like puppies. Then Seth caught her mouth with his, and they kissed long and slow.

"Can you feel how much I love you?" he asked.

"Oh, yes," Calla replied. "But I think a demonstration is in order."

"If the lady insists," Seth said. He kneed her legs apart, grinding his large erection against her already-moist cunt. Calla sighed with pleasure, arching against him. "Let's get rid of these clothes."

They sat up, pulling at their clothes; each drinking in the sight of the other. Calla finished first, falling back against the couch.

"Come and get me, Seth," she said. "I'm ready for you."

Seth lowered himself over her waiting body, carefully placing his length at the mouth of her opening. Then, catching her mouth with his, he slowly pressed his rock hard cock into her. She gasped at the sensation, whimpering with pleasure as he moved within her. Then he stopped moving altogether, and raised his head.

"Thank you," he said.

"For what?" Calla asked in confusion.

"For giving us another chance," Seth said.

"Thank you, too," she replied. Then she pulled his head back down to hers. He started moving again, and the pressure built in both of them. Within minutes, Calla's orgasm hit her. She cried out, squeezing Seth with her internal muscles.

It was too much for him to hold back, and he joined her, shouting out his own pleasure. He collapsed to her side, then leaned up on one elbow to look at the control panel.

"We've missed our launch window," he said idly, tracing a pattern on her face with one finger. "What are we going to do to pass the time?"

"I've got some ideas," Calla said. "Just trust me, I'll take care of it."

"I'll trust you," Seth replied with a smile. "I'll trust you for the rest of my life."

Epilogue

Jess sat in the darkness, idly cleaning his fingernails with a long, wicked blade. It had taken him so long to find Jenner that he'd given up hope at times. Now she was his. She would be coming up to her room soon; when she did, she would see the face of justice. His face.

Calla was dead.

Hari's words had played through his mind a thousand times since he'd returned to Discovery station for his sister. She had been kidnapped, according to the little kitchen slave, or she ran away. There were all kinds of theories, but each ended with the same cold truth. Her implant had been found in the station's recycling pit. No one could survive such a fate. Now it was time for Jenner to die.

He could hear the stairs outside creak as she heaved her massive form up to her room. It wasn't as nice as her apartment at the hostel, but she was lucky to be alive. Of course, her luck was about to change, he thought with grim humor. She'd survived the Pilgrims' disastrous attack on the Saurellians, but she wouldn't survive him.

The door opened, and the light from the hallway outlined her form. She sighed heavily, then turned to switch on the light and close the door. His blaster was already raised by the time she caught sight of him.

"Hello, *Mistress* Jenner," he said tightly, savoring the moment. "I think you should sit down on the bed."

Jenner did as she was told, her snake's eyes wide with fright.

"I'd like to draw this out," Jess said. "I've dreamed about this day for years, you know. All those nights you made me

231

come to you when I was younger? You're going to pay for them now."

Jenner gave a little moan of fear, and he almost felt pity for her. Almost. Then he thought about Calla's lifeless corpse and the pity disappeared.

"Unfortunately," he continued. "I have other business. We'll make this quick."

He tossed her a bottle of pills.

"I've already written a little note goodbye for all your friends," he said thoughtfully. "About how you're so filled with guilt you can't bear to live any longer. I'm prepared to give you a choice. Either take the pills or I'll use the knife."

"You wouldn't dare," Jenner whispered, but she was wrong and she knew it. He could see it in her eyes.

"Oh, I would enjoy it," he murmured with dark satisfaction. "Which way do you want to go?"

"I'll take the pills," she said finally. "I suppose you want to watch?"

"I've seen you stuff your face a million times while those around you were hungry," he replied coldly. "This time I plan to enjoy the sight."

He stood over her with the blaster as she took the pills, watching carefully to make sure that she swallowed all of them. There was enough in the bottle to kill her ten times over, but he wasn't going to take any chances.

After an hour, he rose to check her pulse. Nothing. Jenner was dead. He waited for the triumph to wash over him, but her death left him feeling hollow. Everything left him feeling hollow... Everything except *her*, the woman waiting for him in his ship. She was his love, his life, his prisoner. She was all he had left.

He went over to the window, opening it silently, then crawled out on to the roof. The planet where Jenner'd taken refuge was backward, and security was poor. It had been ridiculously easy to break in and find her. Escaping was just as easy. Within seconds he had blended into the darkness of the streets.

His ship was parked at the edge of the primitive landing field; Nestoria was too insignificant to have a true space port. Carefully checking to make sure no one had followed him, he palmed the airlock open and stepped in.

As always, his eyes flew to her cell in the corner. She was sitting on her little bench, watching him with dark eyes. Still, after all these months, he couldn't bring himself to leave her alone in the ship without locking her in. He told her it was to keep her from sabotaging his equipment, but the real reason was fear. He lived in fear that she would find a way to leave him.

He walked across the small room, pulling out the key to open her cage. She stood with dignity, watching his movements.

"Is it done, then?" she asked.

"Yes," he said tightly. He didn't want to discuss Jenner with her.

"And did it make you feel good to kill her?" she asked in a mocking tone. "Is Calla alive again? Have you stopped being a runaway slave?"

Jess glared at her. Once upon a time she would have been too fearful to speak to him this way. Those times were long gone.

"Please," he said, running a hand through his dark, curly hair. "Please don't. I just need to hold you tonight. Will you let me?"

She stared at him, trying to judge his sincerity. The look on his face must have convinced her, because she dropped her militant stance and came over to him. She wrapped her arms around him, pressing her body against his. It was like coming home, and Jess felt himself harden in response. She was the only person who could make him feel anymore.

"Let's go to bed," she whispered. "We're both tired. We'll think of what to do tomorrow. Tonight let's just be together."

"All right," he said, dropping a kiss on her head. Then she stepped away from him and held out her hand. Taking it, he let her lead him into the bedroom.

Also in this series:

About the author

Joanna Wylde is a freelance writer who worked as both a journalist and fundraiser before finding her niche in erotic romance. In April 2002, "The Price of Pleasure" was released as an e-book and quickly found a receptive audience. She became a full-time writer not long thereafter. Jo is married and lives in north Idaho with her husband, David.

She enjoys hearing from her readers. You can contact her c/o Ellora's Cave Publishing at PO Box 787, Hudson, OH 44236-0787 or visit her online at www.joannawylde.com.